4 12/23 $2-

# Albert and Ettore

by Mark Curfoot-Mollington

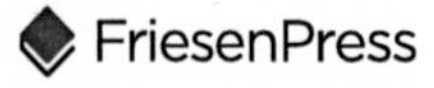

Suite 300 - 990 Fort St
Victoria, BC, V8V 3K2
Canada

www.friesenpress.com



First Edition — 2016



ISBN
978-1-4602-8016-4 (Hardcover)
978-1-4602-8017-1 (Paperback)
978-1-4602-8018-8 (eBook)

*1. FICTION*

Distributed to the trade by The Ingram Book Company

*This book is dedicated to Doug Casey*

This is a work of fiction. All of the principal characters and even those remotely relevant to the story are of my own invention. Granted, certain sections are inspired by unfortunate events and persons in the past. All of these events are, nonetheless, on the public record and appear only as historical background as they were recorded and reported at that time. It is my intent to portray only fictional characters and events which bear no resemblance to anyone living or dead.

What mean ye that ye use this proverb concerning the land of Israel, saying, The fathers have eaten sour grapes, and the children's teeth are set on edge?

Ezekiel 18: 2

The woman was a Gentile, a Syrophenican by nation; and she besought Him that He would cast forth the devil out of her daughter. He said unto her, "Let the children be fed first: for it is not meet to take the children's bread, and cast it unto the dogs".

Mark 7:26–27

I remember in the circus learning that the clown was the prince, the high prince. I always thought that the high prince was the lion or the magician, but the clown is the most important.

Roberto Benigni

# Arturo

April 2012

I am Panducci, Arturo. I live in Casa Alberto, on the Via Miseracordia in the Province of Arezzo and the town of San Leo Tiberino which I recently inherited from Dottor Alberto Stafford who was like a father to me. I never knew my real father. So I currently live here with my wife, Chiara, and our five-months-old son. He is, of course, named Alberto to honour our benefactor.

I recently received a letter from Professor Giovanni Bartolomei at the University of Bologna. I met Professore when he came to pick up Dottore's books and papers. He told me in the letter that you wanted any personal papers related to Dottore's earlier life and asked me if there were any. He said you, Professore Stevenson, were a scholar and would treat them with respect if I sent a copy to you.

The attached journal was found beside Dottore by his housekeeper Maria Pia Meoni when he died in the garden last November. All of the manuscripts for the other writings were in his study. These I gave to Professore Bartolomei for the University of Bologna when he visited as Dottore had requested in his testament.

I watched Dottore write this personal journal over the summer in the garden. His books were all written in Italian, but this one was at least started in English, so I have not read it and can't really say if anything is accurate or not. I did not understand the Italian parts at the end very well. My stepfather, who is fluent in English and who has written this letter for me declined to discuss its contents with me. Dottore did tell me once that it was the first and only personal work he had ever written.

To be honest, when Dottore died, I put the journal away in a drawer and did not think of it until I received Bartolomei's letter. My stepfather says I should also give a copy of the manuscript to Dottore's friend the Contessa Laura Guelfi but only after I send this to you. She will also be aware that I have shared it with you. You might want to ask the Contessa if she is comfortable in sharing any information that might relate to her family. She might not want events in the journal made public. Maybe Alberto did not either. On the other hand, why would Dottore write something over his last summer if he had not wanted it to be read?

Signature: A. PANDUCCI

# ALBERT

## Spring, Summer and Autumn 2011

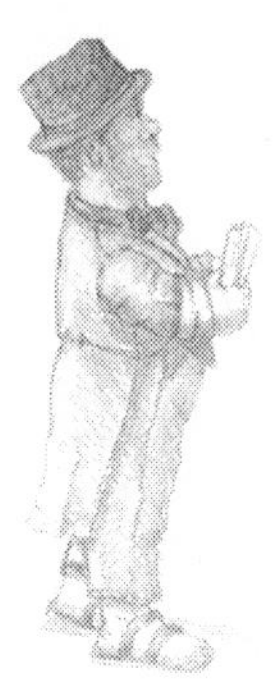

# AREZZO

I am Albert Stafford and I have written many books, historical research, all of them very factual and, if truth be acknowledged, very dull. I have always lived a rather staid sort of existence, even here in a Tuscan town, a conventional life-style in an Anglo-Saxon sort of way. The town of St. Leo Tiberino is a lively source of joy, quick temper and extravagant ceremonies of life to which I have been a foil for over forty years.

When I look back, I see that I was always a stuffy, prematurely adult sort of person, even as a young man studying at the university. Other than two or three close friends here in Italy and one who lives in the United Kingdom, everyone addresses me as Dottore. I wear rather well-cut, yet what appear to be ill-fitting, suits complemented with Windsor-knotted ties, even when I go to the street market. My friend Laura has given me a tie for Christmas for over forty years. They hang in my closet in a straight line in chronological order. That in itself gives the reader some indication of my mindset. Some are wide; some are narrow; all are well matched to each other. There is no spice to any of them, well suited, therefore, to me. I don't think I am grouchy or ill-tempered or even stand-offish, just, shall I be charitable, quite predictable. But life is a funny thing with unexpected turns and unexplainable bouts of serendipity.

It seems strange for me to be writing in English. For a number of reasons, I stopped lecturing and writing in my mother tongue over forty years ago. Now, although I still occasionally write short articles for Italian scholarly journals, I rarely venture up to Bologna to lecture or undertake arcane research. I had pretty much done with writing. Yet, this spring has been unfolding in an unusual manner which for some reason makes me want to record it: hence, I am writing this journal. As to why I want to write something personal, I can't quite put my finger on it. I want to write again in English so maybe that is why I have chosen something personal; my professional life has been all in Italian; perhaps the dichotomy of professional and personal lives is somehow related to the two languages or more precisely my relationship to them.

Things in my rather over-regimented life, I realize as I look back at recent events, came apart at the train station in Arezzo where I got fingered — a term I love, very period and one I don't think I have ever even spoken before. A Gypsy stole my *telefonino*.

The Arezzo train station is one of those post-war, nondescript, meant-to-be-utilitarian structures dotted throughout Italy with platforms level to the main hall. These platforms can only be reached by descending many steps into a dark tunnel only to climb back upstairs, dragging luggage and children to the appropriate track. Unlike my *telefonino*, about which I will add more, and which appears as well-worn silver tarnished to a comfortable patina, the train station is just plain tarnished. No amount of polish will add the lustre or zest of excitement one wants from a train station.

Several attempts by Trenitalia to tart up the main hall by cutting staff at the main ticket counter and dotting the main hall with self-service ticket kiosks have merely added to the general atmosphere of confusion. These new banco-style ticket machines have created scattered queues of confused tourists trying to buy tickets by sticking credit cards into the wrong orifices, while at the same time succeeding only in detaining young people in a hurry. As the minutes count down to the departure of a train, sweaty brows, dropped tickets, slippery euro coins, and tickets for the wrong train turn the whole place into what the Italians would call a "*casino*." One can smell the chaos.

My excuse for being there in the first place was routine and, frankly, bears little on the peculiar circumstances of the events I am about to recount of the coming days. I had driven to Arezzo, our county seat and the nearest town with train access, to meet with two academics, one Italian and one Australian. The Italian was coming along with the Australian ostensibly to interpret. The faculty at the University of Bologna sometimes forgets that English is my mother tongue. Or maybe the young lady-academic, Dottoressa Antonia Berlini, just wanted the chance to get away on her own with the Australian, Dr. Charles Hall, who I concede looks quite attractive in his latest jacket-cover photo — smiling, open-necked white shirt, salt-and-pepper cropped hair. You get the idea.

I waited in the hall while hoards, swarms, packs — call them what you will — of students, harried-looking housewives with baskets of vegetables, and even nuns dashed up the stairs from the tunnel below to fill the main hall. All was over in a second as they arrived and, in one fell swoop, exited the station.

In the midst of it all, however, I was jostled from the rear by a young Gypsy; I remember that clearly. And, I admit — *mea culpa* — that I know it is not politically correct to write, even in a private journal, the "Gypsy" bit. Well actually, in Italy, it is perfectly correct to speak, write or, for that matter, complain, about Gypsies. But since I am writing in English, I admit to feeling the pressure of Anglo-Saxon political correctness despite my acculturation to Italian life. When I took out Italian citizenship many years ago, my motto became "when in Rome, do as the Romans". Or as the Italians say, "*Paese che vai, usanze che trovi*" which, incidentally, makes no reference whatsoever to Romans.

For the most part, that is how I have lived. Now, as I write in English for the first time as an Italian citizen, I must decide whether in general to give the nod to the Anglo ethos or to the Italian.

I debated about expunging the reference to the Gypsy jostler. In the end, however, I decided that if I must write in English, I need not necessarily bow to English-language cultural idiosyncrasies. In my own defence, having lived most of my life in a foreign land, I am perhaps more likely to be sympathetic to the plight of the stranger, the outsider, in this case the Roma, than your average Italian. But like Naomi of the Hebrew Bible with her "whither thou goest, I will go" philosophy, the Italian people have become my people. I will call the Roma "Gypsies".

For the most part, I will indulge myself in this journal to write "that which I sees as I sees it" but I will write it with my own sense of understanding and verisimilitude. In fairness to me, and who better to be fair to me than I, the writer, who is indulging in a personal narrative for the first time, I put the Gypsy jostler out of my mind. It had, after all, not been an unpleasant jostle, just the usual train station jostle, little more than a briefly pressing of leg, groin, and elbow against the various regions of my back. The young man had, after all, excused himself. I thought no more of it. It was, seemingly, nothing which should interfere with the recounting of the tale-of-the-day.

The academics had been so slow in disembarking and walking through the tunnel that my immediate assumption was that they had missed their train. My friends tell me that I have a nasty tendency to assume the worst possible scenario and in this instance they would be correct. When I first arrived in the station, I was basking in the joy of having found a short-term-free-parking spot directly in front of the station. This joy was fading as every last straggling passenger, usually dragging an uncooperative toddler, funneled into view. Now, I conjectured, I would have to move the car and put coins in the parking whatsit. I only had a fifty-euro note. Bank machines in Italy have the annoying habit of giving out only large bank notes something I kvetch about it every time I go to the bank in person.

"Dottore, fifty euro is nothing to-day," I am reassured when I mention this at the bank. It is clearly not "nothing" if you need to feed the parking meter. One can hardly go to the newspaper kiosk and ask to have a fifty-euro note changed.

In my mind's imagination, the academics were sitting unconcerned, sipping prosecco in a first class compartment on another train arriving whenever. I wanted to check for a possible message from them, to which I would reply with a terse text which I was at the moment composing in my mind. When I put my hand into my jacket, however, my pockets were empty.

As already noted, the academics were not ensconced in a first-class compartment; they were just a tad slower than expected and deep in a conversation. They would pause on a stair and speak intently to each other as if their conversation was the most significant, the most erudite, spoken by one academic to another since Abelard chatted with Eloïse. They later told me, with a modicum of too much bravado and self-deification, that they had travelled second class. What this egalitarian cheaper ticket had to do with their slow pace in the tunnel, I have no idea. I took their bags from them and walked to my car in the short-term-free-parking space at quite the clip although I am a good thirty years older than they. Well actually, I am not generally slow by nature just slow to calm down, which walking at their measured pace would not have helped. I was fairly calm by the time we all got into the car to drive the few blocks to their hotel.

All of this meaningless preamble is to say: my *telefonino* was missing.

The academics gave me lunch in their hotel which was just off Piazza Monaco, a totally unmemorable lunch. I kept staring out the window at the statue of Guido Monaco, the monk who developed mnemonics right there in Arezzo. As conversation focussed on the effects of fascism in Emilia-Romagna in the 1950s, I kept going up and down the do-re-mi-fa-so-la-ti of the mnemonic scale in my mind. I had a sneaky suspicion that Guido Monaco's mnemonic hand gestures for do-re-mi-fa-so-la-ti might be being practiced under the white linen cloth by the other two but tried, difficult as it was, to concentrate on the topic at hand. Translations, as I suspected, were not required. As Dr. Hall asked the questions in his Australian thick drawl and brazenly pontificated on his theories, the Dottoressa merely simpered and stared.

When Hall's immediate concerns and questions had been addressed and his lengthy commentaries borne with grace, I left after a quick coffee in the lounge. That is the nice thing about drinking an espresso Italian-style: one quick gulp allows no time for conversation; just one swallow and off you go. The academics, who, I certainly hope, need not appear in this journal again, waved goodbye while, rather rudely I thought, not getting up from the sofa they shared. May they disappear into the nether reaches of the hotel. As to whether this involves one or two rooms, I have neither curiosity nor interest. With their disappearance, the *telefonino*, once again, regains its preëminence in this narrative.

When I got home, the telefonino was not there. My first impulse was to blame the dwarf. When all else fails, blame the dwarf.

The evening before, I had been at the circus in the nearby town of Sansepolcro. For those who have never been to an Italian circus, it is one of those experiences not to be missed. Circuses appear in no tourist guide for Italy of which I am aware. I prefer to think of them, like truffles, as an acquired taste. The big tent in Sansepolcro was redolent of images from the movies, more precisely the sort of grade B movies of the 1940s and 1950s which I remember as a child at Saturday afternoon children's matinees. These films, which starred women like Rhonda Fleming cavorting with men like Burt-Lancaster delighted me then just as the real circus does today. One sits there, at least I do, imagining a young Loretta Young riding the ponies and toe dancing before an inevitable discovery and a rise to the heights. Sadly, none of these circus folks of that previous evening, sequined, pretty, Burt-Lancaster-sort or not, is likely to rise far from the Valtiberina region where I live and they perform.

To be rhetorical: what is a circus without ill-fitting red suits with epaulettes? One size of uniform fits all. The one size, medium, does not, however, fit all men equally, for men were not created equal despite what the clergy and politicians might tell you. The circus owners' sadly have not grasped either of these physiological or metaphysical concepts of human size. At the circus, slighter men pushing brooms, seating the crowd, and selling bottles of water carry out their duties with their epaulettes moving down their arms and fighting their way towards the elbows. The larger men feeding the animals, hoisting the trapeze and escorting the entertainers have epaulettes that choke at the neck like two hands, while their own hands, wrists and elbows are bare. That night, the big tent seemed to abound with these suit coats hanging down from the shoulders of local malnourished Albanians hired for the stay in Sansepolcro, plus one dwarf with the most ill-fitting jacket of them all, although his trousers, which were actually blue jeans, fit perfectly.

There under the big tent I sat watching a fun-loving ring master who was a cross between Stan Laurel and Roberto Benigni. We sat on benches. For an extra five euro one gets an actual seat with a back. There were about fifteen costumed performers who changed costumes frequently to give the illusion of a larger cast. All the ladies assisted in a reptile act with snakes of all deadly varieties, which I could have done without but the children loved. Tightropes and tight-clad legs, twirling identical twin signorinas, faux Egyptian backdrops. All a bit tawdry and I loved every minute (well except the snakes).

Once again, I am going to be completely politically incorrect but truthful. When a well-meaning colleague and her husband took me to the Circle du Soleil as my birthday treat a few years back, I was bored stiff. Putting aside the loud music, I accept the fact that the lighting and general sense-of-the-spectacle was good, but there were no animals. As far as I am concerned: if you`ve seen one Chinese acrobat, you`ve seen them all.

I loved the animals at the local show: dancing horses, camels (I kid you not), a hippo who stood on a stool and opened his mouth on cue, antelope and llamas. The seals stole the show, which they usually do, playing a tune on horns that when I was a child was "God Save the Queen" and conveniently doubled as "My Country, 'Tis of Thee" when the circus crossed the border into the States. These seals played something the children all knew but to me it sounded, a bit incongruously, like "Deutschland über alles". I was a kid again; I wanted to run away and join up.

Little did I know that I and the circus were both about to run away but in a totally different manner.

Anyway, back to the dwarf. He was handing out the programs, more precisely, handing them out for a price. I have always held a soft spot for people smaller than me, the number of whom seems to decrease as I shrink through age. Anyway, he had a sad smile etched in white on his charcoaled face. I bought a program and resisted the urge to pat him on the head. While I was fiddling for money, he had ample opportunity to reach into my pocket and lift my *telefonino*. So when I got back from Arezzo and went over the previous twenty-four hours in my mind, I remembered him. And I blamed him and wished in retrospect that I had patted him on the head, or better, kicked him in the butt.

Of course, I dialled the *telefonino* number from my land line in hopes I could at least yell at the thief, "You little runt! *Stronzo*". Whatever. There was never an answer.

My neighbours, all with an opinion, insisted the *telefonino* was in one of my closets somewhere, too enclosed in a suit coat to pick up the signal. I was dutifully going through my pockets for the umpteenth time when my former neighbour from the country arrived. He drives a small three-wheeled Ape, and is able, therefore, to drive right up the hill and narrow streets in the traffic-free medieval part of town where I live. The man and his wife were neighbours for many years until I felt I was getting on a bit and should move into the town. Not so Mr. Sparrow, who is more than twenty years my senior; he and Mrs. Sparrow continue to live on the old farm where they have lived since the war.

I should explain about the Mr. and Mrs. honorifics. The Sparrows have lived here in Tuscany for well over sixty years. They speak virtually unaccented Italian, frequently to each other, yet everyone in town addresses them and refers to them as Mr. and Mrs. Sparrow — never Signor and Signora Sparrow — and certainly never Geoff and Anne. Even I, after these forty years, call them Mr. and Mrs. Sparrow. In fact, the oldest inhabitants of St. Leo Tiberino, several years their senior, say Mr. and Mrs. although sometimes they pronounce it like characters out of an old Gina Lollobrigida movie pronouncing Campbell Soup.

Mr. Sparrow first came to the region during the war and was shot. He had been an escaped POW and, so legend has it, was severely wounded in a field near the town by retreating Fascists. Two farmers found the bleeding body and carried him back to what then was still a remote, small farm-holding. The local doctor gave him no chance of any sort of recovery but, nonetheless, proceeded to removed seven bullets lodged in various parts of his body. He was unconscious for a month, which is probably what saved him, the equivalent of an induced coma today. When a doctor from the liberating forces eventually visited him, he refused to have Mr. Sparrow moved; moving him, he informed the famers, would kill him. Mr. Sparrow often uses this phrase today whenever anyone dares suggest that he move into town.

Months later, after the troops had long returned to the UK and the soldiers had been demobbed; Mr. Sparrow gradually came alive again. He regained his speech — perhaps it is best to say he learned to communicate in broken Italian. Regaining his physical strength was another matter. It was a full eighteen months before he could walk unaided. Meanwhile, Mrs. Sparrow was still in Dorset running her millinery shop. He refused to return to Britain; she sold up and came to Italy.

So they remain. In all the years since, Mr. Sparrow has never been farther than Florence. Twice a year, on a Sunday around Christmas and again at Easter, they take the train to Florence from that same tarnished station in Arezzo. In recent years, I have usually driven them as the Ape has not kept pace with the traffic or the highway. And I know that if anything happened to them on the road, people would say, "You'd think their countryman Alberto would have driven them". I am not their countryman, except in the Italian context of living in the same country and all three of us having taken out Italian citizenship, but I dutifully take them to the station in Arezzo. I help them through the tunnel before heaving them on board, well especially Mrs. Sparrow, who has substantially broadened over the years in what my Father called "the beam".

They make their semi-annual trip to Florence to attend the very English St. Mark's church, receive the sacrament à la Canterbury, and then walk along the back streets to Piazza del Carmine for lunch at a small trattoria. Then, it is always the same, a train around three o'clock back to Arezzo. Sustained, blessed, whatever, back they come to the farm, the same farm where he was taken in 1944, the same farm where he stayed and worked along with the *contadini*, these two Tuscan farmers, in the fields. When the old men, brothers and life-long bachelors, Mario and Fabrizio Fontana, died sometime in the 1950s, Mrs. Sparrow bought the farm with the money from her millinery business.

Now I digress, but this is a journal and such journals are meant for digression. This digression does, nonetheless, proceed to the events of the day. All to say, I heard the Ape. I also heard him shouting, as it were, to the whole street, "Albert, your telephone is at the *Questura* in Città".

Several neighbours had heard him and also started yelling, *"Alberto, Alberto, vieni; Mr. Sparrow ha trouvato il tuo cellulairio"*.

Maria Pia, Signora Agnèse and Signorina Celestina with rather exultant looks on their faces were leaning, more accurately hanging, out from their windows which overlook the walls of my garden. Well he hadn't found it, although he might as well have had it in his pocket given the praise from the nodding and waving women. It was in their faces, the tone of the voices: Mr. Sparrow had found what Alberto was foolish enough to lose in the first place.

Mr. Sparrow had telephoned me and got the *Questura.* And the *telefonino*, as he in fact had said, unwisely I felt in Italian, was in Città di Castello which in in the opposite direction from Arezzo with about eighty kilometres between them. Città is in Umbria. In the village where I live, Umbria is barely considered part of Italy. And in Città di Castello, everyone knows, they don`t even speak Italian; they speak the Castello dialect, which has only a slight resemblance to the excellent Italian spoken in our town. With warnings from the ladies leaning out the window to be careful in Città, I headed off.

# Città di Castello

Two hours later, after driving round and round the walls of Città, I found the *Questura*. The polite but officious *carabiniero* asked me the make of the *telefonino*. I replied, trying to appear confident, "Sony".

It was a Siemens. But I said it was silver — albeit tarnished — and I knew the telephone number. After filling out several quills of paper, the *telefonino* was returned and the recent provenance provided. Apparently, my *telefonino* had been found on a street near the train station in Arezzo. I surmise it was lifted by the jostling Gypsy hoping from my smart dress that I had an iPhone in my pocket. He evidently jettisoned my worthless, lovingly tarnished *telefonino*, pronto, throwing it down on a nearby street. A deaf man — now what are the chances of that? — found it. When I had dialed it to shout unkindly at the presumed-guilty dwarf, the deaf man, it follows, could not hear it ringing. Sergio — I later learned his name and honorific from my copy of the extensive police report — lived in Città di Castello and dropped off the *telefonino* at his local *Questura* when he returned to town from an outing in Arezzo. Before I headed out the door, the policeman made me promise that I would show my appreciation to Dottore Sergio Ganducca by telephoning him and thanking him. I smiled.

I really was happy, despite the ordeal, to have the *telefonino* back. In fact, I left the *Questura* singing, "I once was lost, but now am found, was deaf, but now I hear".

Strange, isn't it, how such forgotten memories come to mind in such circumstances? My Mother used to have a cleaning woman with the unlikely name of Artemis who used to sing this ditty while attacking the carpets with the Hoover. Well, Mama referred to it as a ditty and claimed she hated the hymn, as she put it, "if it is a hymn at all". It was, nonetheless, her mantra to chant in imitation of poor Artemis whenever she searched for something like a lost button or missing shoe. This entirely meaningless diversion brings us back to the tale at hand.

I backed out of the parking lot in front of the *Questura*. It was getting towards early evening and the roads were pretty busy. I eased into the first roundabout and then it happened. I was rear-ended. A white van that had been following me accelerated for some unknown reason crashing into the back of my car as I was exiting the circle. It wasn't a big jolt; in fact the rosary beads which my neighbour and cleaner, Maria Pia, had draped over my rear-view mirror seemed to me barely to jangle. All the same, I stalled the car and climbed out.

In reality, I suppose I must have been a bit more stunned by the event and slower to exit my car than I first thought. As soon as I was out, the same *caribiniero* from the *Questura* was standing there shouting at passing traffic. Then, he was explaining to two other *carabinieri* who quickly arrived on the scene the sad tale about my *telefonino*, emphasizing that although it was totally incredible: I did not know the make of my *telefonino*. I knew they were thinking "*straniero*! *patso*!". Implicit in the words of the *caribiniero* was that he was not surprised that I would find myself in such a predicament with my car, a small stretch of culpability from *telefonino* to car. Traffic whizzed by; there appeared to be no activity in the white van. No one seemed to take any notice of me. I wanted to sit down but that necessitated getting back into my car.

It was almost as though I had no part whatsoever in the activity going on around me, played no role in the "*incidente*" as the Italians call an accident. I was almost a dizzy bystander as far as the police and anxious drivers were concerned. Two of the *carabinieri*, not the one from the *telefonino* incident but the other two, had pushed my car over to the side of the roundabout. A sizeable crowd had gathered, watching the proceedings but ignoring me; they had stepped out of their cars while they waited for the roundabout to be cleared of traffic so they could continue. Once my car was moved, they mostly ran for their own cars, but a few sauntered and, eventually, all were off.

Finally, the passenger door of the van opened and a woman, I would guess in her mid-to-late forties, popped out. She was wearing Capri trousers and a white frilly blouse that left her midriff bare. She had what my Father would have called "a large verandah" and red hair. Her red hair was not Lucille Ball red but more Cardinal Ratzinger red.

The woman came over to me and shook my hand.

"My name is Sylvia. I am very sorry about all of this. My boyfriend's foot slipped off the clutch and hit the gas pedal."

This seemed quite improbable to me. To slip from the clutch to the brake or the brake to the gas, but how could it slip from the clutch to the gas?

As if she felt the need to give additional information, she went on, "He wears this shoe and it is a bit awkward at times. You must come and meet him; his name is Ettore."

She took my hand and we darted among the cars out to the van. It seemed strange that the police who had worried about my car had left the van where it was. Cars were swerving around it but we eventually made it to the driver's side of the van. The van looked none the worse for the *incidente*. Even the front lights were fine. Instinctively, I looked over at my car with its smashed back lights and pressed-in trunk. Sylvia, meanwhile, had opened the door. At that point, I was certain I was concussed and instinctively ran my hand over my forehead as if to check for cuts.

Ettore was the dwarf from the circus of two nights before, perched there resplendently over raised pedals and sitting on several cushions with a large book of something rather encyclopedia-like at his back; I couldn't help but think "Volume Three: Dwarf to Encephalitis".

I glanced down at the pedals, which had been raised about eight centimetres. His left foot was in a sandal of sorts but on his right foot he wore a huge black orthopedic shoe. It seemed that he used the one foot with the shoe for all three pedals.

Sylvia who was following my gaze explained, "He needs to look at the pedals as he changes the gears. He took his eyes from the gears just for a brief second to watch you going out of the traffic circle and pronto dropped it on the gas instead of the brake."

As for Ettore, he shook my hand as if to apologize for the bother as well as not getting out of the van; it was difficult, Sylvia added, to stand with the orthopedic shoe. He had bits of white makeup around the edges of his mouth, which made him appear to smile, unlike the full white makeup he was wearing the other night which made him appear to frown. On the other hand, perhaps he really was smiling. I felt dazed and was increasingly certain I must have injured myself.

Looking at Ettore sitting there so calmly, I felt at a loss as to how I ought to respond but was, fortunately, relieved of the need to respond by the arrival of the *carabiniero*. Addressing Ettore — again it was as though I were not there — he suggested forcefully that the easiest thing was for Ettore to drive the white van the few metres down the street to the *Questura*. As he left, he turned to assure me that my car had the front lights flashing and would be fine where it was for the time being. He insisted that I allow Ettore to drive me as I looked somewhat peaked.

"Hop in!" Sylvia chimed in.

My reply was slow in coming, "I think I need the air and will walk".

"Don't be silly," Sylvia had opened the passenger door behind Ettore, "you might have a concussion or something".

I stepped up into the van. I lifted Ettore's top hat off the seat and brushed off what seemed to be a lot of dust and dog hairs as we headed back to the *Questura*. I was feeling a bit queasy with all that was happening around me. It was a bit like watching a film that was running too quickly at one point and annoyingly slowly a few seconds later.

Once back in the *Questura*, I sat on a plastic chair three metres from the counter where Sylvia and Ettore stood. Well, Sylvia stood. The policeman had lifted Ettore up and he was sitting on the counter. It turned out that Ettore was originally from Città di Castello and had gone to school with several of the policemen, all of whom gathered around him, slapping him on the back and calling him "*Piccolino*". Meanwhile, not-so-*piccolino* on the plastic chair was sitting there, a total outsider to the proceedings. As they all continued with their laughter, the policeman handed Ettore the office phone and everyone roared with laughter as he chatted to someone at the other end. Maybe it was my dizziness, but I was beginning to believe my neighbours were correct; these people were speaking the Castello dialect of Umbria and it certainly bore little resemblance to any Italian I knew.

Eventually, the policeman called me over and, switching back to standard Italian, told me, yet again, to sign several quills of paper.

"No need to read; just sign!"

Perhaps sensing my inquietude, Sylvia poked me in the rubs, or nudged me with her ample bosom, I can't clearly remember.

"Don't worry, it's all looked after. Ettore's cousin, Maurizio, has a body repair shop. That was him on the phone. He'll be here to pick up your car in a few minutes. He was already driving around the area and spied your car at the roundabout where he gave it a quick look and assessment. He does that sometimes; Maurizio, assesses cars at accident sites just in case he gets a call. 'Saves time,' he says. Anyway, he has agreed to fix it for a thousand euro."

Reacting to my gulp, she continued, "Ettore will pay. It is all agreed-to in the papers. No need to involve the insurance company, just sign and we can all get out of here".

I signed. What choice was there?

After we had all shaken hands with the carabinieri and they had slapped Ettore on the back a few more times, I walked out into the now-darkened evening. I pulled out my *telefonino* but, after being left turned-on for the last few days, it finally needed charging. Chagrined, I stuck the phone in my suit coat pocket, hating the thought of having to return to the *Questura* to ask to use their phone.

I hadn't noticed, but Ettore and Sylvia had already come out and were standing beside me. Ettore spoke directly to me for the first time.

"You need to get an IPhone and get rid of that Siemens."

My eyes widened, "How did you?"

Before I could say another thing, however, I got jabbed yet again by Sylvia. Jabbing seemed to be a precursor to any form of conversation with that woman.

"We all need a coffee; Ettore's cousin Little Nellie has a bar about five minutes from here."

They each took an arm and led me to the van where Sylvia, after helping me into the back seat, assisted Ettore in slipping on his orthopedic right shoe.

I was sitting directly behind Ettore. I picked up the black top hat on the seat and once again nervously started picking off the light brown hairs. I noticed the hairs were also accumulating on my trousers. When we got to the dreaded roundabout, a large man was hoisting up my car. Ettore honked and laughed before abruptly applying the brakes, causing the person behind to swerve and me to slide off the seat. The man, Maurizio, who towered over us, came over while Ettore counted out ten green one-hundred euro notes. The man reached in behind Ettore to hand me a card containing only the name Maurizio.

"Come on Thuesday; I clothe on Monday." He had no teeth and thorta lisped, "Thao, Pitholino; thao, Thylvia". He waved as he returned to my car.

Actually, Little Nellie's place wasn't bad, more like a pizzeria than a bar. Quite well lit, it had fake half-columns and glass-topped tables. Nellie herself, however, was anything but petite. A large, dark-haired woman, she stood well over six feet in her high heels. When she heard what happened, she kept repeating "concussion or whiplash". She sounded like what the Americans call "ambulance chasers". In fact, Nellie started rubbing my neck while a man I presumed to be her husband forced Irish whisky down my throat.

"It is good for the English to drink the whisky in times of stress," she blurted out in amazingly clear English.

"But I am not English," I sort of weakly protested.

"No matter: English genes are in your voice."

Nellie eventually got bored with rubbing my neck, sat down and told the man — who in fact did turn out to be her husband although I never did learn his name — to bring us all Capricciosa pizzas. Actually, that is my favourite pizza so I smiled. It turns out that Nellie and the nameless husband had lived in London for ten years where he worked in an Indian tandoori restaurant in Streatham. I think that is when I stopped trying to understand or determine any degree of logic associated with this family.

After a couple of litres of wine, shared among Nellie, Sylvia, Ettore, nameless husband and couple of waiters, I was feeling better. The waiters kept tickling Ettore as they went by until Nellie shouted, "take your hands off my little cousin; he bites".

This caused uproarious laughter. It seemed every patron who came into the restaurant that night heard about the *incidente*. Every single one also came over to shake my hand as he said he was sorry to hear I had "concussion and whiplash". As if on cue, Nellie would jump up and begin to massage my neck.

When we ended up out on the street, it was after ten o'clock.

"I really must use your telephone," I sighed, half in satisfaction from the wine and half in desperation as to how I was to get home.

Another poke from Sylvia, "we are driving you home. Hop in".

Once again, I held in my lap the top hat with the light brown hairs.

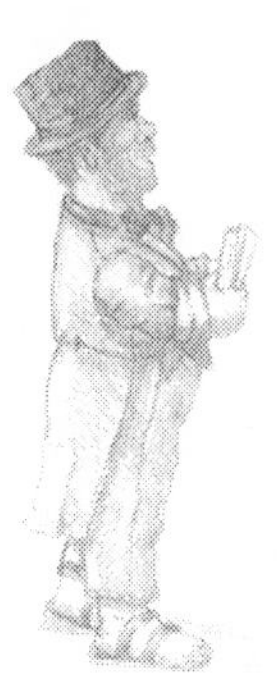

# MY HOUSE

When we got to the village, Ettore and Sylvia insisted that they accompany me to my house, *mia casa* or "*me cesa*" as the locals say in dialect. Alright, blame the wine, but I have to confess that our village also does, in fact, have a dialect but not as incomprehensible as Città's — as we are wont to point out. We wandered down the narrow streets from the parking lot outside the walls. I can park on the nearby Piazza Popolo but, of course, my parking permit was back in Città taped to the windscreen of my car.

Before we had started off from the van, Sylvia had helped Ettore with his orthopedic shoe. I asked her why he didn't wear two such shoes. She explained that if he did, the combined weight was too heavy and pulled him so low in the seat that he often slipped on to the floor. To compensate, she explained, he had a small paddle which he slowly lowered on to the gas pedal as he released the clutch with his right foot before transferring the shoed foot to the gas pedal. The procedure often caused the van to stall but generally they managed to take off, if not smoothly, effectively.

I opened the gate to my garden but fumbled with the house key which Sylvia took from me. She opened the door and went around the house turning on lights. Before I knew it, she had taken three wine glasses from my china hutch and was filling them from a large wine jug I keep near my sink.

"Now, Alberto," she said, "we don't want any arguments. Ettore and I have discussed this and are in absolute agreement. I insist that we sit here for the night for the sake of your concussion."

I admonished, "But I don't have a concussion. I didn't even hit my head; I was just woozy from the sudden shock."

Sylvia shrugged several times before waving her hands, "Ettore insists".

As if there was anything more to be said in my house.

She continued, "Ettore had a nasty concussion once. He was very active in the church as an acolyte, always helping at Mass, holding candles, that sort of thing. They even put a small step ladder in front of the lectern so he could do the readings. One day as he was carrying the collection bags with all the money up to the altar, the thurifer, the man swinging the incense in the brass thurible, hit him right between the eyes. The money scattered all over the church, which had everyone out of their seats pretty darn fast. By the time the congregation all got back into their pews, they discovered that Ettore had been badly concussed and needed to be taken to hospital for observation. That was why he dropped out of the church. Now just tell me where I can find blankets and we'll sit up in these chairs."

She moved easily from discussing the concussed Ettore to the blankets, almost without taking a breath.

Ettore spoke to me directly for the second time that evening, "Sylvia has an eye for the dramatic. I left the church when I joined the *Testimoni di Geova*".

I felt I had little choice. Fortunately, I keep the twin beds in my guest room made up in case a dwarf and top-heavy woman should happen to drop by for the night. I took them through and gave them towels and went to bed. Sylvia insisted on washing up the empty glasses; I could hear her in the kitchen as I undressed. As I lay curled up under my duvet, I had an uneasy thoughts which resembled more a prayer.

"My God, I have two total strangers from the circus staying in my house: a buxom woman and a dwarf who's a Jehovah Witness. The circus has run away and joined me, minus the animals."

* * * * *

I slept amazingly well. The morning light made everything from the previous day seem like a dream. I could hear the noises of morning activity coming from the kitchen so I let out another large sigh.

"My God, it was not a dream."

I slipped on a pair of gardening trousers and an old sweat shirt and headed into the kitchen. There was Ettore sitting up on a stool drinking a cup of coffee, while Sylvia was placing fresh brioches on one of my best plates.

"I've been up for hours. I drove back over to Città to pick up Bartolomeo and stopped by Ettore's cousin's *forno*. Emmanuelle makes the best brioches in Umbria."

Sylvia seemed to be on intimate terms with all of Ettore's relations.

I was about to ask who Bartolomeo was when I looked behind the table. On the floor, sound asleep, was a large Weimaraner. Bartolomeo obviously accounted for the hairs on Ettore's top hat and my trousers. The animals had joined the circus.

Sylvia must have noticed my surprise, "Bartolomeo is usually with us but was at the dog groomers last night. Actually we were on our way to pick him up when the er-um *incidente* happened. Ettore has a cousin Francesco who runs a small pet shop just outside the centre of Città."

I was getting confused at the proliferation of kinship. More relations; I was beginning to believe the little man was related to every living soul in Città di Castello. Meanwhile, the dog took absolutely no interest in me. I doubt he even noticed my arrival, so much at home as he seemed. But, I had to admit, the dog was glorious; I like dogs but have never bothered to get one since my childhood dog died in the accident with my parents.

A nice dog, the smell of coffee and fresh brioche; the day was actually looking up.

As Sylvia was just pouring me a coffee, while commenting that since I had no signs of concussion, we must make our plans for the day, the telephone rang, not my *telefonino*, but the land line. Sylvia answered, "Pronto, Casa Alberto" then immediately passed it to me. Clearing my throat and steadying my nerves, imagining the reaction on the other end of the line after Sylvia's outpouring of "*Pronto*," I answered.

"Albert. Albert is that you? Anne here. That is, Mrs. Sparrow."

"Oh good morning, Mrs. Sparrow." She barely gave me time to get that out before she continued somewhat excitedly and, I thought, a tad authoritatively.

"Geoff, that is, Mr. Sparrow, had a stroke late yesterday. We needed you but you were somehow unavailable, inconsiderately so, in light of Mr. Sparrow's dashing over to your house with information about the missing *telefonino*. I expect this dashing contributed to the stroke. In the end, I rang the *Misericordia*, who sped him away in an ambulance to the intensive care unit in Sansepolcro. I was with him much of the night. I tried you on your *telefonino*, as I know you keep it by your bed, to come and take me home, but got no reply."

"Well how is Mr. Sparrow?" I had to say something.

"Oh, he's alright. I've made his breakfast and I need you to drive me over to the *ospedale*. I tried to use the Ape but can barely fit in; it was an effort with Mr. Sparrow's breakfast on my lap but I finally did get in. Then, I found I was too large for my feet to hit the right pedals."

"Christ wept," I held the phone away from me for a couple of seconds, "a dwarf too short to reach the pedals and an octogenarian too large to get near them".

"What was that? Albert, you must speak up. I have my hat and coat already on and expect you here. I am closing the door now."

"Mrs. Sparrow, I have had a dilemma," I tried not to shout.

"Albert, other people like Mr. Sparrow and I have dilemmas, as we do at the moment. You, on the other hand, live a charmed existence. As you well know, I never lecture. But you might start thinking about other people for a change. There is poor Geoff, Mr. Sparrow, waiting for his breakfast. Albert and dilemmas," she sounded exasperated, "don't speak to me oxymoronically". She cut the line.

I, once again, held the phone in front of me.

"A milliner who uses words like 'oxymoronically'; what other surprise could await? What about my breakfast?" Sylvia just blinked at my English outpouring. I tried the number but Mrs. Sparrow had hung up and was clearly not about to answer.

I repeated this lament to my breakfast, this time in Italian, only to perplex poor Sylvia. "*Carissimo*, it is ready," she was smiling and questioning, "do you take tablets in the morning"?

I knew what had to be done.

"Ettore, could I ask a favour? Would you consider driving a large lady friend to the *ospedale*? Time is of the essence."

"Good God," cried Sylvia, "what are her contractions; are you the father"?

I shuddered before giggling at the thought of us driving up to the maternity ward and the orderlies extracting Mrs. Sparrow on to a stretcher as she shouted about labour pains and broken water. These people, I had to admit, did contribute to a humorous imagination.

"Not exactly, Sylvia, but she needs to get to the *ospedale*."

Ettore wiped his mouth with what I recognized as one of my best damask napkins. Sylvia put his orthopedic shoe on his right foot. "Alberto, you must learn how to do this so we can leave the shoe in the car. Ettore will need your arm to walk in that shoe."

Off we bobbed, Ettore and I, up the small streets and across the piazza, through the gate in the wall and into the public parking.

Saturday is market day. There were the customary stalls scattered around the main piazza with the usual assortment of handbags, aprons, ladies' colourful undergarments, men's undershorts with saucy sayings printed over the crotch, wild garlic and so forth. On market day, everyone comes into town and everyone stared, understandably I thought. Ettore walked lopsidedly leaning on my arm with one leg eight inches higher than the other. He had put on his top hat and tipped it as he passed the ladies. I stared straight ahead.

When we got to the farm, Mrs. Sparrow was sitting on a wooden bench which looked like it had been especially sculpted for her. The view from her house is one of the nicest in Tuscany with the hills and a castle in the distance but she sat with her back to it all. Her purse was on her lap, her hand was grasping a large paper bag and she stared straight ahead. To her left was, not as I expected just the ape, but to my astonishment beside it was a newish Mercedes with San Marino licence plates.

"Is Jack here?" I asked. Jack is the Sparrow's only son.

Looking at me as if I was possessed of two heads, she replied: "He and Elena arrived for the weekend but are still in bed".

"Do they know about Mr. Sparrow?"

I never particularly liked Jack — or his parents very much either if truth be known — but this seemed unbelievable. Jack and his wife were in bed blissfully unaware that their father languished with a stroke in hospital.

"Of course not, Albert, how would they know? I have not told them. Jack is a very important person in Milan with a head office in San Marino. He doesn't have time for minor matters like this glitch in his father's otherwise perfect health. He'll no doubt drive over to see Geoff, rather Mr. Sparrow, when I tell them after lunch. Shall we go now?"

"What happened to your car?" She looked somewhat askance at the van.

When I did not elaborate with more than a "it's a long story," she took up another line.

"And Albert, look at you in those gardening trousers and sports-like top. You'll frighten the nurses."

Ettore had jumped out at this point and balancing on his uneven feet between us we heaved Mrs. Sparrow up into the passenger seat. Actually from his height, Ettore was better positioned to heave from the rear at an upward angle.

If she was surprised at the dwarf, Mrs. Sparrow gave no indication. She spoke to him politely soliciting information about his business connections. When he replied "the circus," she went into raptures about the circus she had seen just a few days previous in Sansepolcro and the dear little dwarf in epaulettes and a top hat. She asked him if he was related to the dwarf.

I coughed and said, in English, that Ettore was the dear little dwarf in epaulettes and the top hat. It made her wax even more eloquently, in Italian of course, on dwarfs and circuses all the way to the *ospedale*.

She told Ettore to stop in front of the emergency.

"Albert, the gentleman and I will alight here and then you go park his van."

I helped them both out of the van and Ettore out of his orthopedic shoe, slipping on his other sandal. I was getting the hang of it. Ettore held Mrs. Sparrows arm. He basically nuzzled in and out of her broadside as they walked towards the emergency entrance. In and out he nuzzled as the electronic door opened for them.

Ettore had left the keys in the van and I managed to drive it, letting out the clutch with my left foot despite the temptation to try using my right foot and the gas paddle. I parked in the visitors' lot and headed to the emergency.

By the time I had reached Mr. Sparrow's room, she had put a table cloth on the bed-side table and was feeding Mr. Sparrow prunes. Ettore was sitting on the other side of the bed. There were several other women in the room feeding their husbands' collations which were a lot more appealing than prunes. I thought of my own brioche, cold and no doubt stale by now.

Once Mr. Sparrow had finished the prunes and before he could utter a word of welcome, she started again: "Albert and Signore Ettore". Then she paused for a few seconds.

She smiled at him and glowered at me. "We must get home at once so I can prepare Jack and that-wife-of-his a nice breakfast".

She put the empty prune jar into her bag.

"You know, Geoff" she continued while folding up the table cloth, "it really was a bit inconsiderate of you to time your stroke when you knew Jack and that-wife-of-his would be visiting".

Then in a voice just audible, she added "and a bit inconsiderate of Albert as well, if you ask me, to misplace his *telefonino* when he did".

Putting the cloth in the bag, she turned to go. Ettore jumped down from the bed and Mr. Sparrow waved rather winsomely as we left. He obviously didn't have any upper dorsal motor effects from the stroke but whether he had any speech impairment, I had no idea. I waved back.

By the time we got home, it was sunny and warm. As I opened the gate, to my horror, I found Sylvia in an improvised chaise lounge wearing extremely scanty shorts and what appeared to be her brassiere. I thought of the neighbours and how this would provide fodder for village gossip. I need not have worried. There were Maria Pia, Signora Agnèse and Signorina Celestina leaning out the window laughing and chatting away with Sylvia as if she were the daughter they never had. I went directly indoors when I heard Maria Pia say, "And who is this handsome man?" as they spied Ettore coming through the gate.

There in the kitchen, I saw my good plate, the one which had held the brioches, sitting in front of Bartolomeo, clean of any crumbs. Sadly, I sat down to watch my day which had seemed promising at one point — unbelievably, it seemed in retrospect — fade into apprehension and anxiety. I longed yet feared to know what was next. I wished for a concussion. I prayed, although not a praying man, to wake up.

Rousing myself, I unplugged my now restored *telefonino*, slipped on a shirt and a pair of decent trousers, grabbed my suit coat and set out for Piazza Popolo through the front door. It was only the second time I had ever used the front door. Everyone uses the garden door, even the Contessa herself, the Lady Laura. I peeked into the garden as I passed the gate hoping they would not see me go by but I need not have worried. Sylvia reclined but with her head turned upwards towards the neighbours' windows was too ensconced in conversation with Maria Pia, Signora Agnèse and Signorina Celestina to notice me slinking down the street. When I got to the square I paid for my *International Herald Tribune* and sat at my usual bar for a coffee.

* * * * *

I looked up from my paper at the sound of snickering, which stopped short-order when I looked up. A second time, when I looked up, the other men in the bar seemed to busy themselves stirring their coffee or gathering crumbs from the counter with their fingers. Maria Pia is a notorious gossip; I suspected word of the arrivals had circulated as quickly as — what my Father would have said — "a dose of salts". I refused to look up a third time. Eventually, I ordered a glass of wine from Gianni, to put off the inevitable trip up the hill to my house. As I sipped it slowly, the *telefonino* rang indicating a text and giving the incoming name as Zanchi. I pressed the appropriate series of buttons to read, "Lunch is ready! Sylvia".

"So her name is Zanchi," I thought, "unless her cellular is hot".

By the time I got up the hill, I found the meal on the table in the garden with my best china and linen. Maria Pia, Signora Agnèse and Signorina Celestina had all chirped in a "*buon appetito*". Sylvia held the chair for me. Ettore was already seated at the opposite end of the table, seated atop my telephone book, the yellow pages directory and three packages of computer paper; he had yet another damask cloth tucked under his chin evidently anxious to begin. Beside the table, I was somewhat surprised to note, was the beautiful Weimaraner. Once again, the dog took absolutely no interest in me or even notice of my arrival, or mercifully the dinner.

It certainly was a meal to remember, a full antipasti course, spaghetti with an amazing ragout sauce, and the thinnest and softest veal scaloppini I had ever eaten; I barely needed to chew. This was served with crisp grilled vegetables and a fresh green salad, all washed down with my favourite Chianti wine. Well, fair enough, she couldn't help spotting the wines in the kitchen. Sylvia had even prepared a dessert of tiny chocolate biscuits in a rich, slightly whipped cream. As I sipped my coffee, she slipped into the kitchen to get cold limoncello. Throughout the meal, Ettore had not spoken. Sylvia, naturally, had chatted non-stop about what I have no recollection. I concentrated on the food.

As I got up to tidy up the plates, Sylvia took my arm and led me to the entrance to my bedroom.

"You must have a *pisolino*, a nice nap. After the concussion, you can now sleep safely.

Well, the wine, limoncello and big meal dissuaded any internal force of opposition from raising a major objection. I dozed and then slept for about ninety minutes.

When I awoke, I found the house strangely silent. I, of course, live alone and the house is always quiet when I rest. There was a warm breeze coming through my window but even it seemed to breath stillness. There was a sense of emptiness, not a foreboding, but a feeling of darkness that comes at the end of a play when the curtain falls and the house lights have yet to come on. I washed my face and headed into the kitchen.

All was tidy and clean. The dishes were washed, not in the dishwasher, and stacked back in the china hutch. I opened the Frigidaire and found there were three little plastic Tupperware bowls with little labels on top reading "*cena*", my dinner for tonight and tomorrow. I walked through the house. The beds in the guest rooms had been stripped. I glanced out the window to see the sheets drying in the breeze.

On the dresser was a note with my name on the envelope. I opened it; it had not been sealed.

"We are off but will be back on Tuesday to take you to Città di Castello for your car. We hope you don't mind, but we have borrowed your cellular as I am unable to use mine anymore."

It was signed S. Panducci and E Ganovelli. So her name is Panducci, not Zanchi. I declined to consider the identity of this Zanchi person.

# The Weekend

The rest of the day passed quietly. I finished the leftovers Sylvia had put away for me in the *frigo*. Tomorrow was Saturday, I noted with satisfaction as I crawled into bed, a day I tend to use to shop, visit the cemetery, have a light supper and then play bridge in the evening. When I awakened it was a glorious morning. I took my first coffee into the garden and wandered about watering the scattered pots of *hortensia*, clematis, azaleas, pansies, as well as the dozens of pots of geraniums along the garden walls. The roses were not yet out and the nasturtium, marigolds and cosmos were not quite at the blooming stage. After a shower, I walked up to the shops, the usual routine of baker, butcher, greengrocer, newspaper shop and bar. There were no snickers as I drank my coffee; life, it appeared, had returned to what life had been.

The cemetery is situated well below the town. To reach it on foot, one follows the small Via Tomba down a winding, almost country-like lane. There are the stately Apennine hills in the distance hugging the blue sky. The serenity of this was shattered by the immediacy of the path with the red of the poppies' dots among the yellow of the broom plants. It is a peaceful walk and the one the funeral processions take. Don Ludovico walks in the front saying the rosary, followed by the hearse, followed by the people, young, old and every variety in between. I have walked this way as neighbour, friend, and in the early hours of grief. It is a path etched in my mind by habit and lately by the flowers of the changing seasons.

Saturdays, especially in the springtime, are the busy time at the cemetery. As Virgil would put it:

*Qualis apes aestate nova per florea rura / exercet sub sole labor.*[1]

It is a time for sprucing up the vases of flowers wilted over the previous week along the mausoleums and planting new pots on the graves. As I walked through the various "gardens", I noticed the same ladies who on a weekly basis, a few assisted by their husbands, fuss over the flowers and chatter among themselves. I had brought a pot of geraniums and paused partway through the cemetery, allowing the old feelings of regret and loneliness to reconcile themselves in the counterpoint of more pleasant recollections shaken into the reality of the moment.

I came down a series of steps, rounded the corner to the massive plot where our *tomba* was situated. To my utter surprise, I saw the *tomba* covered by flowers in vases, pots of plants, small urns of hanging blooms. My first reaction was that the undertaker had mistaken this *tomba* for one just implanted. But mine was a finished *tomba* and the freshly occupied must rest just as mounds of earth for a year. There was a young man busily arranging the flowers. I recognized him at once as the young chap who sells the flowers by the cemetery parking lot. Occasionally, I pick up flowers there; his name, I remembered, was Arturo.

He must have known from my expression, hardly one of gratitude, that I was not prepared for any of this. He pre-empted my questions.

"Maybe, Dottore, we need more lilies?"

I stood there spellbound before responding, "Arturo, I think that is your name, isn't it? I need to know. Who organized this floral extravaganza?"

"Piccolino and my mother arranged all of this." He smiled expecting, I suppose, some sort of joyous expression suddenly to illuminate my face. When my facial expression still just did not

1 Just as work busies the bees in the new summer through flowery fields under the sun, **Aeneid** 1.430–431.

respond, he continued to stammer, repeating his question "Maybe more lilies; what do you think"?

"Arturo, I think I need to know who your mother is."

"Oh, you know my mother is your great friend Sylvia Panducci. I am Arturo Panducci, Didn't you know my name is Panducci?"

"No, Arturo, I did not know your name is Panducci but I still don't understand why the flowers and how did your mother know about *our tomba*?"

"She told me that she and Piccolino have been staying with you. In fact, she called me on your *telefonino* this afternoon. I said I know you and sell you flowers for your *tomba*.

"'Well', she said, '*carissimo*, be creative, fill the *tomba* with lovely flowers and lots of lovely blooms for Dottore'. What do you think? Have I done a good job?"

What did I think? More to the point: what could I say? Out of the corner of my eye I spied Signorina Celestina waving and giving the thumbs-up sign from her parents' mausoleum across the *tomba*. Could Signora Agnèse and Maria Pia be far behind?

"Such a nice boy!" I turned and Maria Pia stood beaming at Arturo.

"I hope," she changed her expression and the tone of her voice, "that you have paid this boy well".

A considerable number of euro poorer, I headed back up the hill into town, still carrying the pot of geraniums. I was frankly numb. Even the dead seemed to connive with these people.

* * * * *

I play bridge each Saturday with three friends. We tend to switch languages, often using French. The aim is that no one speaks a first language; everyone must speak a second. And we meet at each other's houses. Don Ludovico, the parish priest, picked me up. He had telephoned to offer me a lift; it seems the whole town knew my car was in Città. I prefer not to drive with Ludovico, who smokes cigars and is fat. It was, however, Laura's turn to host us, which is too much into the countryside for me to go on foot. The car has a lived-in smell: stale and large-bodied. With my car somewhere in Città, I had no choice. He was already driving Laszlo, a Hungarian writer who has lived in the town since refusing to return to his native country after the war. I did not give either of them any additional details, just that my car was at the shop.

Laura spends the winters in town and the summers out at the Castello di Guelfi, which is not a castle but more of a large, fortified thirteenth-century manor house. Laura is English and came to Italy in the late 1950s as an au pair to the Count Clemente Guelphi. The rest is history straight out of *The Sound of Music*. Laura and Clemente were the funniest couple and much loved. He died about five or six years ago at a great age and she has carried on in the castle. Her general factotum, Riccardo, now well into his sixties himself, organizes the agricultural activity and drives her about in an ancient Daimler that she had shipped over from the UK when her father died around forty-odd years ago. Her children now both live in America; Clemente's son, Giorgio, works in Rome, rarely visiting, so she is quite alone most of the time, except when her brother Cosmo, a former bishop of Sodor and Man, comes over — or "out" as he would say — for several months each year.

A bridge night at Laura's is always a lengthy affair; she insists on serving a late supper despite the fact that she and Riccardo must set out early Sunday morning. Laura is a pillar of the American Episcopal Church in Florence. Unlike the Sparrows, she now refuses to walk over the Arno to the English church. For many years, Riccardo drove her directly to the English church. Age for both of them meant an eventual compromise, the train to Florence and the American church. What the Americans make of her with her English mannerisms and the Contessa rôle playing, I have no idea. Still, she has been a pillar there for many years.

Riccardo now drives them both in the Daimler to that same tarnished station in Arezzo, they climb on board, with Riccardo helping her off at Florence's Santa Maria Novella station and escorting her to the church which is quite close to the station. After the service, he meets her on the nearby piazza and back they go. On the homeward train, Laura takes out sandwiches and an ancient thermos of what, I recently learned when I happened to be on the same train which originates in Bologna, actually contains wine. Week in week out, they follow the same pattern. What Riccardo does while she is at church I have no idea and probably neither does she.

Actually, I have known both Laura and Cosmos for over forty years. I first came to the Valtiberina in the spring of 1967, travelling with a brother and sister, friends from university. Clemente and Laura had been married seven or eight years at that time. They had two small children who, although quite young, were my friends' first cousins, Laura being their aunt. We had been invited to make a summer house party. Ludovico, a young seminarian at the time, and cousin of Clemente was home for the summer and also staying with them. Sometime later when I needed to get away to begin a new life, Laura helped me get started again in Italy. Laura and Ludovico both took me under their wings. They along with Laszlo are my closest friends.

All went smoothly until the second rubber when Laura said quite unexpectedly as she folded her cards, "I hear you are seeing a big bosomed lady, one no-trump".

Ludovico replied, "Well I hear something decidedly kinky is going on these days down on via Misericordia, two spades".

To which Laszlo added: "very nice veal scaloppini is what I'm told, no bid".

"Four hearts", I spoke rather crossly as they all went into uproarious fits of giggles.

"Hearts can be broken," whispered Laura and doubled my bid.

It ended in a difficult contract, which I am pleased to write I made with an over-trick, and nothing more was said on the matter of bosoms or veal scaloppini. In fact, nothing more was said about my recent adventure at all not even when I got out of the car.

"Until tomorrow," was all Ludovico said as if with a premonition.

* * * * *

I did not sleep well that night. I was beginning to grow anxious once again about this whole business with these people who seemed to be circus people on the one hand and not-really-circus-people on the other. I rolled out of bed a little before eight. Sunday is my one morning to indulge in a bit of an Anglo-Northern-Europe breakfast: eggs, *pancetta affunicata*, toast, marmalade and French-pressed coffee. I put on a CD and enjoyed lounging about in my dressing gown. About ten, I realized I had to get going so showered and shaved a bit faster than usual; in fact, I nicked my chin.

Preoccupied with rushing, stopping the bleeding on my chin, grabbing my hat and shutting the door, I didn't notice that the chairs in the garden had been moved. This time fully clothed, I am relieved to write, sat Sylvia.

"I figured you would be heading off to Mass. You strike me as the kind of man who goes to church. Ettore dropped me off on his way to the *Sala del Regno* for the *Testimoni* in Sansepolcro; he never misses. Since we are all going off to Sunday lunch, I thought I would go to Mass with you. Arturo is paying for lunch, incidentally. It seems he made a killing, so to speak, selling flowers yesterday at the cemetery."

She was chuckling at her own joke when the church bells started to ring.

"Oh dear, you have cut yourself shaving; it's bleeding."

She produced a tissue from her purse and applied it to my chin. "Now, press hard and the blood will stop. Let's get along and don't stop pressing."

She took my left arm and kicked open the gate while I pressed the tissue to the wound with my right.

When I say she was clothed, I mean she was not wearing the shorts with the brassiere-like halter thing. Even though it was Sunday and we were on our way to Mass, I don't think that she was even wearing a brassiere, given the way we swayed along the street. Her skirt was quite short but she did have on hose, sort of black lacy ones. The shoes were higher than Ettore's orthopedic one, causing me to speculate how they could ever manage along together with the three elevated shoes. One doesn't like to be critical; I mean she didn't look half bad, not really mutton dressed up as lamb, just a bit blowsy for my taste. Thus, we continued along, she holding my arm and I pressing the tissue to my chin.

I might have anticipated some sort of a reception when I spied Maria Pia, Signora Agnèse and Signorina Celestina going into the church. Celestina is what might be termed "a pillar of the church". When she is not leaning out her window staring at me, or arranging flowers at her parents' mausoleum, she is certain to be found at the church. But in the years since I moved into town and started to attend the *Prepositura*, the big parish church, I have never seen either of the other two darken the church doors.

As we entered, Sylvia reached into her purse and pulled out a black lace mantilla. I have not seen anyone wear a mantilla for over thirty years, except in the movies. The church was packed. Horrors of horrors, Sylvia marched us up to the front row. I could feel my neck kink and stiffen in sympathy with all the heads turning in unison as we passed up the aisle.

"Onward to the Protestant Episcopal and sandwiches with Laura on the train next Sunday," I silently vowed.

The service seemed interminable. When it came to the singing, Sylvia's contralto voice dominated above the congregation, "*Benedetto colui che viene nel nome del Signore*".

I wanted to slip between the pews and sneak out on all fours. I don't take Communion, but Sylvia was first up, almost knocking over several holy ladies, what Barbara Pym would describe as "excellent women". And she was first to walk out, firmly holding me, actually dragging me by the arm. We had, as it appeared, made a statement.

What that statement was, I have no idea, but a statement of some sort it was indeed.

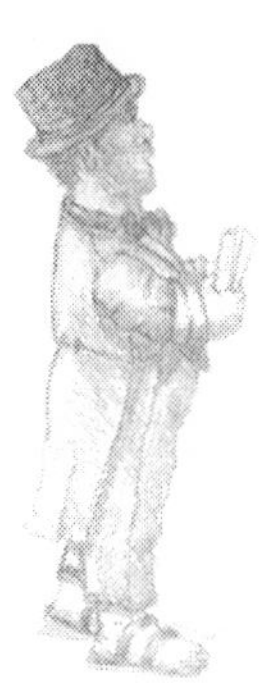

# Caprese Michelangelo

As we went out of the church we were accosted almost immediately by Laszlo dressed in a green linen jacket with a rose in his lapel. He bowed as he took Sylvia's hand, pressing it to his lips.

"Such a delight to meet such a charming lady! I have heard so much about you."

"Laszlo?" I gaped at him. "And just what have you heard?"

When Laszlo's wife was alive, we would have Sunday lunch together once or twice a month. Since her death, we tend to have the lunch on the first Sunday of the month. This was the third.

Laszlo continued, "I was delighted, Alberto, to receive your text message inviting me to lunch with you and the lovely Signora Sylvia, or is it Signorina"?

This was totally out of character for Lazlo.

I started to speak, "And how did he receive a text from my *telefonino*, when . . .". I did not need to complete the sentence.

Before anyone else could speak, the white van wheeled into the piazza. Normally people disperse quickly after church, but today I noticed almost everyone was still there chatting in groups of two or three. Ettore was driving with Arturo beside him with a young woman sharing his seat. Ettore was dressed all in white, looking like he had just made his first Communion rather than returning from the *Sala del Regno* of the *Testimoni*. Arturo was dressed in an open-necked shirt with a silk scarf, the sacrosanct blue jeans and sunglasses.

"Hop in, everyone, we seem to be missing just one person."

I heard the squeal of the missing person approaching. It was not necessary to turn to know that the one missing was none other than Maria Pia. She fawned with "*grazie, grazie, grazie*" to everyone except me, the one actually helping her to step up. With all of us seated inside or, more precisely, on top of each other, Ettore released his foot from the clutch while carefully pushing down on the gas with the paddle. We tore off out of the piazza in a large puff of exhaust, no doubt a fitting climax for the staring villagers' successful morning-out-to-Mass.

"Hey, Piccolino," Arturo was the first to speak, "you need to service this van. Get your cousin over in Città do it for you, the one who is doing Alberto's body work. Maybe Alberto will loan you his car to make up for you driving him around all week."

"We like it the way it is," replied Sylvia.

"Nobody notices us," she turned to smile at everyone, "then when we arrive somewhere we are more or less incognito".

I swallowed a snort and retort, while simultaneously digesting the Alberto-loaning-out-his-car quip.

Sylvia who had not noticed my consternation, continued, "Ettore being in the entertainment business, we like to be unrecognized sometimes".

"I think it's a lovely van and Signor Ettore, if I might add, you handle the wheel extremely well." Maria Pia was half-sitting on me and must have felt my swallowed snort; she shot me a dirty look.

The restaurant was near Caprese Michelangelo, a small, rather alpine sort of town. Its claim to fame as the birthplace of Michelangelo is only outshone by its reputation for seventeen-course Sunday lunches. Ettore stopped abruptly sending everyone careening on to the backs of the front seats. Being in the middle, I lurched forward between the two front seats and whacked my head on the clutch. This time I actually believed I might have incurred a concussion.

"Let's hop to it; our reservation is for one o'clock. The others will already be here." Sylvia was three strides ahead of us.

At the door we were greeted by a rather distinguished-looking gentleman who immediately stooped over to kiss Ettore on both cheeks. Sylvia introduced him as Ettore's cousin Mario and me as their devoted friend of long-standing.

"*Piacere*." I shook his hand.

On his left hand, Mario wore a blindingly large, yellow stone ring which I suspected was a zircon. He was dressed in a casual, linen, open-necked shirt, over which he wore a loose black waistcoat. His hair was slicked down but not in the greasy way, and there was a slight whiff of what I recognized as Chanel's Antaeus. I won a bottle once at a street lottery in Bologna so recognized it at once. Everything about Mario bespoke a certain elegance absent from the rest of his kin I had thus far met.

Mario led us to a large table with a stunning view overlooking several valleys. There were a number of people already seated, all of whom gasped and then gushed over Ettore. Sylvia made the introductions, first of her son, whom they all seemed to know already, and his girlfriend Chiara, towards whom they all seemed totally indifferent. Laszlo and Maria Pia were presented as special new friends. I came last as "our devoted friend of long-standing and our benefactor".

Laszlo, as if on cue, spoke for us all, "So happy to meet friends of our dear Sylvia and Signor Ettore".

Our dear Sylvia! Benefactor!

I was beginning to feel the need to visit what my Father called "the gentlemen's cloak room". Instead, I was taken, rather roughly, by Sylvia around the table to meet the others. An enormous woman sat at the end. Such was her girth, I could not help but wonder if she might have a once been Ettore's colleague rescued from the circus sideshow. She was undoubtedly the heaviest woman I had ever met. Her name was Tiziana, a name I thought more appropriate for "our dear Sylvia".

Tiziana was wearing a red dress, sort of a Mau Mau (or is it moo moo). Frankly, I don't know a lot about women's clothing, and have on occasion been known to mix up the term for the clothing worn by the morbidly obese and the Kikuyu uprising in Kenya. Let it suffice to say that it was a large, meant-to-be-loose, flowing garment.

Tiziana did no more than touch my hand and smile, showing a full set of perfect teeth held in place by some dental glue. She then handed my hand to that of the man on her left. He was introduced as Dottore. Next to him was a petite woman I took to be his wife, named Lucia. Neither Dottore nor Lucia was to speak through the entire meal. It was only once the meal was well underway that Sylvia explained that the couple were deaf-mutes and it was he, Dottor Sergio Granducca, who had found my *telefonino* in Arezzo and dropped it at his local *Questura* in Città di Castello. Until then, I just assumed they were shy or reserved.

We took our seats around the table, with Arturo and Chiara across from the deaf couple and Maria Pia and Laszlo next to them and across from me and Sylvia. Laszlo rather gallantly assisted Maria Pia, who whimpered something as he pushed in her chair. Whimpering seemed so out of character. I was wondering what was happening to everyone around me.

Ettore climbed up to his chair at the end the table. Mario had prepared it with several cushions and books on the seat. Before we started the meal, Ettore spoke with bowed head, "As we approach Armageddon, let us consume this meal humbly as if it were our last".

Cheery thoughts. I was beginning to feel my Armageddon was closer than I thought.

"Now Piccolono Piccolino, my dear little cousin," Tiziana, yet another cousin, it seemed, spoke for the first time. "We are all Catholics here. I respect your *Testimoni* beliefs but let's try to put on a positive and happy spin for these foreign gentlemen — *stranieri* — who may be Mohammedans for all I know."

The thought of Laszlo and me wearing fezzes and facing Mecca several times a day suddenly gave me the giggles. I reached for the *frizzante* water, feigning hiccoughs. I was beginning to enjoy the occasion.

The courses arrived in sequence while the wine flowed. Antipasti: crostini, salamis, prosciutto, three different pastas. We were just staring the mixed grill when Laszlo asked what, on the surface, was an innocuous question, "Signor Ettore, when are you returning to your, how shall I call it, profession"?

Ettore put down his fork, almost composing himself before replying, "The circus has moved on to Todi but we will not be going with the others. I have resigned my post as a matter of ethics."

"Oh, my!" Maria Pia exclaimed clapping her hands. "Bravo! I have harboured for some time ethical concerns about the circus. The welfare of those animals is often on my mind."

Ettore looked at her as though she had flown in from some distant planet. He had that who-invited-you look on his face.

"Signora, I have never been associated with any organization such as a circus that does not treat its performers, two-legged or four-legged, reptile or mammal, male or female, with utmost respect and dignity."

Maria Pia's head dropped. Even I felt for her. I noticed, however, that Laszlo's patting of her hand was eliciting a weak smile from her thin lips.

"I meant," Ettore continued, "that I had differences with the management on personal ethical matters".

He means," Arturo piped up, "ethics related to sticky fingers and the loss of a wad of hundred euro notes".

Sylvia piped up at once, "You know nothing about it, Arturo. I don't know how you can say such things, especially in front of our friends and our benefactor". All the while she continued to pat my hand. This hand patting was, in my opinion, really getting out of control.

Ettore spoke again, "I will handle this, Sylvia". He looked first at Maria Pia and Laszlo and then at me, "My family know me". He paused to take a drink of water.

"My family," he nodded at Tiziana. "And," he continued, "Dottore and Lucia can't hear us anyway. Some vile rumours circulated, no doubt started by that bitch on the high wire, Vera. You will excuse such language." He nodded to Maria Pia.

Quite taken aback for a second time, Maria Pia responded weakly, "Of course, Signore, such, I am certain, unwarranted, dreadful aspersions. Your vexations must not be thwarted."

Aspersions, vexations, thwarted? Wherever did Maria Pia pick up such a vocabulary? I couldn't help myself. "God help us!" I blurted it out in English. Not that anyone at this point was paying attention to me.

Maria Pia had obviously redeemed herself for the animal-welfare remarks. Ettore smiled at her before continuing.

"I have not always had the easiest of lives, as my dear cousin Tiziana can attest. As an adolescent, I was sent away to a special place in Rome, the Regina Coeli. There, among boys of a different background and men of especially low character, I was exposed to many deviant forms of behaviour that no Catholic boy would willingly enter into. The men capitalized upon my stature, teaching me to act out scenarios that were completely against my nature. My height, they claimed, was perfect for performing certain actions. I could walk straight into a man at the perfect height."

This was all getting "a bit close to the knuckle", as my late Father would have said. As far as I was concerned, I wanted to hear no more about walking into men or anything else for that matter. I noticed that Maria Pia was also hoping for fewer details whereas Chiara, from the smile on her face, was obviously hoping for more.

"I was taught," Ettore continued, "to grasp a man in his midregions". There was an audible gasp, except from the deaf Dottore and his wife, who both smiled benignly. I was about to say that there were ladies present, when Ettore quite succinctly and candidly explained.

"I was the perfect height to go into a man's pockets to relieve him of his valuables."

"All this," I sighed out loud in relief, "only to explain that you had been taught the trade of a pickpocket".

Chiara looked disappointed and Maria Pia seemed relieved — indeed almost happy — that Ettore had only been trained as a thief.

All I could add was, “Well, isn’t that a bugger!” another one of my late Father’s favourite expressions.

After pausing for dramatic effect, Ettore continued, “A thief I was; this I sadly admit but that was in my youth. Since joining the *Testimoni* I have led a life incorruptible. But, I do retain an artist’s interest in my former craft and love to reach into a pocket always, and I emphasize always, to return the item almost at once. It is a mere game. Unfortunately, that vile woman Vera on the tightrope was looking down and saw me place my hand in a gentleman’s pocket. The man had been staring up intently as she was twirling, doing mid-air splits while simultaneously ogling the patrons. Vera screamed down to the man to watch but before I could replace the *telefonino* I had taken, I was caught red-handed.

The patron believed me when I said it was all part of an act. No amount of explanation, however, would suffice with the manager of the circus. He put me on probation. I felt as a matter of principle and in defence of my high personal ethical standards that I must resign.”

“Rightly so!” shrieked Maria Pia, who began to clap her hands.

There was a great heaving of the table. I felt that our meat course was about to slide down the table. Everyone grabbed his wine glass as Tizania began to rise, lifting herself by pressing both hands on the table. Eventually on her feet, she raised her wine glass.

“To my dear *piccolo piccolino*, *cugino*, *bambino*, an honest man, the jewel of our family.”

She collapsed back into her chair and I swear the building shook. The restaurant went silent; people were staring in disbelief as Tizania’s waves of flesh settled to a ripple.

I then heard, as I expect others did as well, Arturo murmur sotto voce, “That doesn’t explain the roll of hundred-euro”.

Ever quick to the mark, Sylvia beamed at us all, “The mixed grill is cooling”.

I found it difficult to concentrate on the rest of the meal: salads, dessert, vin santo with *cantucci* to dip into it and, of course, coffee. The thought of Ettore’s pickpocket activities and Arturo’s accusation, albeit unkindly mentioned, were disturbing revelations to say the least. I could not help but remember the roll of one hundred euro notes Ettore had passed to Maurizio the mechanic. I did not speak for the rest of the meal, seemingly as mute as Dottore and Lucia.

Just before Mario arrived with the cheque, Ettore once again spoke to the table, "How fortunate we all are to have our dear friend and benefactor with us who so graciously will accept the bill on our behalf".

There was instantaneous applause even from Dottore and Lucia, which made me think that perhaps they lip-read and had understood more than we thought. I too started to clap thinking the reference was to young Arturo but he was on his feet clapping. And the table almost really did collapse this time as Tiziana rose which got everyone busy up-righting spilled wine, water and vin santo glasses.

As I tucked the Visa receipt into my billfold, I reminded Sylvia of my understanding about Arturo's offer to pay for lunch. She smiled and patted my hand. This hand patting was getting on my nerves. Laszlo and Maria Pia had been doing it non-stop for the last three courses.

"He did offer, the darling, yesterday afternoon when we spoke and such was my understanding until we arrived. Last night, he and Chiara went out with friends. You know how the young are with money."

Everyone was now standing and heading to the cars. As Sylvia and I walked arm in arm to the car, Laszlo caught up with me.

"You are a dark horse," he said. I must have looked baffled as he proceeded to explain, "Maria Pia, your housekeeper. She is charm itself; no wonder you have kept her under wraps."

"I do not keep her anywhere, wrapped or unwrapped. She is not my housekeeper; she cleans once a week. I try to avoid her and her harpy friends as much as possible but she leans over my garden so much of the day she might as well be a live-in domestic."

It was all I could manage to answer. I was also venting my anger at being stiffed with the cheque.

"You protest too quickly, my friend. There is an English expression, I believe, he smirked, 'A nod is as good as a wink to a blind man'".

"Wherever did you learn such expressions, Laszlo? You barely speak the language but I'll teach you another: when it comes to Maria Pia you are 'flying by the seat of your pants'".

Blind man! The deaf! I realized that I had neglected to thank the Dottore for finding my *telefonino*. I turned back but he and his wife had gone out another door and were driving their car down the hill before I could catch up with them. How Tiziana was getting home, I had no idea. I dreaded the thought of her squeezing into the van. She somehow managed to disappear and I did not enquire further.

Too much food probably accounted for the lack of conversation on the drive back. As I headed home on foot across the piazza, Sylvia's words echoed in my head and I expect across the empty square.

"Until tomorrow, Alberto, dear friend and benefactor," she finally let go of my hand, "we have such a busy week ahead".

# San Leo Tiberino

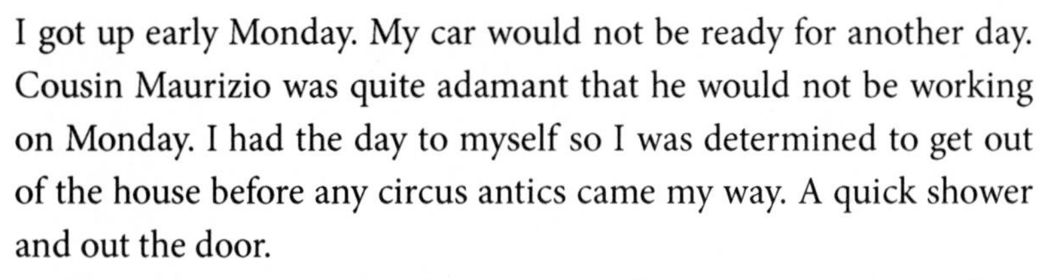

I got up early Monday. My car would not be ready for another day. Cousin Maurizio was quite adamant that he would not be working on Monday. I had the day to myself so I was determined to get out of the house before any circus antics came my way. A quick shower and out the door.

The main piazza was quite quiet, mostly workers stopping off for a quick coffee. I picked up my newspaper and went to my usual bar and ordered from Gianni a *cornetto* with my coffee as a *colazione*. It was peaceful. No academics to bother me and no dwarfs with buxom redheads.

I was startled from my newspaper to see Don Ludovico standing there holding two cups of coffee. I motioned for him to have a seat.

"So you certainly have caused a stir," he was grinning, "indeed I have not seen so many people at church since Easter. Our own local Casanova. And I have heard it said that you are now running a palace of sex and torture."

His face had turned quite somber. "I suppose as your pastor, I ought to be admonishing you".

I began to protest but he held his palms up as his laughter filled the piazza.

"No! No! *Carissimo*, no! I am teasing you. I understand your predicament. But you have lived here for forty years; forty unblemished years. The town has been through a lot with you. I don't think there has been a person who has not shared in your personal tragedy. Just accept that you have brought us a bit of excitement. Alberto, our mild-mannered *straniero*, our import from the outer world, has brought us notoriety, sexual impropriety, at long last, like we always knew he would."

His good-natured humour started to ease my tension. He continued, "It is all too Fellini: dwarfs, hysterical spinsters, buxom red-headed women, theft and intrigue, cemetery flower-peddlers, fat ladies, mutes. Believe me, we've heard it all. Spies are posted on every corner."

He laughed even harder and I managed a sly sort of grin, "Well, when you put it that way".

I had never imagined myself connected with any sort of personal sexual notoriety. When I came to Italy, I left behind my earlier life, scorched by the flames of other people's scandals not my own. We had sought anonymity here; instead of just plain anonymity, we received more of a sanctuary. Notoriety may have eventually followed me even here to San Leo Tiberino but not my notoriety of my own making.

"Of course," he continued, "Laura is a bit more circumspect and has been worried about you. You are her local family. With her children gone abroad and Cosmo only here for short periods, you are central to her life. She and I are the only ones who know your history and the circumstances which brought you here, and have shared your confidence for over forty years. So she telephoned me last night and put me to work."

I really did not know what to say so let him continue.

"Tuscany is Tuscany and Umbria is Umbria and never the twain shall meet. No one here knows anything about Ettore. They may have seen him at the circus but he comes from Città, which is in Umbria and only twenty-five kilometres away but might as well be Naples. I do, nonetheless, have an old friend who is a retired doctor in Città. I telephoned him and he knew the family.

"Ettore's family name is Ganovelli, but I expect you have learned at least that by now. He comes from a large family none other of whom seems to suffer from achondroplasia. It could have been caused by other factors. And this is what is interesting: Ettore's mother was not Italian. According to Luigi, there was little discussion or reference made of her by any of the family — some veil of mystery. His father returned alone from Sicily where he had been for many years. His wife had died there and he returned with the boy Ettore who spoke only English. So Ettore lived alone with his father who himself was one of eight boys. Ettore although motherless and an only child had lots of cousins in this large extended family."

"I think I have met them all."

"Oh no, I doubt that; lots more, I am sure of that." Ludovico was enjoying all this. "They are a pretty rough bunch, yet surprisingly, some of them have done quite well; a few of the more successful ones have moved away, even out of the country. Ettore was a popular boy at school; his dwarfism didn't make him at all shy. Luigi, my friend, said that they lost track of him when he was finishing his adolescence; dropped out of sight for three or four years."

"Regina Coeli in Rome," I started to speculate but not for long. I heard a cough behind me. It was Mrs. Sparrow.

"Good morning, Don Ludovico, Albert. She nodded at each of us. "I want to thank you belatedly, Albert, for the luncheon invitation. Geoff, Mr. Sparrow, and I would have loved to attend. He was discharged from the *ospedale*; it seems it was only gas. Oh, I beg your pardon, Don Ludovico."

Her sense of propriety made Ludovico add another packet of sugar and stir his coffee with gusto.

"We got the message today, not Saturday. For the life of me, I cannot understand what is getting into you, Albert, sending us a text. We always phone each other. It is generational; we do not text invitations. So, we were unable to attend what might have proven to be an interesting outing in Caprese Michelangelo especially for Geoff, Mr. Sparrow, after his ordeal.

"Although," she continued without pausing for a response, "I belatedly again say thank-you, Albert, albeit from what I hear, you have certainly lost any sense of propriety. Whatever is coming over you? Well, we all have an idea about that, I'm sure."

She walked away without an *arrivederla*, adieu, or by your leave to either of us.

Ludovico continued as though Mrs. Sparrow had been but a passing phantom, like Mr. Sparrow's gas, "You were saying, Albert, about Regina Coeli. That might just fit. Luigi said there had been some sort of trouble. But then about twenty years ago, Ettore joined the circus or a series of circuses, pretty much travelling around the country but turning up in Città every once and a while. He has been associated with the woman, named Sylvia for a couple of years. No one, however, seems to know much about her, except she has a *Napolitano* inflection in her voice. Her son works here for the florists on the square, Roberto and Mirela. I visited them to see if I could find out anything. I had to be a bit circumspect. It cost me eleven euro to have flowers sent to Laura."

I couldn't resist the temptation, "Miss Marple in a cassock. G.K. Chesterton breathes new life: Don Ludovico Brown will be sticking his camera out from hedges or bugging the font, or better the confessional, before we know it."

"Do you want that I should continue or not?" Ludovico made as if to get up.

I knew that to say nothing and let him go would greatly offend him so I nodded weakly, "Proceed".

Nothing succeeds like a procession to the confessional.

"It seems the woman's son, Arturo I believe he is called, has worked for the florists for a couple of years. I have encountered him a few times at funerals; he seems pleasant enough. Anyway, Mirela was in the shop this morning and she sings his praises. He is quite creative, a good floral arranger, and respectful with the cemetery crowd. Once Mirela gets going, there is no stopping her.

"She mentioned his mother; I don't think our Mirela quite approves of Arturo's *mamma*.

Well, in the first lace, it doesn't help that Sylvia is a Nepolitana, somewhat even lower than Umbrians around here. Mirela can convey a lot just by innuendo. But she was quite clear on one thing:

she referred to this woman as having her claws into you. Now don't get upset."

He finished his coffee.

"The boy was in the Valtiberina first. He said his mother travelled a lot for her work. No mention of the circus or Ettore. Mirela's only complaint is that his girlfriend, Chiara Ventura, hangs around too much in her shorts and bare midriff which Mirela feels are not suited to the funeral business. She also confided that Chiara's parents are not enthralled with the budding romance."

He placed the cup and spoon on the paper napkin.

"So all in all, nothing to suggest any espionage. I do not want to impute sinister motives where no such motives appear to exist. You may, therefore, proceed with your romance with the church's blessing."

Ludovico is a bit rotund; I thought he would convulse off the chair.

"You are not making any of this easier," I almost moaned. "They have taken my *telefonino*. I am not certain where my car is in Città. One of the myriad of cousins has it. Plus, they refer to me as 'their friend and benefactor'. They just take over. Ludovico, I must be getting old. Could we talk about something else? Why not start your investigation of the budding relationship between Laszlo and Maria Pia?"

That started the convulsions again. "I love my job," he gasped.

That night as I lay in bed, the thought of the upcoming day did not enthral me. I felt my life was slipping out of my control. My grasp on reality must be eroding. On the other hand, the whole business was turning into an adventure over which surely I could exercise some control through some effort of will. Surely.

# Sansepolcro

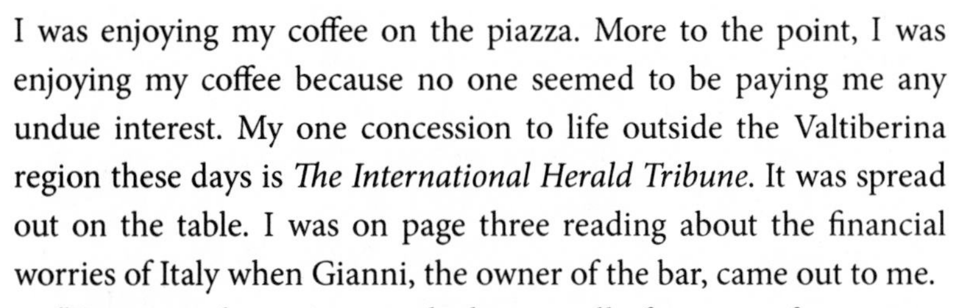

I was enjoying my coffee on the piazza. More to the point, I was enjoying my coffee because no one seemed to be paying me any undue interest. My one concession to life outside the Valtiberina region these days is *The International Herald Tribune*. It was spread out on the table. I was on page three reading about the financial worries of Italy when Gianni, the owner of the bar, came out to me.

"Dottore, there is a telephone call for you from your own *cellulario*."

The calm of the morning dissipated as I walked inside.

"*Pronto*."

"Maurithio," he lisped.

"Oh, Maurizio," I replied. "I was hoping you would ring. My neighbour here will drive me over to pick up my car."

My heart sank as he told me that my car was already en route to me, driven by Arturo and Sylvia with Ettore following behind. He suggested that I go home and prepare some coffee. I could hear Sylvia in the background shouting to be sure to pick up some brioche from Gianni.

How did she know about Gianni? One could almost believe that the world was conspiring against me.

I gathered up my newspaper, asked Gianni to pack me some brioche and cornetti before heading up the hill. I sat in the garden waiting. A half hour later, they poured in through the gate. I was quiet but the three sisters from Macbeth cackled out their welcomes. Sylvia said she would make the coffee and in she went.

Ettore was carrying a large duffle bag, which he opened to take out four large pins which he started to juggle. Arturo was doing push-ups down by my roses as Sylvia came out carrying a large tray of coffees and brioches and cornetti.

The three-ring circus had come to town; all we needed was the tent.

At that point, the cellulario rang in Ettore's pocket. Recognizing my ring, I said, I realize now in retrospect, more than gruffly than was warranted, "*Piccolino*, please hand me my *telefonino* at once".

Ettore let the pins drop and spoke directly to me for what was probably only the third time since I had known him.

"Have you any idea how offensive that term is?"

He was speaking in perfect English.

"How would you like it if I called you beaky, slack arse, baldy or some other reference to your ugly aged physique? Sure, my friends and my cousins call me *Piccolino* but they care about me. From you, the word is an insult."

I was taken aback and could only utter, "You are speaking English".

"My Mother's English. Isn't she? But you probably know that I am only half Italian."

I couldn't really answer that. Through all this, the *telefonino* continued ringing. Ettore continued,

"For me English is the language of deceit and abandonment. My mother sends me a birthday card every year. She has never missed since I last saw her at the age of seven. And she writes 'Happy Birthday from Jean.' I think 'Happy Birthday from Jean'— not even 'Mother' — is such a lovely English phrase that it rates as abandonment."

He pointed at me, "And you Dottore, represent the English deceit in two ways".

I was unable to reply.

"One," He held up his small finger.

"You are sneaky in your deceit. Telephoning Dottore Luigi to check up on me. Luigi is not the most discrete. When he hung up, he told his cleaning woman, Loredona, who was dusting in his study, that questions were being asked by a gentleman in your town about me. In addition to not being discrete, he is very old and forgetful. He has forgotten that Loredona is my cousin. She had heard him saying not very complimentary things about me and my family background. If you want to know about me, why not ask me face to face like a man. I have already told you about my time in Regina Coeli and what it's like to be a little person there. But then you don't think of me, the dwarf, as a man. I am just a part of your circus fantasy."

I stood up but before I could speak, he went on.

"Two," he held up one finger on each hand, "you are trying to take my girl away. I love Sylvia. All my life, I have dreamed of a beautiful girlfriend and you think you can have her with your fancy linens, your cheap sarcasm spoken in English which you think no one understands, and your tall, slack arse body."

He started to cry and slammed my *telefonino* on the table in front of me.

I went to go around to him but tripped over the duffle bag. I heard my shoulder crack as I landed on the terracotta terrace. The last thing I remembered was the sound of breaking china as Sylvia dropped the tray and Maria Pia shouting "*Madonna alla bicyclette*".

* * * * *

The *ospedale* in Sansepolcro is old, the legacy of a bequest from a local girl, from our village actually, known affectionately as the Leonessa da San Leo. The Lionessa left our village and went on to become the madam of a large whorehouse in Vatican City. The *ospedale* has large wards occupied by four patients at a time. Despite the four patients per ward, there is lots of room and about five metres between the beds. The wards also have large terrace windows which actually open.

Several days later, I was propped up on my pillows in the same bed Mr. Sparrow had occupied. The surgeons had operated and placed a pin in the shoulder somewhere. But, as they put it, "The bones were finished, the operation was really cosmetic".

"Very sad," was all the chief medical examiner said by way of diagnosis and I didn't pose a single question.

There were two large bouquets of lilacs beside my bed by the windows which Laura had brought, well, more accurately Riccardo had carried, walking two paces behind Laura. The Sparrows, Laszlo with Maria Pia and her two weird sisters, Ludovico, plus half the town had driven over to the *ospedale.*

But at this point, Ettore was sitting on my bed, reading my *International Herald Tribune* that Gianni from the bar had brought over. My French teacher, Madame St-Jacques, had brought me some grapes which I was eating and enjoying. Arturo and Chiara were sharing my other fruit which did not tempt me.

Sylvia was chatting away, "They said you can go home in an hour. Ettore will drive and Arturo can carry these lilacs, no point in wasting them."

"Leave them for the others," I replied. "We have lilacs in the garden. Maria Pia has already complained that they were making her sneeze."

I was holding Ettore's hat, twirling it before putting it on my lap.

Sylvia went on, almost without pausing to hear my replies, "I have the meat for dinner slowly cooking. Maria Pia said she would go in and check. All the things you like."

She patted my hand.

"I am even managing to make pastry on your granite counter."

I was getting used to the hand patting. Everyone who visited had done the patting.

# Under the Small Tent, Then the Bigger Tent and Finally the Even-Bigger Tent

This summer has proven to be the happiest I remember since the lazy hot summer of my first visit to Italy with Laura and Cosmo and all the family some forty-five years ago. My shoulder did not heal; my health has generally declined. Most days, I sit in the garden with papers, journalistic and personal, strewn about. Arturo has been amazingly attentive, helping me to walk out, arranging pillows, even designing a wooden device that helped me to hold the cards for bridge.

Since mid-May, Arturo has occupied the small bedroom at the top of the house. What he did with it by way of decoration, I have no idea. I could no more manage the steps than ascend bodily to the moon. True to form for me, I suppose, I drew the line when it came to Chiara. Old habits, like prejudices, die hard. Perhaps, I dreaded the thought of her parents suddenly arriving at the garden gate. In any event, she was not allowed up beyond the ground floor. Not that it mattered much as by late May, Chiara was, as my Father would delicately have put it, "in the family way". Or, when I think of it, he might well have used a more earthy expression if my Mother was not around.

I guess some might call me hypocritical, but I was not so prudish when it came to his *mamma*. Sylvia and Ettore occupied what had long been my guest bedroom and bath. The room opposite remained closed and locked as it has been, unbelievable now to fathom, for several years. Time passes quickly; memories and associations fade more slowly. Some doors figuratively and literally remain locked. In any event, Ludovico must have fessed up that it was he who had telephoned Dottore Luigi. Ettore reconciled himself with me although he never spoke English to me again.

In the lazy period after lunch, as I relax on my lounge in the garden, Ettore does his daily practice hour of juggling. Not only can he juggle the pins, but also wine glasses, small pots of flowers, in fact, almost any small objects. A rather strange man, named Signor Pernicci, who interestingly enough is not a cousin of Ettore and who always wears a seersucker suit, pops in three times a week to train Arturo in tightrope balance. Together, they stretch a taut wire from one wall to the other, directly over my roses and herb beds, in order that Arturo can walk across it while holding my large Burberry umbrella. As if to complete the three rings of the garden, Chiara frequently undertakes a routine of small tricks with Bartolomeo.

Twice a week, Ettore drives to Sansepolcro to pick up my French teacher, Madame St-Jacques. It is the only time I feel I can have a one-on-one conversation without its being heard and filed away by everyone in the garden and those overlooking the garden. She often brings French pastries, which she makes herself and which Arturo seems to enjoy.

If Mohammed can no longer walk to the mountain, or more precisely the piazza, the mountain comes to him. Gianni runs up with my *International Herald Tribune* around eight each morning. Laszlo pops in almost daily for a glass of wine before lunch. One morning, he lowered his voice, speaking almost conspiratorially, to inform me that he and Maria Pia were officially "walking out".

"Walking would be about it," I responded coyly, "for someone ninety if he's a day".

Laszlo graciously took my outburst as teasing. I shook his hand. It had been so long since anyone confided such a thing to me, I no longer remembered the correct responses. Perhaps I ought to have slapped him on the back.

Laszlo went on to tell me in great detail that he was about to become my neighbour. Some days previous, he had signed an agreement to sell his small house on Via Cavour to Mr. and Mrs. Sparrow. It seemed that the Sparrows' absent son, Jack, had convinced his parents of the need to move into town. Got the wind up Mr. Sparrow, so to speak. Mr. Sparrow adamantly refused to sell the farm or give up the Ape, so a small adjustment was to be made to the walled garden at Laszlo's to accommodate the Ape, thereby enabling the old man to drive out to the farm each day. I was thankful Laszlo's house was on the opposite side of town. As I lifted my glass to a toast, I swallowed a small laugh at the thought of Laszlo sharing Maria Pia's window and peering down into my garden in harmony with Signora Agnèse and Signorina Celestina.

Laura, if not in quite the guise of "lady-bountiful", comes regularly. I accept that we have been each other's close friends for so long that she has concern and wants to visit, but the bags of fresh produce carried by Riccardo, the requisite two paces behind, although appreciated by Sylvia, seems a bit over-the-top. Arturo usually whisks the bags from him. Sylvia, the frugal housewife, manages to use up all the produce preparing truly gastronomic delights for summer dining — as the food columnists would put it — I confess, to my great delight, given my declining appetite.

Laura, first and foremost, always asks after Chiara who tends to slip away discreetly when she hears Laura approaching. And one always knows Laura is arriving a good two minutes before she actually squeezes through the gate. She chats with everyone in the street or piazza in her not-quite-lady-bountiful voice. I think the girl is clearly frightened of her. Reclining in the garden, some days I am frightened of her.

Upon her arrival, Ettore always kisses Laura's hand, addressing her as "Contessa". What can I say? Laura likes the lot of them. Occasionally, she can be persuaded to stay for a gin and tonic, after which things sometimes get a bit raucous. Where Laura learns some of these off-colour stories, I have no idea. As she leaves, Laura will bend over and kiss Ettore on both cheeks and tell him he is henceforth to address her as "Laura". Once, I swear, I heard her corset snap as she bent and thought that it would be wiser to have Riccardo just pick Ettore up to lip level.

Laura insists on leaving the weekly leaflet from the Episcopal Church in Florence. My spiritual welfare has suddenly seemed to take on an annoying importance.

"Laura, please," I respond in vain.

"Ludovico is my dearest of friends," she confides and slightly swells, corsets expanding, "but he and his church are not the same as our own".

"Laura!"

I sometimes get quite angry with the woman.

"I went to church for the child's sake and now as much for habit and tradition as any sort of actual faith; I like going to church but don't read too much into it. I have not been a communicant of any church since childhood, and even then not your church. My parents were Presbyterians, Church of Scotland not England, old-fashioned Calvinists. Don't you think it odd for me to somehow now become fervent?"

At moments like this, I have developed a habit of reaching down under my chair for the reassuring presence of Bartolomeo.

All to no avail as the leaflets keep coming, more fervently pressed into my hand. And it seems Laura is not alone. Ludovico has intensified his visits. I know he is about to broach the subject when he balances his frame precariously on one of my wrought-iron garden chairs. I have difficulty reconciling his girth with the svelte young seminarian friend of my younger days. He annoys me by uncharacteristically veering the conversation towards realms spiritual. In retaliation, I veer spiritually left and plod straight to the realm secular. Remarks about sexual misconduct on the part of the clergy usually do the trick and we'll be back on to the weather before you can say "Bob's your uncle." And of course, Bob was my uncle, Dad's brother.

As if Laura and Ludovico aren't tiring enough, a steady stream of *Testimoni di Geova* have started arriving in pairs. In their pressed black trousers, they insist on standing in the background as Ettore flings his juggling pins about. It is almost eerie the way they just stare at me while holding copies of *Awake* and *The Watch Tower* in English as the pins are tossed into the air. Through it all, day after day, I often have an awful premonition that something is afoot. Arturo, for example, seems to be molding things with papier mâché which illogically disturbs me.

I don't usually dream at night, but in the late afternoons, dreams come to me, especially on those occasions when Arturo gives me a small shot of morphine. Or are they dreams; sometimes I can't tell with any certainty? One memorable recollection is fixated on that papier mâché Arturo was molding. It was so clear, frightening and yet not frightening.

I was in the garden in white linen trousers and a white Nehru shirt. Suddenly, the gate opened to a small procession. Laura's brother Cosmo entered first wearing the papier mâché mitre and a purple cope. Arturo followed, as an acolyte, in a lace cotta and the black tights of an acrobat. He held an enormous orange ombrellino that seemed to cover us all. Ettore was a thurifer, also in a cotta that almost reached the ground. He was juggling three silver thuribles all belching out incense. Standing in three different parts of the garden, yet seemingly under the orange ombrellino, were Sylvia in her black mantilla holding Laura's hand, Ludovico in his cassock and the two Testimoni in black suits.

Cosmo reached into the pockets under his cope and pulled out a large communion wafer. Ludovico began to sing the Regina Coeli and the Testimoni began to chant "Awake".

I awoke. I wanted no more religion then; I want no more religion now.

Somewhat disconcerted, I questioned Arturo about the papier mâché the following morning. He passed the whole thing off as an attempt to make a flower arrangement container for Mirela. I kept the vision, if that is what it was, to myself.

Through all of the summer, the bridge games have continued each Saturday, with the difference that they are now always held at my house. The only change to my usual bridge nights is, with all deference to Laura, a superb supper afterwards. Sylvia really outdoes herself and strangely Laura doesn't seem to mind. We all sit outside enjoying our wine, eventually the five of us once Cosmo arrived from the UK. Cosmo claims not to play bridge but I have always suspected he likes the game far too much and plays it far too well to be bothered with the four of us.

Cosmo also comes over a couple of evenings each week to play chess. The two of us sit quietly at the small chess table which Arturo brings out. The table, beautifully inlaid by a local furniture maker, had been a gift from Cosmo and Laura for my sixtieth birthday. Arturo carries it with almost a degree of religiosity which I put down to the presence of Cosmo whom he addresses as "*eminenza*". Arturo sits on a small stool and watches the playing. He is becoming a crack player in his own right. The boy and I play several times a week in the afternoon while the rest are enjoying a *pisolino*. The chess pieces hold a strange sort of mystic association for him, maybe it is just the thoughts of knights and kings and queens and dreams of Arabian Nights.

One evening Cosmo rather deliberately put down his chess piece and spoke slowly, rather unexpectedly.

"Bertie, I want to ask you something and I don't want to upset you. Most of all I do not want you to be angry with me. Laura and I have never asked you this straight out in forty-five years. But please, given our relationship with her mother and even more so with you, I think we need to know. We know what you have always said was the truth — what all the principal players have said is the truth. And what was sworn in court you again say is the truth. But we have always harboured a small hope in our heart that the truth was otherwise."

He sipped his wine as if seeking courage.

"There were the five of us, all young, here that summer. Ludovico was a seminarian and still too much in love with his church. Besides, he was too busy sleeping with me. The second was her brother. You were the third and we could all see you were in love with her. Truthfully, did you love her? Was there even the remotest chance, despite what she believed — what we all have come to believe — that you could have been the child's father? Has this nightmare any chance of lightening a bit? Why have you never once shared a feeling, an emotion, any sense of normal personal emotion — hurt about her — with either Laura or me?"

I waited a full minute before responding.

"To answer your cruel question: emphatically, no! You are free to read what you like into it all: her, the events, me, the whole pathetic mess that has been my life. I thought you would have understood. Again, it seems, I have chosen an inappropriate friend."

I looked into his face with anger, which I think rather frightened him; I know the remembrance of it frightens me. I have, on occasion in my life, expressed grief and fear but never rage. I wanted to reach across the board and claw his face, spit out all I longed to say, have longed to say, for decades. I merely sat there mute and tipped the chess game to the ground, frightening Arturo but saying nothing. As the boy scrambled to pick up the chess pieces, just watching the boy made my anger fade.

Arturo, simply and instinctively searching out the pieces under the table and strewn across the patio, pressured me, or more accurately calmed me, into putting things into perspective. Cosmo had been my friend for forty-five years. No one had been more supportive to me when we came here, almost like refugees, than his sister Laura. I watched as the old man covered his face with his hands. All he sought was what I had failed, no, refused, to give him: a brief respite, something to hope for in making sense of what were, no less for him than for me, the worse events of his life. My anger shattered the one spark of possible redemption in the whole sad tale that linked me with him and Laura.

"Ettore," I continued, looking straight at Cosmo, anger gone, "told me once that English was the language of deceit and abandonment. He was right. The past, our past, Laura's, yours, mine is rooted in our Anglo history played out in foreign lands. I have hidden truth, concealed facts, and lied even to you and Laura, most regretfully to the child, and in the end, to myself. And to what benefit? Deceit and abandonment."

Cosmo was still, his expression fixed as I continued, "But this garden will from now on form my history and my history will exist only in the present, in an Italian garden surrounded by my exotic family. My family is now a dwarf with a buxom girlfriend, a young boy and girl expecting a baby, a fat priest, a love-struck nonagenarian Czech, three harpies looking from above, an English crone and a tiresome reprobate of an old English bishop."

I stared at him, "Cosmo, I will never speak English again nor allow it to be spoken here in this garden by you or anyone — we have all had sufficient deceit and abandonment".

And I have kept true to this; I have not spoken English since. This journal is now written in the language of Dante. I have even gone so far as to have Gianni bring me the *Corriere della Sera* instead of my dear *International Herald Tribune.*

* * * * *

August has been matrimonial. In early August, Alberto and Chiara had a quiet secular wedding at the *Comune.* Her parents invited them both and Sylvia for a pizza on the piazza afterwards. Ettore and I, meanwhile, opened a very expensive bottle of wine and toasted their health. The cost of our bottle of wine unquestionably exceeded the wedding supper! Chiara has now moved into my house officially. Maria Pia, embarrassingly dressed in white, married Laszlo and was whisked off to Leriche on the Ligurian coast for a honeymoon. The less thought about this, the better, especially when it comes to consummation and wedding nights. To my knowledge only Signorina Celestina and Signora Agnèse were at the church for the ceremony; the question remains as to whether they were actually invited.

As the summer moved into late August, we had the big wedding. Sylvia, holding Ettore's hand, announced one evening in the garden that they were going to get married and hoped I could host a small gathering. A week later, men arrived to install an enormous marquee that seemed to cover the entire garden. Ettore's cousin Mario from the restaurant in Caprese Michaelangelo came to inspect the kitchen and bring a variety of portable gas stoves, all the while flashing about his zircon ring and smelling of Antaeus. Maria Pia and Sylvia spread square metres of white cloth all over the sitting room and the hum of Maria Pia's Singer sewing machine hummed the air.

On the last Thursday of the month at ten minutes to ten on a clear morning, Sylvia and Ettore walked into the garden for an inspection. She wore a rather flamboyant white dress, which appeared to be floating away from her bosom at every angle. In fairness, she was stunning. Ettore was in a morning suit, impeccably cut, he told me, by his cousin Mauro in Città. He was also sporting a new black top hat, imported from Savile Row he assured me. Arturo and Chiara presently joined them. She wore a very tight–fitting, turquoise, sequinned dress which her growing tummy lifted to an almost indecent level. Arturo was wearing a shiny blue suit with a white tie. He held three red roses, one he pinned on Ettore and the second on me, before pinning the third on his own lapel.

There was a commotion at the gate: the bridesmaids had arrived. Maria Pia, Signora Agnèse, Signorina Celestina and Tiziana were all dressed in pink: Maria Pia with freshly dyed red hair — rather resembling the Virgin Queen on her last appearance down the Thames — and Tiziana cavorting about in about twenty-five square metres of material draped in bunches from each of her amply-fleshed arms and all the while flashing her denture-smile at everyone. Since Sylvia had never actually been married to Arturo's father and Ettore, albeit a frequenter of the *Sala di Regno* in Sansepolcro, had been raised a Roman Catholic, Ludovico had raised no objection to a church wedding. Ettore's one request was that there be no incense, at least near the bridal party.

I was unable to make it up to the church. Arturo had organized two white horses with white and gold plumes to pull the, well, small carts up to the church. They just fit into the narrow streets. He had covered the carts with flowers, every available bloom in the area. I pictured all the bare graves in the cemetery for weeks to come. The first cart was to take the bride and groom, plus Arturo and Chiara. The second would have only the bridesmaids; given Tiziana's size, I felt for the horse. Arturo wanted to organize a third cart for me. I can imagine the reaction that would have stirred. Better to stay out of the circus parade. I rested in the garden with Bartholomeo.

The garden reception was truly a feast. Large tables had been placed the length of the garden. Everyone, it seemed, was there: Mr. and Mrs. Sparrow, she wearing what appeared to be a hat left over from her millinery days before the war; the smiling and nodding Dottor Ganducca and Lucia; Laura; Cosmo and Riccardo; and the cousins. Ettore's father, remember, was one of eight sons, all, apparently, with offspring. In addition to Tiziana and our chef for the evening, Mario, there were the ones with whom I had some degree of acquaintanceship: Maurizio (the mechanic, who was actually wearing his teeth and hence did not once lisp throughout the evening), Little Nellie (from the restaurant, with no-name husband), Francesco (the dog groomer), Mauro (the tailor), Emmanuelle (in the bakery), and Loredona (the housekeeper for Dottor Luigi, who was seated to her left). But there were also twenty-three other Ganovelli cousins: Fausto, Andrea, Vetruvio, Americo, Hortenzia, Cinzia, Luca, Lorenzo, Zelinda, Rosa, Vincenzo, Pietro, Palmiro, Clementina, Loretta, Ascanio, Vasco, Lina, Letitia, Rita, Beppa, Ermido and Fiametta. All had arrived with a partner or spouse; I learned not to ask. One, Fausto, was there with both a wife and mistress. Another, I think Vasco, was accompanied by what appeared to be a boyfriend.

There were several other new faces. Signor Pernicci, Arturo's tightrope instructor, introduced me to a snake charmer, a bareback rider, a ventriloquist with a puppet named Mia Nonna, and the identical twins I remembered from their twirling at the circus, both dressed in purple sequined dresses. Partway through the meal two young people from Montréal arrived with a viola and cello. The girl, of Korean origin, and the boy, sporting a Mohawk cut, were travelling in Italy. Gianni in the square had sent them up to play as his gift to the happy couple. All through the dinner, a magician who called himself Dottor Caramello Gelatina worked the various tables. He pulled twenty silk handkerchiefs from the bride's bosom and handcuffed me at one point to Laura.

And happy everyone was indeed. Ludovico and I sat at the table with the happiest of couples, as well as Chiara and Arturo, and also Laura and Cosmo. Bartolomeo sat under the table at my feet. Laszlo and Riccardo, the only men at the table with the bridesmaids and Madame St-Jacques, exchanged grimaces at periodic intervals. I kept thinking that Laszlo was having second thoughts about his matrimonial commitments and Riccardo thanking his lucky stars for having remained celibate.

Mario had out-done himself with the food and wine. The party got louder as the evening wore on. After the dinner, Ettore got out his accordion and everyone sang. The puppet Mia Nonna sang what sounded like "God Save the Queen". The circus people got up on the tables once they had been cleared and performed several acrobatic feats. I passed a message to Ettore to remind him that under no circumstances was the snake charmer even to consider performing. There was dancing and lots of toasts. Arturo gave the official one to the bride and groom, adding in special thanks for the festivities to their "benefactor and his adopted father". Yet another first for me. Where once I would have worried, I laughed and ruffled his hair when he bent to kiss me.

* * * * *

Ettore and Sylvia left on their honeymoon for a week in Sicily. Bartolomeo, Chiara, Arturo and I settled into a quiet September. If the summer was glorious, the autumn has been brutal. Cold came quickly by the end of the month. One rare sunny day, I had Arturo open the window to my garden. Maria Pia, Signora Agnèse and Signorina Celestina were discussing the weather. They agreed that a hard winter was coming, which would, as they put it, "carry folk off".

"I expect old Bruno won't make spring," Agnèse piped up, no doubt characteristically shaking her head, "or Lisa, up with the nuns at the Misericordia".

Maria Pia, never one to be slow at holding her own on the misery-end-of-things, chirped in, "Alberto certainly won't make spring, or Christmas for that matter".

There were great hushing sounds from the other two. Maria Pia grudgingly changed the topic to the appropriate name for Arturo and Chiara's baby.

I am not really too keen, in any event, on another Christmas. Since Clemente died, Laura has insisted on a traditional Italian meal with one concession to English tradition: all of us wearing silly paper hats. I am reminded of Christmas at my Uncle Bob's house with my Father's annual recitation, well the rude version, of *It was Christmas Day in the Work House*, in which he would tell the worthy master to take his Christmas pudding and stuff it up his Royal Canadian, or words to that effect. This preceded my Mother's yearly pronouncement "really, my dear, enough is indeed enough especially in front of Albie".

I can do without these Christmas rituals.

A true St. Martin's summer has come in mid-November. Today is a glorious day. Arturo lifted me out to the garden before heading out to arrange some floral tribute. Ettore and Sylvia are over in Città, no doubt visiting some cousin or other. Chiara is up in their room, no doubt avoiding Maria Pia, who has been house cleaning.

Maria Pia came into the garden a while ago.

"I don't suppose I could trust you to pay the man when he comes with the eggs?"

Whether such statements are actually exclamations or rhetorical questions, I have long given up trying to figure out.

"I must run down to the shops. I have left ten euro on the *frigo*; you are to get five euro back. Here is your *telefonino*, you can call any of us if you need anything."

I assented with a small gesture. As the gate closed, I nodded off but was awakened soon after as the gate opened again. Oddly,

Bartolomeo, who was at my feet, didn't react. A tinker had come into the garden with a large pack. He was quite olive-skinned; I was used to Africans coming door-to-door. I let my surprise express itself.

"You are not a *vu cumpru*, more a Gypsy."

"Yes, a Gypsy. But that is not a nice term for a Roma, nor for that matter, is *vu cumpru* for an African. Maybe you can just make amends by buying something?"

I was too tired to argue or, for that matter, pay much attention to the wares he was setting on my table. I nodded when he pulled out a black doormat with a very yellow Tweety Bird on it.

"That", I thought, "will irk Maria Pia when she gets back".

"How much?"

He said, "Seven euro".

"I will pay five."

I was dropping off again, so very tired.

"You will find ten euro on the *frigo*. You can bring me the change."

I dozed even with the pain which was almost too intense. I wanted Arturo back quickly. I seemed to have slept.

I startled, looking up as he leaned over to place the five euro under my *telefonino*.

Close to my ear, he softly whispered, "Aren't you glad I returned your *telefonino*"?

# PROFESSOR STEVENSON

DECEMBER 2011 – JANUARY 2012

Parton Terrace,
Grove End Road,
London NW8,
December 8th, 2011.

Professor Sean Stevenson,
Department of Psychology,
Sidney Smith Hall,
Toronto, Ontario, M5S 3G3,
Canada.

Dear Professor Stevenson,

You write that you hoped your letter would not be too much of an affront. It certainly was.

The only mitigating factor was your reference to Guy Paris. In addition to my surprise that he is still living, is that you refer to him as Father Paris. I would have thought he would have packed all that business in a long time ago. I am almost ninety and we would be about the same age. I ceased the practice of medicine twenty years ago. I should have thought he would have abandoned the Church years ago. He could be reclining on a beach in Florida, which I believe retired academics in Canada tend to do. He could have made some poor spinster or comfortably-off widow very happy in her later years.

You seem, on the surface, to be interested in events which occurred a long time ago. But things on the surface, I find, have little face value. You want a great deal more. I am not certain I want to give you more. I am, or rather was, a pathologist by profession so tend to view things more in black and white terms than the psychologist and his shades of grey. "The dead are dead so leave them dead, accept it and get over it" is, in my opinion, a very good way in which to conduct one's life.

You want me to resurrect events in my family following from tragic events that took place in Toronto in the 1960s. Those events, as I am sure you know perfectly well although you carefully fail to mention this fact, have had ramifications on my family for over forty years. My wife has grandchildren in Canada who regularly use the word chutzpah. You certainly have that in spades.

And I do not believe you when you write "for research purposes". I do not trust psychologists, to be truthful, any more than I trust clergymen, the exception perhaps being Guy Paris. I can smell a salacious book featuring photos of me and what few elderly relations I have left on a jacket cover.

The short answer is simple. No, I will not help you in what you really want, what you are requesting. I will not provide a publishable memoire. Of the events in Toronto, Guy can give you all you want. We attended the public inquest together. I will not spend the next months writing out my recollections, organized and edited in for want of a better word, "memoire". Nor will I meet with you.

But I will do something for you, out of respect for Guy, who obviously values you. And, I did ring him to ascertain the veracity of what you have written. He assures me that you have "impeccable integrity and are a devout Catholic". The words integrity and devout Catholic both make my teeth grind. I know Guy used them just for that very effect.

If, as I intend to do, decline to provide a full memoire, I will, nonetheless, agree to contribute to a larger narrative of events coming out of the tragedies in Toronto. There are four of us who have intimate knowledge of different periods from the 1960s to the present. The other three are my siblings, Laura Guelfi and Cosmo Neagle, and their friend Ludovico Calli. I am considerably older than both my brother and sister. She is about ten years younger and I was almost ready to enter university when Cosmo was born. My sister rambles around a large Italian manor house, what they call a *castello*. She will be the one to organize things, if, of course, all three agree. Laura has the time and, I am quite certain, will have the inclination to take the lead once she learns of this undertaking.

I will suggest to her that each of the four of us cover a time period and that our accounts be sent to you unedited and unread by the others. This will allow us room to be frank about each other should we so chose. That way, you ought to be able to make some sort of chronological sense of things. We are, in spite of our dotage educated people.

I always thought my memoire, if ever written, would involve the dead, how they died, and why they died. So, in an ironic twist, it seems that is what I about to do after all. I am not happy about doing this. Early on, I decided to divorce myself from it all. I am not looking forward to dredging everything back up.

I have two requests. First, I ask that you never contact me again. Second, I ask that you refrain from contacting any person still living whom we may mention in our narratives; this is especially true of the people in Italy. I promise, in return, to ask the others to be open and write freely. The knowledge that you may respect these requests will make the task easier.

Yours truly,
Harry J. Neagle

Castello di Guelfi,
Locanda San Lorenzo,
San Leo Tiberino, (AR), 52035
January 14th 2012.

Doctor Sean Stevenson,
Department of Psychology,
Sidney Smith Hall,
Toronto, (Ontario), M5S 3G3,
Canada.

My dear Dr. Stevenson:

I am so sorry to be slow in replying to your letter which was forwarded to me by my brother in December. As you might expect, the death of our friend Albert Stafford affected us greatly. The past months have been a period of great loss. Your letter, I must be blunt, added to that loss by raising matters going back over forty-five years, matters that I initially felt were best left alone.

My brother has suggested that we cooperate with you. This quite astonishes me as he has categorically refused to discuss anything to do with this whole unfortunate mess for a generation. Age, perhaps, is mellowing him. It is suggested that we change with age. Not me. I have always been the soppy one in the family so it is my nature to comply even when against my better judgement.

In the weeks subsequent to the arrival of his letter and a copy of your letter to him, I have discussed your request with the local priest here, Don Ludovico Calli who has been a constant throughout the entire period of your research. At Christmas, my brother Cosmo Neagle was here and the three of us had a long discussion. The outcome was that we all believed that we could no longer hurt anyone by being open with you through the sharing of our recollections.

My younger brother and his late wife were childless and obviously Don Ludovico has no children. Well, you know how my older brother feels. Harry, who has re-married and focuses his life on his new family, obviously feels they will not suffer from our "confessions". Harry, nonetheless, told us that although he no longer has any interest in the events of the past, he will share what information he has with you. How can we refuse to do otherwise?

For myself, I did feel that I must consult my stepson Count Giorgio Guelfi who lives in Rome. He has recollections of the parties but as he put it, "Although I liked Alberto well enough and Angela, I have only vague recollections of her mother and uncle. As far as I am concerned, you are free to do as you see fit. You will in any event."

I need not have quoted the final caveat but if you are to know about us, maybe it is best to know the more-than-enough about us, our inter-relationships, warts and all. My own children are living in America, one on each coast. Nothing I write could possibly interest them; they live in their own worlds. I find Americans tend to live this way.

The only person who would have suffered through our participation in this enterprise would have been Albert Stafford. Had your request come a year earlier, we would all have declined. He is dead now and one hopes past being hurt by these events in his unhappy life.

I accept your attestation that you are interested in the tragic events for "research purposes only" and that we shall not have our photographs plastered over the tabloids. We have all had enough of the gutter press. I also appreciate your offer to come and interview each of us personally. We have all agreed, that is, Ludovico, Cosmo and I, to decline being interviewed. Strangely, Harry said to us, although he wrote that he too declined to be interviewed, he actually had no objections to a personal interview, with the proviso that the discussion be directed to his recollections of the quasi-judicial hearing he attended and not his personal relationships with his children or grandchild. Well, he must be going through some sort of geriatric metamorphosis.

Each winter, I move from the country into town where it is warmer and more comfortable. It is here and not the castello where

I shall write my recollections. I know you proposed providing us with a list of questions. It sounds too much like psychoanalysis for us folk. We three, that is Cosmo, Ludovico and I, have decided to prepare individual narratives and forward them to you while simultaneously sending copies to each other. I know from his correspondence with you that Harry plans to proceed differently. I doubt whether Harry will relent and send us copies of his narrative; he was never one to share.

I have offered to edit Don Ludovico's but the others vetoed that suggestion, no one more vehemently than Ludovico himself. We do not want there to be any hint of collusion. Our narratives, therefore, may seem to contradict each other from time to time; you must remember, we are, to be candid, getting on and many of the events took place almost half a century ago. But then, isn't that the nature of historical research? Sometimes conflicting points of view? You answer that, Professor Stevenson. You are, after all, the psychological researcher.

Our individual styles might not be to your liking. You wanted to provide questions. We chose to reply through narration. The four of us have agreed to endeavour to provide you with in-depth background information on persons and events as we recall them. You must endeavour to put these narratives together in some sort of a chronological order and make sense of them. We have all sworn to each other not, willingly, to withhold information. We all, of course, will. Isn't that human nature? It becomes your job to decipher the essentials, as you see fit, from what we have provided.

Finally, I understand that you have in your possession a journal prepared by Albert Stafford during the final summer of his life. I was unaware that you, or more precisely your agent from Bologna, had contacted the new owners of his house directly. His heir, Arturo Panducci, had withheld this document from us until after he forwarded a copy to you. Perhaps, in fairness to Arturo, he thought these scribblings unimportant, which, having read them, they certainly are. I shall address this further in my narrative.

Suffice to note: Arturo was part of a collection of unfortunate attachments which Albert formed towards the end of his life.

My narrative will arrive in the weeks to come. Don Ludovico, Harry and Cosmo have told me that their narratives will be completed in a similar time-frame. I look forward, in a perverse way, to what they will write, at least Cosmo and Ludovico. There will be no opportunity for us to refute each other. Another challenge for you!

In conclusion, I wish you well with your research which I expect will result in a book. Sad as it has been for all of us, now it is perhaps the time for a fuller story to be told. I have no objections.

Yours truly,

Laura J. Neagle Guelfi

# DON LUDOVICO CALLI

1967

Albert Stafford was a rather retiring and serious man. He was like that as a young man and remained that way until shortly before his death last year. In the spring before his death, he was involved in an automobile accident in the nearby town of Città di Castello. His car was hit by a small van and he apparently knocked his head causing or possibly accentuating brain deterioration. This combined with a bone cancer and heavy doses of morphine administered by an untrained hand seemed to inflict, although this may be the wrong words in English, some sort of personality adjustment.

Over this last summer, Albert went from being his reserved self to one uncharacteristically sarcastic. *Molto molto sarcastico!* As the summer progressed, he changed again, perhaps mellowed is the term, into a character of gregarious outpouring of conviviality. Your English words delight me.

Albert became outwardly vivacious, at times even affectionate. His grip on reality, of course, slipped significantly as the summer wore on. Mind you, he still managed a good bridge game; the Countess, his friend Laszlo and I played each Saturday at his house, usually in the garden. He would, however, speak of people, like his former neighbours Anne and Geoff Sparrow who died a dozen years ago, as though they were still regular visitors. He spoke constantly about imaginary friends from the circus as if they were intimates of all of us. His poor housekeeper, Maria Pia, a rather prim spinster, he drove to distraction claiming that she was married to his friend Laszlo.

Most surprising was Albert's having a young man, whom I believed at the time to have been of somewhat questionable motive, Arturo Panducci, move into his home along with a girlfriend to act as a sort of general factotum. The young man's mother was frequently at the house causing people to suggest Albert had entered into some sort of relationship with her. Utter rubbish! There was no, as you English, say "hanky-panky" as far as I am concerned. Ah, another one of your wonderful English expressions. In fact, she was involved with a man from Città di Castello with the name of Ganovelli from a somewhat notorious family. Suffice to say, he was a graduate of one of our better *riforrmatorio* in Rome. Ganovelli was as diminutive as the woman was voluptuous.

Towards the end of his life, Bertie took to referring to Panducci as his adopted son. In fact, he left the boy his house. Italian inheritance law is much less favourable to this sort of thing than your English common law. The testament could have been successfully challenged but who was there to challenge it?

The young man looked after Bertie extremely well and, through it all, the end of Bertie's life was possibly his happiest time. Cosmo, Bishop Neagle, Laura's brother, would play chess with Bertie in the afternoon with Arturo seated beside them, studying every move. In fact, during one of these games, Cosmo gained a glimpse into the depths of Albert's hitherto unknown feelings regarding this whole unfortunate business. In the end, I signed a legal document to say Bertie was of sound mind with, to my knowledge, no living relations at the time he signed his final will. There was also a legacy to his housekeeper, Maria Pia, of course, and money to fix the antique organ in the Badia church on his street, while I received the executive copyright to all his publications.

As you are aware, Albert had kept a daily journal throughout the period after the accident. I have read it: It was sheer fantasy. Oddly, partway through, he had switched to Italian. As with his speech, he used only the Italian language in the last months preceding his death.

You may find it strange that I write all this. But Albert, Alberto, Bertie, you must forgive me if I switch them about. We all used them interchangeably, that is, all four or five of the people who addressed him as something other than Dottore. Please understand he has lived as a young, middle-aged, and elderly man through what he came to call "forty-five years of abandonment and deceit" with quiet dignity as a retiring individualist. This individualism, some would call conformity. But conformity to what? Certainly, he conformed to nothing normal in our frame of reference in a small Italian town.

His quiet, almost austere nature, his scholasticism, and utter respectability stood firm. This release of fancifulness towards the end of his life suggests to me that there was a potential for joy, humour, and the acceptance of love latent within Albert. Had these early events which the four of us are about to recount been different and had the burden of responsibly not been thrust upon him, these traits might have been part of his very nature all his life instead of confined to his last months. In the events about which I am writing, there are many tragedies, many tragic figures, none I fear greater than that of Albert Stafford.

Albert first came here to San Leo Tiberino in 1966 with Joanna and Christopher Neagle, the young niece and nephew of my friends Cosmo and Laura. Laura had married a widower, Count Clemente Guelfi, by whom she had two young children. Some years earlier, Laura had come to Tuscany and the Guelfi *castello* to teach the Count's older son by his first marriage, Giorgio. Clemente was the most un-count-like of people. Totally irreverent, he made us all laugh and was delighted to fill the house with young people that summer. In addition to the nephew, niece and Albert, there was also Laura's brother Cosmo, younger than she by about eight years, who was studying for the church at St. Stephen's House, Oxford. I was a distant cousin, what you Anglo-Saxons call "a poor relation" of Clemente and a seminarian.

Castello di Guelfi was much more accommodating and inviting to younger people in those days. Today there are just Laura and a family retainer living there. Then, however, the pool was open; we had tennis courts; and we even had a few horses to ride. I was considerably younger than Clemente and he encouraged me to spend time with our guests if for no other reason than to perfect my English. Those were different times and Laura had lots of help with her children which afforded her time to spend with us. Clemente's older son, much as he would to-day dismiss it, was thrilled with the attention the others bestowed on him. As I mentioned, we had lots of help about the castle, all gone now except for Riccardo who was then an apprentice gardener and who now virtually runs the place for Laura. Maybe she should take a leaf from Bertie and adopt him.

The weather in the summer of 1966 was hot and idyllic, in itself a season to remember. Joanna, Christopher and Albert arrived by train in early May and stayed the whole summer. I don't think Laura had seen her young relations since they were adolescents and had not prepared us for how beautiful they were. Chris was tall with dark curly hair. Joanna affected the Julie Christie-look which was popular at the time, with her long blond hair and blue eyes and pouty lips. They eclipsed everyone around them.

It would be unfair to omit writing that Albert was also very attractive but in an understated way with straight hair and glasses. It is strange, the glasses are the first thing that comes to mind when I remember him arriving at the dreary train station in Arezzo. As I noted, he was not unattractive; he was quite handsome, actually, with his light brown hair worn slightly long and a dark tan which I attributed to hours on the tennis court. In addition to an old duffle bag, he was carrying a tennis racket. If people didn't notice him it was simply that the other two had an electric appeal, like sparks flickering from one to the other. Eyes went to them and not Albert. Yet, Albert maintained his looks; in fact, had he not been so prudish and self-righteous, he could have had all the women in town swooning after him right up to the end.

Joanna and Chris laughed uproariously from the moment they climbed into the car; Albert just smiled. I think it was only with this smile that I noticed him beyond the glasses. And so went the summer, with the brother and sister laughing and Albert smiling. Albert, Laura, Cosmo and I provided the perfect foils for the young cousins. And Clemente seemed delighted with it all.

Harry Neagle, Cosmo and Laura's older brother and Joanna and Chris's father, had taken them to Toronto when they were about midway through their secondary schooling. Their mother had died from an accidental overdose of prescription drugs about which little was said, at least in my presence. Harry thought it would be good for them to get away from Britain for a while. He was a pathologist and took a two-year assignment teaching at the University of Toronto. After the two years, he returned to Britain. Chris and Joanna insisted that they be allowed to stay to finish their senior matriculations, which is what I believe was equivalent to Britain's sixth form. (You must realize that forty years of conversation with Albert made me quite conversant with odd bits about Canadian educational and religious practice.)

Harry, perhaps unwisely in retrospect, had extended the lease on the house, so the brother and sister lived there together alone until the following year when they moved into university residences.

I understand Harry was furious that they were not returning to study at Oxford. They just simply refused to leave and in the end it was not his choice; they were eighteen. I wouldn't say that they were used to getting their own way. Based upon my opinion of them formed that summer, I would say they just did, in this instance, what they wanted to do. They also had access to the money their mother had left them which made any opposition on Harry's part inconsequential.

Chris and Albert lived, at one point, in the same house in the residence at Trinity College, I believe it was called. After graduation, Albert had remained on as a don while he pursued graduate studies. All his friends, or whatever friends he might have had, had moved on. When Chris arrived on his floor, the friendship blossomed. Meanwhile, Joanna lived across the street in St. Hilda's College, the women's component of Trinity; she took exactly the same courses as her brother, so other than for meals and sleeping they were virtually always together. It is strange how I remember the names of the colleges, so English and so un-pontifical; I have always enjoyed the British tradition of naming colleges after theological concepts such as the Trinity.

Albert came from a small Ontario town, Collingwood; the name has a delightful English ring to it; one does not forget it. I remember him telling me once of going with his father to watch the launching of boats. He was an only child whose parents had died in an automobile accident. His father had one brother, if I remember correctly, who was a medical doctor and his only living relation. Albert rarely referred to either of his parents, his uncle, or his childhood, which is why the boat launch and the name Collingwood remain so clearly in my mind.

The three were clearly adrift: Albert with no family and Chris and Joanna across the Atlantic from their father, uncles and aunt. They formed, instead, a close almost family-like bond among themselves. That was evident from the moment I first met them at the Arezzo train station, an understanding that strengthened over the summer. At times, Albert seemed the older brother, and at other times, the younger.

By the time they came to us for that summer, Bertie was well through his doctoral studies and Chris had entered a theological college. You might have gathered that the Neagles were a fairly churchy sort of family. Harry, Laura and Cosmo's father, still of course living at the time, was a clergyman with the wonderful name, at least to an Italian, of Swithin; their paternal grandfather, had been a canon in a some provincial cathedral. All the Neagle men embraced the church except Harry. For whatever reason, he had chosen a different profession from that of the other males in the family. Cosmo, Chris's uncle, was about to be ordained in the church; it seemed only natural that Chris would as well.

What was not natural, at least to Cosmo's and my way of thinking, was Chris's choice of seminary. That summer, as young theologians, Cosmo and I both vied for who could be the more ceremonial. We were both Catholic by tradition, if not by allegiance. Both Cosmo and I were astounded when Chris told us that he had intended to pursue his vocation at a "Low Church" college like Wycliffe in Toronto. Chris's grandfather, Swithin, was very Anglo-Catholic and Cosmo was at St. Stephen's House which was very, very Anglo-Catholic. We both, rather pompously, I see now, begged him to reconsider. I remember the debates we would have well into the night, with Albert just smiling benignly and Joanna sitting on the floor with her head on her brother's knees.

It became clearer throughout that summer that Albert was in love with Joanna. He didn't fawn but his feeing was visible in his eyes. Joanna knew, of course, but seemed neither to encourage nor discourage, for that matter, his attention. What struck us all at the time was that Chris and Joanna seemed more the lovers, while Albert remained fixed in the rôle of brother. Often, at breakfast, Albert would be alone while the other two were out riding. Albert and I were partners in tennis doubles against the brother and sister. While Clemente, Albert, Laura and I played bridge and Cosmo read in the evening, the other two would disappear for long periods. The summer passed gently, but the turbulence from the summer was to last for forty-five years. Joanna went back to Canada pregnant.

+ LUDOVICO CALLI

# HARRY

1967

My name is Doctor Henry Neagle, Harry to my family and friends. A retired pathologist and lecturer, I currently live in St. John's Wood in London. My first wife and I had two children, Christopher and Joanna. I had married quite young when I was on leave in London during the War, to the Honourable Frederika Cantly, known to all and sundry as Freddie. Her father was a viscount, who thoroughly disapproved of a marriage to the son of a country parson. Freddie rarely saw her family as a result; this estrangement, and who can say with certainty, added to her increasing sense of isolation. After the War, I returned to my studies and when I was still a houseman, my son was born. My daughter followed a year later.

We had my family's flat, where we lived while I was carrying out my studies and completing my RCPS. Although I continued to work in Oxford, we eventually bought a house in King's Sutton, a beautiful Northamptonshire village with a magnificent Norman church about thirty kilometres from Oxford. It was a move I have long regretted. If the verdict is out on the effects of the estrangement from her family, the move, in retrospect, without question contributed to Freddie's decline.

It is easy to view the past in the present. I know, from the point of view of to-day, I ought to have sent the children away to two different public schools. On the other hand, I felt that having them near their mother seemed a good idea from her mental health perspective. There seemed no reason for me to have assumed that they were anything but perfectly well-rounded children who could not in any way be injured through neglect. I just assumed Freddie would remain active in their rearing. They were bright children and I thought they would keep their mother up to the mark.

As a pathologist, at least during those early years, I worked very erratic hours. There was a small flat attached to the morgue in

Oxford and I often spent the nights there. It was not unusual, therefore, for the three of them to spend the evenings alone, shut up in the large house with Freddie nursing a bottle of scotch. Maybe I was, as Freddie was so fond of pointing out, "better at understanding the dead than the living".

The lack of proper stimulation in the house, Freddie's increasing withdrawal and my absences threw the children together more than would be the case with normal siblings. They were not at all toffee-nosed or standoffish — far from it. They were extremely polite, thoughtful and well liked at the local school and in the village. It is just that they preferred each other's company and they preferred to stay at home. Their usual sports were those which the two of them could enjoy together: tennis, cycling and hiking. In summer, they would take their bicycles and head out into the countryside. Summer evenings, they would go to play tennis around tea time when the courts were pretty much deserted. My attempts to encourage them in team sports or Girl Guides and Boy Scouts failed miserably; these were the only occasions when they pouted or complained. I eventually gave up. Then, their joint disposition returned to its usual upbeat manner.

The only group activity they seemed to enjoy when they were a bit older was singing in the choir at St. Peter and St. Paul's, the parish church. From the age of eight, they went hand-in-hand to the children's choir practice. As they grew older and Chris's voice changed, they went to the adult choir practices on Thursday evenings. On Sundays, they sang at the morning Eucharist as well as Evensong.

As the black sheep of the Neagle family, I used every ruse to avoid church. My job has brought me face-to-face with death on a daily basis. Over the years, I have tried to console hundreds of grieving families, often in the most gruesome of circumstances. In only the rarest of cases, did I find a religious faith to be of any substantive value to the grievers. I came to find the idea of any sort of a beneficent being almost an anathema to me. I, nonetheless, learned very early on that it was best to keep these views private from the rest of the Neagle family.

So, I conformed in public. Besides, I recognized that it was good for the children to have an interest outside of the home and each other. When I was in King's Sutton for the weekend, I would attend the church on Sundays, often both services. The parish, mercifully, was Anglo-Catholic with good music. I would often look around at the others in the pews and wonder how many of them shared my atheistic views but were outwardly practising for the sake of family and appearance. Maybe, I was too cynical about them and their spirituality, or lack thereof, especially poor Freddie. She never missed. I knew it was fairly easy to sober up for the morning service, but she eschewed any offer of a luncheon drink on Sundays so she could appear sober at Evensong. I suppose it was the one occasion when she could assume her daughter-of-a-viscount rôle. And people always did smile at her, not because she was a viscount's daughter, but because she was a drunk and they pitied her.

When Freddie died, succumbing to a lethal mix of pills and booze more than likely deliberately ingested, the children were fifteen and sixteen. Joanna had been pushed forward a year at the local comprehensive so they were both in the same form. I realized that they needed to get away. Christ Almighty, I needed to get away. It was to be our one chance as a family to put back the pieces of normal family life. And in some ways we were successful, at least initially.

I was offered a visiting professorship for two years at the University of Toronto. I rented us a fairly large house in the old Rosedale section of the city. It backed onto a ravine where the children rode their bikes on the many pathways. They had a final year to complete at secondary school when I completed my two-year stint. I was invited to stay the third year but before this offer, Oxford came through with a much better offer, one too good to refuse. The children pestered me to allow them to complete their final year at the local collegiate, and I extended the lease on the house for an additional year with the understanding that they would return to Britain for university.

Against my wishes, they stayed on in Canada for university. I protested, threatened, all to no avail. Freddie had inherited some money from her mother. God knows the old viscount had precious little. And she padded bank accounts in the children's names with enough pounds to enable them to live independent of me at least for a few years. It would seem she was trying to compensate for her failure at mothering but I suspect it was an attempt to get back at me, strip me of any leverage in their later years.

They both completed four-year honour degrees in French literature at a small Church of England affiliated college at the University of Toronto. Apparently, the competition to enter the college was fierce but they had both excelled at the collegiate (one of the reasons I had relented and resigned myself to their staying) and actually won scholarships. Chris lived in the Trinity College residence and Joanna at the college's women's residence at St. Hilda's College. They did fairly well, if not brilliantly, in their studies, corresponded with me regularly and even came back to Britain for a couple of visits. We were on as good terms as I can remember by the time they finished their undergraduate degrees.

Joanna took a part-time job at a small French-language high school and Chris, against my advice, entered a theological college. Remember, I had taught at the University of Toronto and knew the reputation of Wycliffe College, as it was called. Academically, it was alright for Hebrew, Greek, Old Testament studies, and so forth. It had, unfortunately, a bit of an evangelical tendency. The church's theology, in general, was pretty abhorrent to me; in my family, however, one learned to live with all manner of religious abhorrence. But the evangelical stuff just enraged me. I'm afraid I told Chris how I felt and thus began a bit of a chill in my relationship with both my children. After his first year, they came to Europe, only landing in London, taking the train at once, and heading for my sister and brother-in-law's in Italy. They did not come up to Oxford nor did they suggest meeting in London at either leg of the journey.

Now let's move to the facts on the Toronto tragedy as I have come to view the events that took place after I left Canada. They were also the events that would eventually foster my return to that country. So although I was not present for all of them, I have a pretty fair understanding of what transpired, some of it from first-hand encounters with the principal players. My siblings and Ludovico suggested that I might want to concentrate my narrative on these events about which they have basically hearsay and anecdotal information.

Initially, much of what happened will relate to your major area of research. You, in fact, will be much more familiar than I with the incidents inside St. Matthias's rectory and the subsequent scandal. I have, perhaps, more pertinent information on the activities of its daughter parish, St Bartholomew's, Givins Street. These events, unlike those at St. Matthias, were never the focus of the press or other public scrutiny, yet affected me directly. I am assuming that what you will have read, as I am also assuming you are too young to remember the events first-hand, will confirm that when the press broke the story of the events in St. Matthias's rectory, the city of Toronto was in shock.

I have held onto the newspaper clippings. The headlines were quite sensational. The front pages ran:

**Banned Anti-Devil Cult Goes on in Gloucester Street**
(*Toronto Daily Star*, September 2, 1967)

to, just three days later, in the same newspaper

**16 to testify on anti-devil cult girl**

The headlines would become even more salacious once the inquest was held later in the same month.

By the end of the first week in September, St. Matthias's had become a household word in the city and across the country. Indeed, the rector rivaled anyone for front page coverage. Canon Moore Smith was a priest who had spent the past twenty-some years in an old Anglo-Catholic parish with a small collection of downtrodden Anglos-Saxons. The neighbourhood, Bellwoods, was a down-at-heel part of the city which had become demographically primarily Polish and Portuguese Catholic. Moore Smith became involved with what was, in my opinion and politely termed, a spirit-based group. Part charismatic, part primitive animism and part simple emotionalism, the theology of faith healing and its twin sister demonism crept into Moore Smith's motley parish under his leadership. Except, he didn't really lead the congregation, if what we read was to be believed.

You will probably concur that it was Father Douglas Tisdall, a handsome, bright and colourful cleric, a recent ordinand with a young family, who was the real clerical force behind the motley crew. Except, they were hardly motley. The woman deemed by some as "high priestess" and regularly by the press as "the leader of the cult" was Mrs. Marjorie Rogers, the wife of a well-respected and well-liked professor at the University of Toronto. Many in the congregation were what my old Irish nurse would have called "quality people" from the better parts of town and, let us not forget, the university, They drove to the Mass Sunday mornings and stayed on afterwards for "other activities".

My understanding, and you will have a more definitive knowledge, was that there were allegations of a sexual relationship between Mrs. Rogers and Father Tisdall, but whether that was before or after the death of the girl, or if in fact such rumours were true, I have no idea. She was a powerful woman and certainly held sway over a sizeable group of followers.

How Tisdall could have exerted such force over Canon Moore Smith, I can only speculate as a pathologist who has seen so many similar tragedies unfold. I suspect the older man was flattered by the attention of the younger man. Decades of living and working among the Anglo-Saxon poor would grind down the strongest of us, and I suspect Moore Smith was a less-than-strong man who may easily have been swept away by the flattering interest of a younger, richer cleric. Evidence later came out that the former bishop had known of Tisdall's charismatic practice of glossolalia[2] but had, despite his own misgivings, ordained the young man at the insistence of Moore Smith.

---

2 Speaking in tongues.

Canon Moore Smith was tall and thin, his thinness exaggerated by his circular Protestant clerical collar. To-day, with his round glasses we might say he looked like an aging Harry Potter. Yet he and his children seemed bright and were scholars. His followers all seemed to participate in the rituals of the cult while at the same time displaying a certain degree of empathy towards the poor in the community.

According to my friends in Toronto, everyone knew the juicy bits and relished discussing them on the streetcars and at lunch counters. In St. Matthias's rectory, an eighteen-year-old girl, Katherine Globe, had been "spanked" by four men, including her brother, fiancé, and the two priests (Tisdall and Moore Smith) to force the devil from her body. She died of meningitis without receiving proper medical care. Even after she died, the priests, in full liturgical regalia, performed a strange liturgy at the morgue to raise her to life again. The failure to act as rational people are expected to act, in itself, was not malevolent but terribly misguided. Still, they must have been cruel — were cruel — and the girl undoubtedly suffered terribly in the final hours of her life.

I still have the clippings from the *Toronto Star* and other newspapers. A friend from my teaching days at the University of Toronto sent me the first clippings. She and her husband had been members of St. Matthias's who had left the parish, as she put it, "when the sour had turned to the surreal". She carefully avoided any suggestion that I might have a connection. I suspected, nonetheless that she had encountered my children and had an inkling that something was amiss in their relationship with the triumvirate of Moore Smith, Rogers and Tisdall.

My actually suspicions were really triggered by the first clipping about Gloucester Street. It suggested to me there was trouble. I had recently received a birthday card from Joanna, simply signed Joanna. There was no salutation or term of endearment just her Christian name. The return address was a house on Gloucester Street.

One other clipping stood out and led me to believe Chris and Joanna might indeed have a connection to this group at St Matthias's.

This clipping affixed a photograph of Fr. Tisdall and Mrs. Rogers with a group of supporters and well-wishers standing behind. It was a bit grainy but there was no mistaking Chris and Joanna in the background.

As has been mentioned, Chris was a student at Wycliffe College and, I suppose, came into contact with Fr. Tisdall there. The dead girl, Katherine, had a brother who was also a student at the college. Her fiancé, moreover, Canon Moore Smith's twenty-six-year-old son, was a University of Toronto student. Joanna, on the other hand, may initially have become involved, albeit indirectly, with St. Matthias's through Mrs. Rogers and her husband. Professor Rogers was a French literature professor at Trinity College, where even after graduation Joanna continued to take classes. By this time, the Rogerses had returned from a stint in Paris and quite soon after he befriended her. I remember Joanna writing to me, when she still wrote, of his kindness and I believe on all accounts that in addition to being a kind man, he was a good scholar and well-respected academic. It is conceivable that Joanna, through her association with the Rogerses, began to attend St. Matthias's and eventually, when the proverbial you-know-what hit the fan, transferred her loyalties to St. Bartholomew's.

Chris, when we had last communicated, did tell me that he had taken a student placement at St. Bartholomew's, Givins Street. St. Bartholomew's was, as I mentioned, a daughter parish of St. Matthias's and, I understand, somewhat high church. Now this seemed strange to me at the time, and probably still does, that both Chris and Tisdall, coming from Wycliffe which purported to be evangelical, would have appointments in these parishes, Tisdall at St. Matthias's and Chris at St. Bartholomew's. Chris subsequently confirmed that he had been given lodgings in St. Bartholomew's parish house and he had been living there for some period of time since shortly after their return from the summer in Italy. Joanna, he said, would be joining him there eventually.

My Father was in his final illness at the time, so I asked my sister Laura if she could come over from Italy to stay at my flat in Oxford and look after him. Relations between me and my children, especially Joanna, had really become strained after she reluctantly wrote to me about the baby. I am far from a prudish man but it was more her cavalier manner about the whole business that I found a bit irresponsible. And I told her as much.

I flew over, arriving two days before the coroner's inquest into the death of Katherine Globe. I declined offers from friends to stay in their houses, thinking perhaps I should be available should Joanna agree to see me. My evenings, for the most part, were quiet and gave me more than enough time to reflect. I was perturbed to think that my two offspring were only a few blocks away and yet that they might well be attracted to, even closely involved with, this bizarre cult and the death of that girl. The whole notion, quite frankly, made me sick. I had to confess to myself that not only did I know little about my children's association with this group at St. Matthias's, but I also knew little about my children.

In later years, I would often go over the events of the inquest with Laura and my brother Cosmo before I refused to discuss the events any longer. My second wife and I also shared our perspectives on the events. The players in the bizarre drama that was to unfold, those who testified and those who witnessed the testimonies, as well as the reactions of the Moore Smith group of family and friends astounded me. The spellbound gazes of my fellow courtroom observers remain as clear to me to-day as all those years ago.

Later that same month of September, the coroner's inquest was held in the old town hall in Toronto, a large neo-Romanesque building which dominates the downtown of Toronto's business district with its large clock tower. Built in the nineteenth century and impressive as it is on the exterior, its courtrooms on the west side of the building reflect an age of wood and gloom. Dr. H. B. Cotnam was presiding. Cotnam and I had become acquaintances during my tenure at the University of Toronto. He, of course, could not meet with me privately. For me to have approached him would have been a clear breach of professional etiquette both proscribed and personal. So many times over the years, friends have approached me

final night
latest sport

# Toronto Daily Star

all star ★★★★★

PLUS THE CANADIAN & COLOR COMICS SECTION

## BANNED ANTI-DEVIL CULT GOES ON IN GLOUCESTER ST.

NEW HEADQUARTERS OF "DEVIL" CULT

A new slogan STUDENT POWER comes to Canada

By ANDREW SZENDE
Star staff writer

TOM FAULKNER, U of T student president, favors equal faculty-student power at university.

See A NEW SLOGAN, page 22

Packing in 460,000 students

## 2,300 specialists quit Quebec medicare in revolt over fees

From our Quebec bureau

QUEBEC—The Quebec government and 2,300 doctors confront each other today in the biggest rebellion by the medical profession against government medicare since the Saskatchewan doctors' strike in 1962.

See MEDICARE, page 22

## Tory fund-raiser quit Bramalea firm 'to avoid conflict'

See PRICE, Page 12

### CUSTER'S LAST TRENDEX?

CARRYING PRAYER BOOKS, Canon Moore Smith, rector of St. Matthias Church, today enters the church building. Right Rev. George B. Snell, Anglican Bishop of Toronto, said he had ordered Smith to desist from the practice of trying to eliminate "evil spirits" from distressed people and had warned of dangers involved.

## Tory donnybrook could erupt over '2-nation' Quebec theory

By WALTER GRAY
Star staff writer

See DONNYBROOK, page 4

## Girl killed on wedding eve six children hurt in crash

Special to The Star

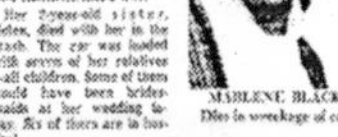

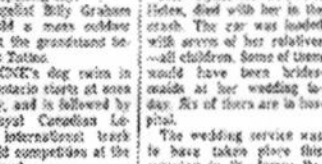

MARLENE BLACK

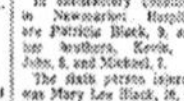

YOUR BIG SATURDAY STAR

THE CANADIAN PLUS COLOR COMICS SECTION

### The Tory leadership race — and its dark horse

EXCLUSIVE

### LIBERALS LEAD IN CNE VOTE

## A sunny holiday weekend

## Palmer quits world golf tourney

By KEN McKEE
Star staff writer

ARNIE PALMER

on my cases, hoping to influence me or at the least obtain information not made public. I would never have considered placing Cotnam in such a position. At the most, we exchanged pleasantries on the few occasions we passed in the corridors. Although I knew he was aware of my presence every day in the courtroom and the possible involvement of my children in the cult, in kindness, and he was an extremely kind man, he never made any reference to the proceedings.

I consoled myself that Chris and Joanna had been in Italy when the girl died. They could not be directly indicted in any verdict but their names could appear in the press as part of the overall "spiritual awakening" which had occurred at the church. I was also worried that they might attempt to testify, or be called to testify, about the working of the cult. Other similar circumstances which might not have resulted in actual death could come to light, other events in which they might have been involved.

Cotnam was fair in his chairing of the inquest and his directions to the five jurors. But, the whole things was bizarre albeit, at times, spell-bounding. Several of the witnesses, notably Mrs. Rogers, dubbed, as I previously noted, the "leader of the cult" by the popular press, seemed almost convincing, as if the casting-out of devils was a normal everyday activity. Mrs. Rogers, in her suede flat shoes, seemed the epitome of a middle-class professor's wife which until her involvement with the St. Matthias's crowd she undoubtedly had been. Her performance, for clearly that is what it was, was without doubt rehearsed. She avoided direct answers by falling back on the Bible; it happened in the Bible ergo who was she to question. When asked point blank, for example, if she believed a person can be inhabited by evil spirits, she replied, "The Bible says so and I believe the Bible".

It was all so unbelievable as to be funny at times. The courtroom burst into laughter when a Mrs. McClintock, the wife of a reformed church minister, sat clutching her purse and testifying that Canon Moore Smith had said "that I! that I was possessed by a devil". One couldn't possibly imagine anyone more unlikely to be possessed by

METRO WEATHER

Friday rain and cold. Low 40, high 48. Details page 2.

ESTABLISHED 1892

# Toronto Daily Star

Thursday, September 28, 1967

THOSE CLOSEST to Katherine Globe, 19-year-old who died in rectory of St. Matthias' Anglican Church, are at inquest into her death. Left, her parents, Mr. and Mrs. George Globe, sit with their parish priest from Burlington, Rev. R. J. Stackwell. Right, Canon G. Moore W. Smith, rector of St. Matthias, arrives with his wife. Canon Smith was Miss Globe's adopted daughter; Mr. Globe denies R. Colt believing in exorcising demons was reported operating at church.

## Ottawa increases mortgage rate to record 8¼%

By TOM HAZLITT
Star staff writer

OTTAWA — An unprecedented one per cent increase in the maximum interest rate under the National Housing Act will go into effect next week, touching off another round of increases in the whole mortgage field.

The new NHA rate—a record 8¼ per cent—was announced by Labor Minister J. R. Nicholson amid boos and gasps of surprise in the House of Commons last night.

The increase, to take effect Oct. 1, will mean:

### New rate won't help housing crisis here say Metro builders

See NEW RATE, Page 8

See OTTAWA, Page 7

Problem of survival'

### Question of unity worries Pearson

By WALTER GRAY
Star staff writer

See PEARSON, Page 2

### COLDEST SEPT. 28 IN 125 YEARS

### Evil spirit inquest opens death incredible: Cotnam

See EVIL SPIRIT, Page 3

### $50 pension increase for widows urged in compensation report

### Help Wanted with Ron Haggart

### Would Viet Nam GIs like girl pen pals?

More HELP WANTED: See page 7

### It was a dark day for Nixon

By EARL McRAE
Star staff writer

See BAD DAY, page 9

### Chlorine leak kills man, injures 46

### New French station

### Mexico poison traced to 50 bakeries

a devil than this woman who sat there bobbing her hat and jowls in indignation. If nothing else, it put Satan's credibility to the test. Dr. Cotnam threatened to clear the courtroom and a policeman had to call us to order.

Words such as demons, witchcraft, devils, and spirits slipped with such fluidity from the lips of the Crown Counsel and witnesses, and even Dr. Cotnam, almost transporting us back centuries. The cult had a jargon certainly hitherto unknown to me. Over the course of the inquest, I heard terms like "discernment," "up the flue," "atmosphere" and "high." My favourite was "potting out," which I gather meant the sudden movement into a trance. One witness described Mrs. Rogers "potting out and howling like a dog".

Their favourite location for much of this was in the nave of St. Matthias's church where they would lie in the aisles, presumably to be closer to the altar. At times Douglas Tisdall, according to testimony, was seen actually lying on the altar. As Dr. Cotnam was to insist in his charge, although cult members denied the term "exorcizing" actually meant the casting-out of evil spirits and demons, "the prayer they used suggests they do believe in such things".

Strange behaviour, almost laughable had it not been for the cloud of sadness, not just over the possibly needless death of a young woman but also the families wrenched apart, not least my own. The girl had been taken from her family and put under the wardship of Canon Moore Smith and his wife, Violet. Several other testimonies spoke to families rent asunder. Even Mrs. Rogers had become estranged from her husband and mother. Testimony showed that her husband, Professor Rogers, had send a lawyer's letter to Moore Smith banning him from their house and that Mrs. Rogers had actually ordered her mother from her house.

Over each of the four days of the proceedings, the three Neagles would sit in the courtroom: Joanna, Chris and I. Their friend, Albert Stafford, often sat nearby his friends but I was a distance from them. Chris and Joanna, starting to appear pregnant by this time, sat near the front, often holding hands, directly behind the Moore Smiths. Again, although it became increasingly clear that there was

Special to The Star

PARIS— President Charles de Gaulle has ordered his ministers going to Canada not to visit Ottawa while there.

METRO WEATHER
Wednesday mainly sunny and warm. Low 58, high 78. Details page 2.

ESTABLISHED 1892

# Toronto Daily Star

four star ★★★★ edition

Tuesday, October 3, 1967—56 pages

## A drippy, drippy day...then marooned girl, 16, died

CARLA CORBUS
'I want to be rescued'

See DIARY, Page 5

*Remanded 2 weeks*

## Foster mother demands trial

See FOSTER, Page 8

## 'Boy' sent to Peru is a blue-eyed girl

"We did not adopt a boy," said Mr. P., a lawyer in Lima. "We got a girl. We call her Barbara."

See BOY, Page 18

## Formosa PM cancels visit to Canada

TAIPEI (AP)—C. K. Yen, vice-president and premier of Nationalist China, has cancelled his visit to Canada as a result of two-China statements made by Canadian officials, the foreign office announced today.

**Toronto Daily Star**

**Snow on Clairtone's screen**

There's trouble on the screens of Clairtone color TV sets—at least temporarily. The company that began as a brightly colored success story for two young Canadians has had to be bailed out by the Nova Scotia government again—this time to the tune of $7,000,000. A special report appears on Page 17.

## LIBRARY HIRES BOOK CHASER

VANCOUVER (CP) —

AN EVIL SPIRIT can inhabit a person, Mrs. Marjorie Rogers told jurors at the inquest into the June 21 death of Katherine Globe. She denied saying the 15-year-old girl should be exorcised before receiving medical attention.

## Witness believes evil spirits can 'inhabit' human body

See WITNESS, page 2

## Sharp hints he'll refund part of sales tax on materials for housing

By WALTER GRAY
Special to The Star

See SHARP, Page 4

## Nixon's dash in vain Robarts not sharing TV

## Buddhist nun in fiery suicide

## Test Hanoi with halt in fighting: Senator

## Fuel firm could close airport

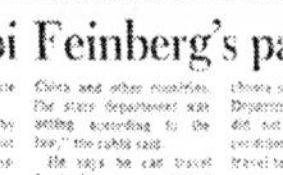

## U.S. revokes Rabbi Feinberg's passport

RABBI FEINBERG

no question my children would be called to testify on these events, they clearly were intimate with those who were present at the death. When the day's proceedings ended, the brother and sister would leave with one or another of the Matthias's crowd. Joanna would walk by me without a nod.

Chris and I had dinner once but he behaved sullenly, uncharacteristically non-communicative, throughout. I had selected a small French restaurant on Charles Street. They brought round a trolley of hors d'oeuvres which I thought might be a distraction if things got uncomfortable. Uncomfortable? They increasingly were, from the moment they arrived. I write that, in the first place, because Chris refused to come to see his father alone. He was accompanied by a Polish doctor friend who was a gynecologist working at the Women's College hospital. I knew that institution well but clearly could not imagine them employing such a person. Quite frankly, I though him bonkers and offensive, his comments unwarranted, in fact his very presence totally insufferable. All I had planned to do was simply beg Chris to return to Britain with his sister.

"Dad," he kept repeating, "you don't understand, you have never understood, I am afraid you never will. You just don't understand."

"Understand what, for Christ's sake," I shot back after the fourth or fifth time he said this.

It was then that this doctor who Chris called Broni basically told me to shut up.

"Stop badgering your son. He and his sister have moved beyond you and your secular understanding of life. Chris has told me you are an atheist. I would, having now met you, go a step forward and say you are a force of evil in these young people's lives."

At this point, Chris just stood up and, without a further word, walked out of the restaurant. I never spoke to my son again. The Polish doctor, who I was later to learn was Bronislaw Wieszkowski, followed him. As Wieszkowski took the door from Chris who slipped out ahead of him into the street, he held back a minute to turn and grin at me. It was a smile I shall never forget, which actually sent a shiver up my spine. Wieszkowski was undoubtedly mad.

I had a few meals with Joanna and Chris's friend Albert. Albert was also a friend, and favourite, of my sister and brother-in-law in Italy. I remembered that he had accompanied my children the previous summer on their trip. Albert was a very serious young man, not without a sense of humour, but focused on things that mattered, like his studies and his friends. Albert was clearly upset about what was happening in his friends' lives. But, whether through a sense of misplaced loyalty or what have you, he shed little light on what was going on. Although I was certain he had insight into their behaviour, I could not break through this shell of reticence. Yet, although I felt sorry for him, I wished he had had more backbone and had stood up to them. On the other hand, the lines of communications were still open for him, whereas they were irrevocably broken for me.

The power of the cult distressed me greatly. On several occasions at the inquest, I sat next to a well-dressed woman who seemed almost anxious to chat during the breaks. It was as though she needed to share her opinions and, more importantly, her personal story. She was, as it turns out, Douglas Tisdall's mother-in-law. She made seemingly flippant remarks to me, which, nonetheless, suggested that the events presented at the inquest were perhaps only the tip of the iceberg. Remarks such as, "They'd love to get me up there on the stand; could I tell them stories," had a chilling effect. She also clarified the money aspect of the cult. How could a poor inner urban parish afford the stipends for two priests? The woman explained that Douglas Tisdall was the son of Dr. Frederick Tisdall, one of the co-developers of the children's cereal Pablum. No shortage of money.

The mother-in-law confirmed that there had been a conspiracy by church officials to ignore the activities at St. Matthias's. There had been an indisputable attempt to cover things up, whether through benign neglect of responsibility or an attempt at collusion with the clergy at St. Matthias's. Initially, I was uncertain about the degree of awareness church officials actually had. That is not the case now: they knew; they did nothing. And although I hate to write this, I believe they lied even while sitting in the box.

I shook my head in disbelief on the final day, when even more bizarre statements seemed to be tumbling out one after the other. An older man in a tweed jacket and woollen-knit tie had seen me and came up to me at the lunch break. He introduced himself as Father Guy Paris, an Oblate priest teaching at the university's Catholic college, St. Michael's. He reminded me that we had met several years earlier at a dinner in the home of mutual friends. He asked me to join him for lunch.

We walked over to a restaurant on an upper floor of a nearby department store with the memorable name of Arcadian Court. Amidst the splendour of this Art Deco dining room and surrounded by sixty or so ladies-who-lunch, Father Paris tried to make some sense of the whole business. I had admitted to being an atheist but from a church family. As a pathologist who had seen almost every sort of human depravity, I told him, I was resigned to being at sea as I witnessed testimony such as that we had endured that morning.

"You must accept, Harry, that for many, and not just the uneducated, the immediacy of blood, suffering, and direct encounters with the spiritual realm are necessary. And don't forget the voices and apparitions that are mostly but not exclusively a phenomenon of the Roman Catholic Church, although St. Matthias's is probably more ceremonial than your average Catholic parish to-day. The ones we hear most about are modern: Lourdes, La Salette, Fatima, and Medjugorje. There are, however, many interesting earlier ones, with the voices of Joan of Arc being a fine case in point; all the more interesting in that Joan was generally quite down-to-earth and not in the least triumphant or suggestible. The relentless questioning of the learned Church lawyers, eager to make her slip up and bring in some minor detail that would link her voices with the well-developed and highly imaginative demonology of the period proved to be a total flop. In the end, they had to condemn her in great part for wearing men's clothing."

He paused to take a sip of his wine before continuing.

"What, you might ask, has all this in common with our St. Matthias Pablum rentiers and their dabbling in diabolical possession?. The short answer is the fact that all of this makes religion feel real, alive, now. Events are happening. Something, good or bad, is happening right now, happened last week, or last year, right over there. The statue cried real tears. The possessed child turned his head right around 360 degrees and delivered himself of a volley of horrendous blasphemy in Hebrew. Mrs. Rogers goes into a trace and howls like a dog.

"Otherwise, everything happened two thousand years ago, Salvation, the Resurrection and all that. We are supposed to believe, appearances to the contrary notwithstanding, that events in the first thirty-three years of the Common Era changed everything about life on earth.

"The average Christian, Anglican, Roman Catholic, Reformed, certainly one here in the West, lives comfortable in the in-between time. We have been saved, possess Holy Scripture and the Sacraments, and have only to be very, very good and wait for Christ to return. Totally bloodless and very neat, but honestly not too satisfactory for the group at St. Matthias's who can't and won't wait. They need the search for the existing spiritual right here and now. So demons are easy prey for them!"

He laughed as he said this, a large booming sort of a laugh. Several ladies turned their heads but not, I am pleased to note, three hundred and sixty degrees. Then he said a strange thing.

"You know, Harry, sometimes I envy your atheism."

As we headed back for the final session of the inquest, I shared my initial astonishment that so many people had testified under oath that they had approached the bishop with their concerns. All of this had convinced me, and Guy completely agreed, that the activities surrounding the death of Katherine Globe were only the visible evidence of a much wider problem within the churches in the inner city. He told me that the evidence when linked to his conversations at the inquest convinced him, unequivocally, that the St. Matthias's group was only a small part of a wider, more extreme web. Its members had merely moved from the fringes of the more benign St.

Matthias's congregation to other welcoming churches. My fear was that they had taken Chris and Joanne with them.

Guy and my suppositions were collaborated when the verdict was read. As the rather condemning headline in the *Toronto Daily Star* of October 4, 1967, read:

**Inquest verdict: Canon and wife negligent in girl's death**
**JURY WANTS ALL CULTS PROBED**

Meanwhile, throughout the inquest, Princess Margaret shared the front pages with Canon Moore Smith, Mrs. Rogers, and Father Tisdall. As she visited Toronto, I wondered what she thought about the goings on in the church over which her sister nominally presided. This Brit, I do know, was sickened.

I stayed on in Toronto after the inquest was adjourned, for what reason I don't really know. For one thing I was enjoying the company of Guy Paris. I had taken a long leave from my work so no one was pressing me to return. Perhaps I believed Chris and Joanna would make some effort to contact me once the pressure of the inquest had died down and it appeared no criminal charges were to be laid. Maybe because they were my children and I as a Father just refused to believe two bright young people like they would succumb to such nonsense; maybe it was my own vanity; whatever it was, I stayed on. Surely my children would eventually recognize by my very proximity that I cared? Only when my own Father died, did I returned to Oxford for the funeral.

During the inquest, however, I had met several families who had been in similar circumstances. Several of them I met through the chatty, well-dressed mother-in-law. One particularly sympathetic couple, Lawrence and Helen Wilkinson, invited me to their home for dinner one night. I felt sorry for them; they had contacted the bishop's office on several occasions about the St. Matthias's group but on each occasion had been rebuffed. Lawrence and Helen were the antithesis of me. Whereas I reacted with frustration and eventually spontaneous outbursts of anger, they had unlimited patience

METRO WEATHER [illegible]

ESTABLISHED 1892

# Toronto Daily Star

closing markets

*Inquest verdict: Canon and wife negligent in girl's death*

# JURY WANTS ALL CULTS PROBED

SURROUNDED BY SPECTATORS, principal witnesses Mrs. Marjorie Rogers (right foot at left) and Canon G. Moore Smith stand outside old city hall courtroom after inquest jury into the death of Katherine Globe retired at 12.30 p.m. today. Earlier the jury heard Dr. H. B. Cotnam, Ontario's supervising coroner, sharply criticize members of the St. Matthias' Church group for ignoring the 19-year-old girl's basic human needs as she lay dying June 21 in the church rectory. "No one checked her basic needs —those of fluids, food, bowels or clean bed clothing," he said. —Star photo by [illegible]

Canon G. Moore W. Smith and his wife were negligent in not providing proper medical care for their ward Katharine Globe who died in the rectory of Canon Smith's church June 21, a coroner's jury found today.

The jury recommended Canon Smith's "faith-healing" cult at St. Matthias' Anglican Church, Bellwoods Ave., be "further investigated"—and it asked that "other, similar" groups be sought out and investigated also.

The jury's verdict, read out by the foreman, attached no blame to the medical profession in the 19-year-old girl's death from meningitis and rupture of a brain abscess, after an ear infection.

Specifically, the jury urged a thorough investigation into the "actions and practices of this faith-healing group, especially the involvement and influence of Canon Smith, his assistant, Rev. Douglas Tisdall and Mrs. Marjorie Rogers."

The latter was identified in evidence as leader of the cult.

The three rushed off to [illegible] with their lawyer, Gerald [illegible], declaring they would have nothing to say immediately.

Advisers to the bishop of the Anglican diocese of Toronto were expected to rush the verdict to him.

'REASONABLE'

"I feel this is quite a reasonable verdict, based on the evidence," Dr. H. B. Cotnam, Ontario supervising coroner, told the jury, composed of two house-wives, an engineer, a public relations man and a newspaper executive.

[illegible]

See JURY, Page 7

## U.S. believes Con Thien seige broken

CON THIEN, South Viet Nam (Reuters)—American military commanders believe they have at last broken the back of a three-month North Vietnamese artillery barrage of this besieged marine post.

Sources said reconnaissance indicated what could be the beginning of a North Vietnamese withdrawal from around Con Thien, one mile south of the demilitarized zone and from Gio Linh, another marine post seven miles to the east.

Massive raids and raids on the North Vietnamese artillery by giant B-52 bombers seemed to have broken the siege, the sources said. B-52 strikes have been launched almost [illegible]

## Holdout: No 'home-for-home' deal

Toronto's Board of Control was told today that one of the four Don Mount home-owners resisting expropriation had found a new house and was now happy.

But Mrs. Rilda Hughes, 58, turned nearly white with anger when she heard about it. "It's not true. I haven't got anywhere yet," she said.

The board was told by Real Estate Commissioner David Alexander that Mrs. Hughes had bought a house on Pape Ave. for $12,300 and that she had been offered $12,000 for the home on Matilda St. in which she has lived for 30 years.

Controller Fred Beavis said: "She's getting a better house than the one she's moving out of. Show the pictures to the press."

But Mrs. Hughes told reporters later she only knew of a house on Pape Ave.

See HOLDOUT, Page [illegible]

## Stock Market ★ Capsule ★

Toronto stocks pulled out of a six-day decline today, but gains were of a token nature. New York moved indecisively.

Laura Secord paced the local board, rising 1½ to 12. Salada Foods has raised its bid for Secord to $23.50 a share from $[illegible]. Ahead a point or more were Bow Valley, [illegible], Levy Industries and Canada Cement. Western oils were stronger but golds sagged.

Stock tables Page [illegible]

## *Marijuana sold in schools: Ross*

By MICHAEL KAPRAL
Star staff writer

Professional criminals operating out of Yorkville are selling marijuana to high school students across Metro, Chairman William Ross of the Toronto Board of Education said last night.

Ross said he has called a special closed meeting tomorrow with officials of various agencies in an effort to halt "what I think is almost an epidemic."

An RCMP spokesman said he wouldn't "agree or disagree" with Ross, "at the moment," but declared that use of marijuana by high school students is "approaching epidemic proportions."

He estimated that teenage use of marijuana has increased [illegible] to [illegible] per cent in Metro this year.

[illegible]

See POT, Page [illegible]

## MAFIA DID FEASIBILITY STUDY ON YORKVILLE

By DAVID MARX
Star staff writer

Agents of a Mafia-style mob conducted a feasibility study of Yorkville 2½ years ago and decided against a move to control marijuana traffic in the village.

Both Metro and RCMP drug experts have repeatedly said there is no organized or professional syndicate behind the area's booming drug business.

The U.S.-based gang sent agents into the village for a study that might anything done by a major industry.

They studied all aspects of the situation and then determined the financial possibilities of the area were limited.

The only known criminals close to the village are about 30 young, small-time and part-time thieves.

All are known by police and all have minor criminal records.

They move on the fringe of the hippie crowd, most making regular use of marijuana, LSD and teenage girls.

The organized gang made contact with several members of this loose fraternity and in at least three cases offered to set some members up as the gang's Yorkville representative.

[illegible]

## Toronto Daily Star

## 'It's good to be a Liberal'

"It's a good thing to be a Liberal in the province of Ontario right now," says Liberal Leader Robert Nixon. "... The province is ready for a change." Nixon was taking part in the first of three interviews in The Star with leaders of the main political parties contesting the Oct. 17 provincial election. Interviewers were three members of The Star's editorial board, Mark Harrison, Robert Nielsen and Val Sears. Their conversation is on page 8.



*After elections*

## Provinces to be invited to housing crisis talks

By WALTER GRAY
Special to The Star

OTTAWA — The federal government will meet with the provinces to discuss housing problems later this year, Labor Minister John Nicholson told the Commons yesterday.

His announcement was followed by an Opposition non-confidence motion on the government's housing policies which the Liberals defeated 112 to 98.

Nicholson, who is responsible for housing, said the conference, first announced in last spring's Throne speech, has been delayed by the provincial elections in Saskatchewan, New Brunswick and Ontario, and by the recent change in premiers in Nova Scotia.

Nicholson said that as a result of his conferences with provincial and municipal leaders, and representatives of financial institutions earlier this year, the government now is considering four new programs relating to housing and urban growth:

- Establishment of new satellite communities in urban areas in which Ottawa would provide special incentives.
- Comprehensive planning of urban regions and the acquisition of lands for transportation corridors and the open spaces needed for urban growth.
- Housing programs to serve as an integral part of other combined federal and [illegible]

See OTTAWA, page 4

## Pipe bursts man dies in scalding steam

[illegible]

## Two bodies in plane

STRATFORD (CP)—[illegible]

## French minister postpones visit

(From our Ottawa bureau)

OTTAWA — French Agriculture Minister Edgar Faure has postponed his trip to Canada, Agriculture Minister J. J. Greene told Commons today. The visit was scheduled to begin tomorrow. See also page 47.

## *Cards beat Sox 2-1 in Series opener*

Special to The Star

BOSTON—Lou Brock had a World Series' baseball record by getting four straight hits and scored both runs today as St. Louis Cardinals edged Boston Red Sox, 2-1, in the opening game at Fenway Park.

Righthander Bob Gibson, who missed much of the 1967 season because of a broken ankle, pitched superbly for the Cards. He allowed only six hits, one of them a home run to Boston pitcher Jose Santiago for the Sox only run.

Details on Page 18

with their son Peter. Peters was living in the same house as Chris and Joanna.

They had convinced Peter to join us. He was a soft-spoken young man who had graduated from McGill University in Montreal where he had taken a second degree in Social Work. Although his parents told me he had been a good athlete, he seemed pale and almost gaunt. The dinner proceeded quite calmly and we all chatted freely on a number of topics.

I remember Helen's recounting a funny incident at a reception she had attended for Princess Margaret. Peter had laughed, "My mother would wear a hat if she thought Princess Margaret was flying over in an aeroplane".

We all laughed. The atmosphere was convivial and I liked Peter.

The topics remained light until inevitably we came to St. Bartholomew's. All through the inquest, my focus had pretty much been on St. Matthias's and my children's attachment to that cult, but I was increasingly aware that an analogous situation was developing at St. Bartholomew's. Peter sanctioned my worst fear, not so much by what he said, but what he didn't. Peter did, nonetheless, affirm his friendship with Joanna and Chris as well as confirm my fear of their deep involvement in the parish.

It was clear throughout the discussion, that the young man was exceedingly troubled by the death of Katherine. He seemed genuinely remorseful of any possible rôle he may have played in the death, however indirectly. His parents kept reminding him that he had been working at a residential clinic for disturbed children and so had been away from the rectory for most of the time of Katherine's illness. He seemed to accept this on one level but insisted that he still must be loyal to the group, his friends, and share their responsibility and culpability. He made it clear, quite gently I thought, to his parents that although he loved them, he would not be moving home.

Over coffee, he once again told me that he was a friend of both Joanna and, particularly, Chris. He said that Joanna was usually in her room, even going so far to remain there for meals. On the other hand, he and Chris played tennis together at a nearby indoor court several times a week. Two days after the dinner at his parents' home, Peter and I met in a small lounge in my hotel. He was a shy person who worked with troubled children, to-day what they call "children at risk". In the course of his work, he had crossed paths with Moore Smith and started to attend the church. After McGill, he had worked in Vancouver where he eventually broke up with his girlfriend. Without her, he said he felt adrift in Vancouver and so moved back to Toronto. He didn't want to move back with his parents, but he recognized the need for some sort of surrogate family, hence the church connection.

All this he freely admitted. As I have noted: he knew Joanna and Chris quite well. It was through him that I learned some details about their initial affiliation with St. Matthias's and eventually the cult at St. Bartholomew's Givins Street. At first he had been slow to betray too much information. By the end of our discussion, I had the impression he had revealed far more than he intended and certainly far more than the cult leaders would have sanctioned. I had appreciated his frankness but it had not been a comforting conversation by any means.

When I returned to my hotel that night, there was a message from Laura and Cosmo telling me that our Father had died in Oxford. I booked an aeroplane home for the next day. I made one last attempt to contact my children. I had the taxi stop at St. Bartholomew's parish house. When I rang the bell, it was answered by a blond Polish-sounding woman I assumed to be Dr. Wieszkowski's wife. I told her that Chris and Joanna's Grandfather had died. She curtly replied that Chris was at the university and Joanna was unwell but she would inform them. The door closed. I rang the bell again but it was not answered. I lacked the patience of Lawrence and Helen Wilkinson; I turned and got back into the taxi.

Some days after the funeral, my sister who had been staying in my flat returned to her family in Italy. For all intents and purposes, I had pretty well washed my hands of my two children; we never made contact again. I also made up my mind on another matter. I refused categorically to have anything to do with the child Joanna was carrying.

My wife was dead. My children were as good as dead to me. My sister lived in Italy. My brother, newly ordained, was posted in a diocese miles from me. I was alone.

I shudder every time I write the word "cult" but that is fundamentally what it was. That it caused the great tragedies in my children's lives, I have had to accept. Other than the stark details, I knew nothing of what actually transpired in Toronto for some time. Laura kept her confidences. I knew no one else prepared to discuss the tragic events. Your interests are in the facts of the case not the emotional reactions of peripheral players like me. So I will not elaborate on my own feelings. I feel no compulsion to write an apologia for my actions. Suffice it to say, I made no further attempt to contact my children again.

About three years after my trip to Canada, I received a letter from Helen Wilkinson. Lawrence had died earlier that year. Their son had left the cult, utterly rejecting them, and had eventually moved home with them. He had accepted a job in Vancouver and, when he returned, married the East Indian woman, his former girlfriend. In her chatty way, Helen told me the girl's family were immigrants from Uganda who had read the handwriting on the wall and left Uganda ten years before the general expulsion of East Indians by Idi Amin. Both Peter and his wife were working at a centre for refugee youth. Lawrence Wilkinson had been extremely fond of his son's wife, whom he met before he died. Helen, although saddened with her husband's death, seemed a woman with no regrets. In fact, my acquaintanceship with Helen grew exponentially through correspondence.

Peter and his wife had been invited to share their professional experiences in Vancouver at a refugee centre with a similar organizational structure in London. They were going to be in Britain for ten days and had invited Helen to join them. Helen wrote that Peter had felt very close to Chris and felt he had one last thing he had to do before he could be completely free of the cult which was to speak to me.

I met Peter in St. James's Park. He said he felt he could speak more easily if we walked rather than sit in a pub or restaurant. I came down from Oxford the night before and we were able to meet at nine in the morning and walk. We walked much of the day.

Peter told me that around the time I left Canada, the group became more and more insular. He was discouraged very strongly from visiting his family. He said he now regretted not to going into greater detail when we had met in Toronto about the practices of the group other than to confirm that they had intensified from the days at St. Matthias's. He made just the one remark, several times.

"I am ashamed, Harry, utterly ashamed."

In the evening I had dinner with Peter's wife, Asha, and Helen. It was to be only the first of many such evenings. Never, however, have the events I had learned earlier in the day from Peter been discussed again by Peter, Helen and me. A curtain had been dropped, to be melodramatic about it, never to be raised. As my Latin master would say all those years ago: "and here Virgil draws the veil".

* * * *

It had been my intension, Professor Stevenson, to relate the events of my children's lives, after I left Canada until an appropriate point for my sister to continue. At this point in my narration, however, I would have had to base virtually everything on my conversation with Peter during that long walk all these years ago. But hearsay of hearsay is never the best. So, I renege, therefore, slightly on our original agreement and I do so unbeknownst to my siblings. Some weeks ago, I asked my step-son to recount the events himself. Peter is now a man in his sixties living with his wife in Vancouver with grown children. His recollection will be clearer than mine. He lived the events; I heard about them only once on a long walk in St. James's Park over forty years ago.

I have read Peter's narrative; my siblings have not. They have never met Peter nor my wife Helen for that matter. I am affixing his narrative with mine and also another newspaper clipping which, having read Peter's narrative, I feel fits with his chronologically.

As I conclude, I realize, with hindsight, how difficult all this misfortune must have been for Albert. As I left Canada, he was preparing for his thesis defence and needed to focus on his work while having serious concerns about his friends' well-being. I admit now that I had underestimated the man, his compassion, but mostly his loyalty. Sadly, I think from Albert's perspective, he must have formed and retained a negative opinion of me. The total antithesis of this man, I had made it clear I wanted nothing more to do with my children until they "grew up".

My unyielding attitude I recognize did little to make life easier for Albert. He is dead. I regret to a degree the manner in which my family treated him. Christopher and Joanne treated him childishly and irresponsibly. Against his advice, they entered into the cult as educated adults. But, Albert, possibly naïve, also was an adult capable of making informed decisions about the future direction of his life. There are no devils out there directing our lives; we make our decisions and life-choices.

I never saw my grandchild. And I never heard from my son or daughter again. I veritably forbade Laura in her chatty way from any reference to my grandchild as she grew. The whole business surrounding the sordid circumstances of the child's birth disgusted me then and does to this day. In much the same way, the death of my first wife disgusts me.

Use whatever you will of what I or Peter have written as it relates to your research. I quite frankly don't give a fiddler's whore what people think of my rôle in all this. I have a new life and family. I am glad to be finished writing and to be done with the whole affair.

H. J. E. Neagle

# PETER

1967-1968

My step-dad has asked me to relate what I told him so many years back in that park in London. My wife Asha also encouraged me; she more than anyone helped me with my rehabilitation, if that is the right word. Besides, Harry has been so decent to my Mother and a terrific grandfather to my kids. I could not refuse him, much as I dislike remembering. He quotes me as saying, "I am ashamed, Harry, utterly ashamed". I remain that way. But I have been asked not to atone for the past but to recount the events after Harry left Toronto.

Eventually, Albert was never allowed to be with either Chris or Joanna alone. Whenever Albert encountered Chris on campus, Chris would return home in an agitated state. Joanna, as far I could tell, rarely went out of the house during her "confinement," except to activities at the church. My Mother used that word "confinement" and it still had some resonance in 1967.

I remember Albert would try to visit the parish house whenever he could although his visits were not especially welcomed by the other cult members. In fact, we were all encouraged to avoid anything more than a perfunctory acquaintanceship with Albert.

One evening about eight o'clock, when Joanna was well into her second trimester, Albert came to see her. I had answered the door and quickly led him upstairs. It was quite dark and we found Joanna sitting alone without any lights but staring out the window onto the street. She turned when Albert came in.

"Bertie, I am glad it is you. Do you remember when we were in Italy in the summer how much better my tennis had become?"

I found this an odd remark and remember a pained look came over Albert's face. Joanna, although it was late November and quite cool in the house, was wearing a free-flowing, sleeveless summer dress, so as Albert approached her he commented on bruises on her arms and red marks on her wrists. She reached out and grabbed both of his hands and started to whisper although at first I had trouble hearing her.

"Bertie, I am going to need your help."

Albert spoke slowly in staccato-like sentences, "Joanna, let me take you out of here. You can stay with me. Just for a few days. I promise to bring you back."

Her only response was a slight shaking of her head.

Albert continued, "Joanna, I don't think you are well. Are you actually seeing a doctor?"

"No need. One of the women here, Stanie, who used to be a midwife, looks after me. She is Broni's wife and he is a doctor. If I follow their regime I will be fine. But quickly, before she comes back, I must ask you a favour. First, you must swear you will not hate me for what I am about to ask."

Albert must have hesitated for she asked him a second time to swear not to be angry. He squeezed her hand which encouraged her to continue.

"I need a father for my child, one whose name I can write on the forms. Please let me put down your name. I can't tell the truth. Please may my child be a Stafford, not a Neagle."

I knew the rote well enough. We had all been instructed that Joanna was not to be left alone with anyone outside the group, especially Albert Stafford. But I felt sorry for Albert and had stayed in the room, not going immediately to summon the "duty" caregiver which was the erstwhile mid-wife Stanie. In any event, the woman arrived fairly promptly without being summoned.

Before Albert could answer Joanna, the woman entered the room.

"What are you doing here?"

For many years I have always referred to this woman as "she," "her," "the true leader of the cult". Quite frankly, I think I am still almost frightened to use her name; the very mention of it seems conjured up evil. At first like most of the others, I had always assumed that Mrs. Rogers perhaps still called most of the shots. But it seemed the Tisdall-Rogers duo had been usurped, at least at St. Bartholomew's, by Dr. Wieszkowski and his wife, Stanie. Joanna, by this point, had been an intimate of the entire group. She recognized authority.

After the verdict at the inquest, the press had hinted obliquely that there were other powerful forces, especially another powerful woman in the background. Whether Albert had picked up on this before this evening, I don't know. He quickly read the situation as he faced the woman. But such anger, anger as I have rarely seen in this life, welled up in the woman when she spoke to Albert.

The woman demanded that Albert leave immediately. He naturally refused. She shouted at him and almost immediately three men entered the room, one of whom was Chris.

"I asked you, Mr. Stafford," she shouted. "now I am commanding you: Get out in the name of God. You are polluting this handmaiden, you are polluting this house, you are polluting all of Christ's servants here in this room, in this house. I command you to leave."

She almost at once turned her anger onto me, shrieking "Useless backslider, help them get him out of here".

I was frankly amazed despite his anger how calm Albert remained and how resolutely he remained by Joanna although she had pulled back her hands from him.

The woman continued, "My brother Christopher, I command that you remove this man, this agent from the other side".

Chris approached him and gently, considering the oppressive hostile atmosphere of the room, took Albert's hands.

Then Joanna spoke, "Albert was here to coach me on my tennis game, to get me in form for the summer. But Albert, dearest Bertie, please go now. I must rest for later tonight."

She stood up and walked away from him towards a bedroom behind her.

The others parted so Chris, Albert and I could pass out into the hallway and down the three flights of stairs. When we got to the door, Chris was already telling Albert "It is best that you not just drop by like that as Joanna likes to prepare herself for visitors".

With Joanne away from us, Albert was quickly losing his calm. "Chris, these people are mad. Did you hear that woman? She is a character from a bad movie. For the love of God, man, look what they are doing to Joanna; she is almost catatonic. Are they giving her drugs? These bruises on her arms, how do you account for them and her wrists? And you, Chris, her brother, allowing all this. Chris I am your close friend, we can talk, if not here, anywhere you chose."

Chris only smiled. "Albert, these people are my close friends, look at Peter here, friends who love Joanna. Do you think him mad, a social worker helping kids in the slums? Stanie a nurse? Broni a respected surgeon? These friends are good Christian people, real Christians, who are seeing to Joanna's needs both physical and spiritual morning, noon, and night. You are reading too much into all of this. This is not St. Matthias, you know. Go home and concentrate on your defence next week. I will phone you when it is over and we can have tea together with Joanna."

With that he shut the door. Albert was left alone on the street in the cold November night.

At that point, I realized that I was probably mad, possessed, as we had been instructed to describe such a state, "engulfed in the madness of a spirit". I moved out later that evening. While the others ranted and wailed about Albert and the encroachment of evil into their sanctuary, I slipped into my room, gathered my clothes into two plastic garbage bags and slipped out unnoticed.

I smile when I think of my "escape". They probably thought I was taking out the garbage.

Like Albert, I stood alone on the street but I had no idea where to go. I had lead my parents a dog's life lately, I didn't wish to go there. But I had in my pocket a calling card which Albert had surreptitiously given me with his phone number. I telephoned Albert. True to what I came to discover was Albert's way, Albert took me in.

Although I pronounced myself "cured of any attachment to the cult life," I, nevertheless, still suffered in remembering the events of that evening, that evening especially. And I had seen other things which frightened me. The period of adjustment to living with Albert was difficult, probably for both of us. Albert was about to defend his thesis but Albert, being Albert, had his thesis well written and knew his subject inside out. He admitted that he was stressed over the recent events but recognized that he needed to approach the examining board calmly.

We had discussed approaching the diocese but agreed to do so only after the defence of the thesis. I became increasingly agitated at the idea of approaching church officials and told Albert that I wanted no part of the church ever again. So just after his defence and when I was at work, Albert telephoned the diocesan office and asked to make an appointment with Bishop Snell, I believe he was called, on an urgent matter.

A day or two later, I answered the telephone when Albert was out and took a message. A secretary asked if I knew the purpose of the meeting Albert had requested. I told the secretary it was a follow-up to the St. Matthias business and that Mr. Stafford had new information that he would like to share, especially since it concerned a theology student from Wycliffe.

An hour later, by which time Albert had returned home, there was a second call, which Albert answered. I surmised it was the bishop's office when I heard him repeat the time as eight o'clock that evening and say that he thought it was an odd time for the meeting. Only sometime later, was I to admit, somewhat shamefacedly, that I had not told him about the earlier call. I had not wanted Albert to ask me again to accompany him to the meeting. Albert, perhaps recognizing my reticence about the whole plan to approach the diocesan office, went out directly at seven-thirty without telling me where he was going.

I remember visiting the cathedral in Toronto once when I was a child with Mom and Dad. It is an imposing structure with a very high spire, the highest I think I have ever seen even in the UK. It is quite imposing so I expect the bishop's office was probably quite impressive as well. I have no idea. Albert eventually told me that when he got to the door of the diocesan office, he was met by a secretary, a young woman with a British accent, who lead him into what he assumed was the bishop's office. After a brief wait, a short heavyset man wearing a stock and collar but no jacket came in and introduced himself with the improbable name of Canon Ivor Bangor, a chaplain to the bishop.

"I was given to understand that I would meet with Bishop Snell," Albert replied when he was told that Bangor was to conduct the interview.

"The bishop is in Peterborough for Confirmations. He wanted that the meeting proceed, so he asked me to meet with you."

"Surely, Bishop Snell knew he was to be in Peterborough when the appointment was made. Only this afternoon, I spoke with his office. I mean, a Confirmation is usually scheduled months, not a few hours, in advance."

"Ah well, yes," replied the chaplain, "shall we say a clerical mix up"?

The man actually chuckled at his own joke. Albert apparently did not find the humour in it.

"What about Bishop Hunt, the suffragan bishop? May I meet with him? He attended the St. Matthias inquest and gave rather improbable comments when he testified. I am certain he might be interested in what I have to say."

"That will not be possible. Please, Doctor Stafford, do sit down. May I offer you a drink? Sherry? Perhaps something stronger, scotch?"

"It's still Mr. Stafford, until my doctorate is actually conferred."

"You are being modest, Mr. Stafford. May I call you Albert? I understand you made a brilliant defence of your thesis."

He held up his hand as Albert tried to speak.

"I keep up on these things. That will that be a scotch for both of us, I think?"

He poured the drinks. Albert felt that everything seemed too scripted. He oftentimes over the following months would refer to the meeting and Canon Bangor and the great sense of uneasiness he felt almost from the moment he discovered he would not be meeting the bishop. The whole conversation seemed carefully, too carefully, rehearsed on Bangor's part. Albert used the words "scripted" and "rehearsed" many times. I think it's why I remember Albert's reaction so well.

"In fact, Albert, we were expecting your call. I expect you waited until your defence was over and you could prepare your story. Dr. Wieszkowski, the church warden at St. Bartholomew's, telephoned me shortly after your visit last week to the parish house."

Albert reluctantly accepted the drink.

"In addition to being the church warden, Dr. Wieszkowski is an attendant obstetrician at the Women's College Hospital. He was concerned that you had been filling his patient Joanna Neagle with strange ideas. Perhaps some small prevarication on your part? Here, let me top up that scotch, you seem to have finished it quickly."

Albert started to speak but slurred his words. He felt he was slipping down more into the chair.

"I am extremely concerned there might be a repetition at St. Bartholomew's of what went on at St. Matthias. Dr. Cotnam warned that this might be the tip of the iceberg. I know you have had a Commission and all that, but I am telling you, this casting-out of demons, faith healing, whatever you want to call it, is going on still."

"Albert, you are confusing a number of things. You arrived when Joanna Neagle was in an extremely upset state. It might surprise you to learn that she has a drug problem. It is necessary to sedate her at times. If she is not restrained, she goes out to buy illegal substances that might be of danger to the baby."

Canon Bangor sipped his drink.

"I think, Albert, you feel you have some sort of a mission."

Albert was astounded.

"Mission for what? That is preposterous and what is more preposterous is that you would believe these people. This woman, Stanie, spoke of evil and my polluting Joanna, the handmaiden, and everyone in the room. I have known Joanna for many years; she is no more a drug addict than I am."

"Well, everyone was concerned about your behaviour. Stanie Wieszkowski's English is, at times, not that good, her phraseology erratic." He placed the palms of his hands together and pressed them against his mouth before continuing. “So, let’s leave it at she doesn’t always express herself too clearly in English. She was obviously concerned about her patient and close friend.”

“Canon Bangor, I only want to avoid a repetition of what happened with Katherine Globe. I am worried over the health and safety of a dear friend. But I am not going to sit here and argue about these deranged people. You are obviously prepared to side with these idiots. I heard the same thing time and time again, both in testimony and chatting with people at the inquest. Bishop Snell did not care to hear such things, neither, it appears, do you.”

Before Bangor could reply, Albert stood up and turned to the door.

“I afforded the church the courtesy of first speaking to Bishop Snell. I ought to have gone directly to the police or, better still, the newspapers. Good evening, Canon Bangor.”

The corridor outside the office was dark. There was no sign of the secretary. He headed towards a light over a door. Albert told me that as he walked away from the building, he was glad of the cooler November air. He was angry but increasingly dizzy. Canon Bangor had doused himself in a perfume which was overwhelming. He wanted to get home. Two scotches on a fairly empty stomach could be bad but surely not that bad. He hailed a taxi. He had difficulty managing the stairs to the apartment and threw himself onto his bed. I had wanted to avoid him so had left him a note to say that I had been called to help with a crisis at a youth residence and might not return until morning.

* * * * *

But it gets worse than the dizziness. Later, in the middle of the night, Albert was awakened by banging on his apartment door. He heard only Chris’s voice but opened the door to Chris and three men. The light had been turned off in the hall so he only got a glimpse of their faces before he was shoved to the ground. A large man stuffed a handkerchief into his mouth and two others bound his wrists after stripping him. The man spoke with a Polish accent, telling him to rest easy and that they were here for his benefit, not to harm him. Then he gave an injection from a syringe into Albert's upper arm.

When Albert regained consciousness, he just lay there, naked but not cold, perfectly aware of everything but unable to move. There were a few candles lit but it was too dark to identify anyone clearly. He knew, of course, that Chris was there and he could hear him quietly chanting the Te Deum, "Holy, Holy, Holy, Lord God of Sabaoth" or some such canticle. He could distinguish the white band of a clerical collar on a short man who sprinkled holy water. The Polish man seemed definitely in charge, but it was the short clergyman who took the lead. He placed a crucifix in Albert's hand before starting some sort of a litany. Once again there was the cloying smell of perfume.

I recognized the ritual at once when Albert repeated the bits he could remember. I never really doubted Albert but when I heard those words, I knew Albert had experienced an exorcism. They were the same words I had heard used on Joanna.

I was dumbfounded. My look must have startled him. Albert said, "You don't believe, Peter, there was any way I, even drugged, could have imagined the rite."?

I shook my head.

Albert continued. The men began with some lengthy litany of saints and a psalm. My God, it was one I had heard many times. I began to shake.

"Albert," I was finally able to say, "There are a bunch of these rites, all much the same. I know this one which we usually used. I was supposed to learn it by heart. It was the normal one you heard."

As if there could have been anything at all normal about this nonsense.

I looked it up again last night; I found it fairly easily on line. So I am including the last part which contains the bits Albert remembered. Had he not remembered it I might have given less credence to the use of this particular rite and the perpetrators. I wished I could have dismissed the whole thing as a drug-induced dream. It was no dream:

> *Priest: And lead us not into temptation.*
>
> *Men: But deliver us from evil.*
>
> *Priest: Save your servant (insert name).*
>
> *Men: Who trusts in you, my God.*
>
> *Priest: Let him find in you, Lord, a fortified tower.*
>
> *Men: In the face of the enemy.*
>
> *Priest: Let the enemy have no power over him.*
>
> *Men: And the son of iniquity be powerless to harm him.*
>
> *Priest: Lord, send him aid from your holy place.*
>
> *Men: And watch over him from Sion.*
>
> *Priest: Lord, heed my prayer.*
>
> *Men: And let my cry be heard by you.*
>
> *Everlasting who once and for all consigned that fallen and apostate tyrant to the flames of hell, who sent your only-begotten Son into the world to crush that roaring lion; hasten to our call for help and snatch from ruination and from the clutches of the noonday devil this human being made in your image and likeness and called by the name of (insert name).*
>
> *Strike terror, Lord, into the beast now laying waste your vineyard. Fill your servants with courage to fight manfully against that reprobate dragon, lest he despise those who put their trust in you, and say with Pharaoh of old: "I know not God, nor will I set*

*Israel free." Let your mighty hand cast him out of your servant, (insert name) so he may no longer hold captive this person whom it pleased you to make in your image, and to redeem through your Son; who lives and reigns with you, in the unity of the Holy Spirit, God, forever and ever.*

*I command you, unclean spirit, whoever you are, along with all your minions now attacking this servant of God, by the mysteries of the incarnation, passion, resurrection, and ascension of our Lord Jesus Christ, by the descent of the Holy Spirit, by the coming of our Lord for judgment, that you tell me by some sign your name, and the day and hour of your departure. I command you, moreover, to obey me to the letter, I who am a minister of God despite my unworthiness; nor shall you be emboldened to harm in any way this creature of God, or the bystanders, or especially any handmaiden of their possessions.*

You may rest assured they inserted Albert's name each time.

It was then that I confessed to Albert: first that I had left hours early for work because I did not want to see him after his meeting with the diocese; then, I told him that I really was appalled that he had to undergo such a primitive ritual practised upon him in his own home. And finally I confessed to him and myself that I was even was more frightened of some sort of retaliation attack on myself.

The worst part for Albert was accepting that he had heard his friend Chris participating. Unable to move, his head pounding, he found himself alone with the Polish man. The man lifted Albert and placed him on his bed. What actually struck terror into Albert was that he took out a surgeon's scalpel and placed it on his throat.

"If you are still possessed of evil, evil over Joanna and the baby, I will be back with this. I will silence you for eternity. You have been our enemy, an agent of the anti-Christ. In kindness we have given you a chance. If you, as you threaten, go to the authorities or the newspaper, there will not be a second chance."

I found my friend naked and sweating on the bed when I returned in the morning. Other than the unusual sight of Albert naked on the bed, there was no sign that anything was amiss in the apartment. Once Albert awoke, he was able to move about with ease. He had no headache but was ravenous for food.

I asked Albert why he hadn't contact the police. Albert, clearly mentally ravished, replied, "I don't want to hurt them, Joanna and Chris; they were my life, my friends and the only family I had known for a decade. I feel there may be other options."

But, by the end of the day, Albert had, nonetheless, admitted defeat and said "There are no other options and I have had enough Peter and agree not to seek out Chris and Joanna again". In fact, I know he wrote to Chris to tell him that.

* * * * *

Christmas came and went with no news from Chris or Joanna. I think we all secretly hoped Joanna would have written, somehow acknowledged the season. Albert sent her a card but said he also heard nothing. He kept busy tidying up affairs at the university in preparation for his move to Oxford and his post-doctoral studies. His degree had been conferred at a small ceremony at the end of the autumn term. I was his only guest.

Albert had a fairly large apartment with two bedrooms. Over time, we seemed to fit well together. And, more importantly, our friendship grew. Towards the end of February, Albert received an envelope, his name and address written in Joanna's handwriting. Inside, were a British passport, two passport-sized photos of a newborn and a notarized copy of a certificate of birth. Angela Frederika Laura Neagle was born on February 21st to Joanna Mary Neagle and Albert George Stafford. The attending physician was listed as Dr. Bronislaw Wieszkowski. There was no note attached and no return address on the envelope.

I was there when he received the package. He went into his room and closed the door. I heard him cry, inconsolably. He must have known that I had heard; he eventually told me he had felt emptiness even greater than when his parents and his dog died so tragically. He had been nine years old. I suspect he had not cried since then if, in fact, he had then.

You must consider that for a man like Albert to admit such a thing was totally out of character. In fact, it was the first time I had ever heard him make reference to his parents. That he also mentioned his dog make it all so much more poignant. We all knew that he loved Joanna, but to be named the father of her child took him to the edges of unbearable grief. As I look back, I doubt any of us realized how vulnerable a man he must have been under this composed austere veneer of the academic. We were all ready to dismiss him as just "a far too serious a young man".

The next day he dealt with the practical aspects of Joanna's strange request. He knew what needed to be done. His first stop was the British consular office where Albert registered Angela as a British citizen born abroad. Earlier that year, in preparation for his move to Oxford, Albert had claimed British citizenship through his mother who was born in Edinburgh but had immigrated to Canada with her parents as a young child. He gave the officials his British passport and Joanna's and had little trouble with the registration. He also arranged to have Angela as a minor attached to his passport. He told me, afterwards, that it was the two passport photos that convinced him of Joanna's intention. I wondered at the time if what he actually did was what Angela wanted but kept that to myself.

I do believe, in spite of what he said, I was not convinced. He must have understood Joanna intention that Angela be added to her passport and not his. Whether she even knew that he had acquired a British passport was by no means a certainty in my mind. Albert had travelled on his Canadian one the previous summer. I think he surmised that Joanna was intending to make a surreptitious trip to England with the baby. He put the baby on his passport, not hers, to ensure that he would have to accompany her.

Nothing more was heard for several weeks when an invitation arrived in the post for Angela's christening. It was addressed to both of us. So if there had been any doubt, it was confirmed that they knew I was living with Albert in his apartment. At the least, it would be a chance for him to see Joanna, return her passport and perhaps begin planning for the trip.

The baptism was held in the chapel of Wycliffe College, which I remember from my walks with my Dad around the University. We would laugh as we past. Dad, an architect, said "Wycliffe College looked like a Victorian red squash cake prepared by a mean Auntie".

The service was quite well attended although I certainly did not go. I had had enough religion to last lifetime. Many of those in the congregation, Albert had assumed, were students and faculty, one of whom was Canon Bangor who shook his hand when Albert entered the chapel as if they were old friends. There was a smattering of the St. Matthias-types he remembered from the inquest, looking quite subdued. All of the gang he remembered seeing at St Bart's parish house were there in smart dresses and dark suits. Chris and Joanna took turns holding the baby at the font. The godparents were Stanie and Bronislaw Wieszkowski. If he had taken this as a slight, Albert didn't say. But, it must have been hurtful. Otherwise, there was nothing unusual in the service. Albert, the historian, called it "a normal christening from the 1662 Book of Common Prayer".

At the tea afterwards, the college Principal who had conducted the baptism was the only person to speak to Albert. Albert told me that cleric seemed a decent sort of person who, he expected, had no knowledge of anything much going on in the world or his college, never mind the activities at St. Bart's. Chris and, naturally, none of the St. Bartholomew or St. Matthias crowds acknowledged Albert's presence. Generally, as he put it, "It was as though I had the mark of Cain tattooed on my forehead".

As Albert prepared to leave by the porter's lodge and was putting on his overcoat, Joanna came out from the reception, holding the baby on her hip and shook his hand, no kiss, no smile.

"Thank you for coming, Bertie."

She opened her purse, obviously for him to slip in the passport. He congratulated her on the baby and said Angela was on his passport and she need only contact him.

"We must get together for tea one day," was all she said before turning and walking back toward the reception.

* * * * *

Albert received a telephone call two weeks later. It was Maundy Thursday. The apartment was almost empty, with the bits of furniture sold and the books shipped to Oxford. I was moving back to my parents' place in a couple of days quite soon after Albert's departure. A flight had been booked for London for Easter Sunday. The call was from Chris, asking if we could both come for tea the next day, Good Friday, in the mid-afternoon.

"He sounded as he had always in the past," Albert smiled, "almost jocular". Chris told him that they had a new apartment on Spadina Avenue near the university.

After putting down the phone, Albert said, "I have agreed to go but would prefer not to. God help me, Peter, but I have been through enough".

For my part, I answered, "Wild horses couldn't drag me". Then added, "in fact a date with wild horses would be tamer".

It was a sunny day. I agreed to accompany Albert part way and we headed off on foot towards the Kensington Market area of the city where Joanna and Chris lived. The market had seen a series of ethnic communities in transition pass through, Jewish, Portuguese and by then Asian. All left their stories and history behind as each in turn moved up the social ladder and away to the suburbs. I told him I would walk him there for "moral support".

When I turned to head back up towards the university and Albert headed down Spadina towards their apartment, I had a change of heart. So, I shouted to Albert that he should wait and I would go inside with him.

I really did felt sorry for Albert. He had been so kind to me. The man looked totally rejected. If I am honest, I had been afraid that Dr. Wieszkowski or that woman might be there. I, however, also knew that eventually I would have to stand up to these people or spend the rest of my life in fear. So in the end, I agreed to go inside but only stay for a short while.

I joked, "Better for two Daniels to go into the lions' den".

The apartment was in an old building with a shop below, a Chinese grocery or something. We rang the bell and Chris, dressed in black trousers with a freshly starched white shirt, opened the front door in the small hall with the stairs directly behind leading up three flights. The three of us shook hands before climbing the narrow stairs to the first landing where a door was open leading into Chris and Joanna's flat.

The place was fairly basic, pleasant, freshly painted and modestly, yet comfortably, furnished. There were no pictures or photographs on the walls and although the flat had been freshly painted, this plus the lack of any ornamentation suggested the temporariness of a motel room. There was only one small painting, hanging just inside the door of the small kitchen, a print of Christ with coloured rays emanating from his heart onto a small kneeling nun. I saw it at once when I went to help Joanna bring in the teapot and asked about it.

"It is St. Mary Faustina Kowalska and the Divine Mercy." Joanna smiled, seemingly pleased that I had commented. "Stanie gave it to me. She brought it with her when she and Broni fled to Canada from Poland. It has powers she said would help me gain back my strength. I keep it in the kitchen with me as I am afraid it rather upsets Chris. Of all my possessions, I treasure it most."

I carried in a large teapot. Joanna had set out some hot cross buns with a pot of jam on a small wooden table with four cups. The four of us sat silently as Joanna poured out the tea. The baby, meanwhile, was asleep in the bedroom which was directly off the living room. The bedroom was small with the double bed taking up much of the room. At the foot of the bed was a small white bassinette where the she slept.

I said little as they chatted about the most inconsequential things: how Billie Jean King would fare on the tennis circuit, that sort of thing. Tennis, once again, was the neutral topic and one to which they could all relate. They asked me about my work and Chris said that his studies were going well and that he had a new student placement starting Easter Sunday in a church in North Toronto.

"Lots of hats," Joanne joked.

And we all laughed. If there was no real thaw, at least there appeared to be a softening of the ice.

Nothing was mentioned of the events at St. Bart's. After half an hour of small talk, Chris got up and said that he had to go. There was a special performance of *Stabat Mater* at the new parish and he was expected to attend. I said that I also had to be off. The three of us men shook hands as Chris and I left. Joanna and Albert were alone. It was the first time that Albert had been alone with Joanna since their trip to Italy the summer before.

As Albert told me later, he sat there quietly with Joanna for several minutes. When she spoke, it was, once again, with a strange request. She asked Albert if he would take the child for a walk. She was tired and had a few things to prepare. A half hour, she said, would allow her to prepare all she had to do. Albert suspected that she was planning to leave with him for Britain and that when he returned her bags would be ready.

Joanna carried the baby downstairs as Albert lifted down a pram which was folded up beside their door. He walked for about twenty minutes away from the Kensington market with its stalls and crowds. It was a beautiful warm day. He walked up by the Connaught Laboratory and by the College of Education. The sidewalks were full. The baby rested quietly. When he returned, he did not need to ring for entry, the door was open. He pushed the pram into the entrance hall, closed the door and dashed up the stairs to get Joanna to help lift the baby which he had left in the pram. The door to the flat was ajar. When Joanna did not answer his call, he noticed two envelopes and a sheet of paper on the small table that had held the buns and teacups. One was addressed to him:

*My dear friend,*

*I have been a foolish woman and a bad friend to you who has always been so faithful. I hope you will forgive me; I have done a sinful thing today, probably rendering me to who knows what. I am so confused about these things. No longer do I know what I believe, what is true and what is truly madness. I feel what I am doing is what is best for Chris and for the baby. I cannot bear one more session at the church and the thought that my only friend will be thousands of miles away is unbearable. While you were here in the city, I could console myself that I had a secret refuge. If I had the courage, I would go with you back to England; I no longer have the will.*

*I have a favour, the greatest favour a mother can ask. Take the baby at once; get out of here before anyone arrives. There is a bag on the sofa of the baby's things. Take her anywhere, but take her away from all of this. I beg you, Bertie. I believe you to be my only friend. My father refuses to speak with me. There is no one else who can protect her.*

*Do not go into the bedroom. Stanie and Broni Wieszkowski will be here soon. Let them find me. They always come to check on me when Chris is out. He lied about Stabat Mater; he has one of his gruesome activities at St Bartholomew's. He will have told them that you are here, which will hasten their arrival. Nothing much has changed; we only pretended this afternoon. Things will only get worse.*

*You are legally the child's father; that is really why I asked for your name for her; they cannot stop you from taking her away.*

*God bless you, my dear Bertie. But hurry. They will try to prevent you from taking my Angie and I do love her so much, as I love you.*

*Joanna*

Albert sat down on the sofa afraid to open the bedroom door. He noticed a letter addressed to Chris and the Wieszkowskis but it was sealed. There was a short note on the table addressed to the police basically stating that she had taken her life freely, that she felt that she would be an unfit mother, and that the baby was with its father in England where it belonged.

He saw a suitcase and a white carrier bag on the sofa. The door to the bedroom was closed. Slipping his letter into his pocket, he pushed open the door. Joanna was hanging from the ceiling, an electric cord wound about her neck. Her face looked grotesquely bloated, her eyes, as if about to pop from her face, stared at him from a face no longer capable of expressing either regret or joy, only death. On her chest, tied on with a piece of blue ribbon looped over her shoulders was the print of St. Mary Faustina Kowalska and the Divine Mercy. Albert knew. There was no uncertainty. Joanna was gone. There was nothing he could do.

Shaking as if in a fever, Albert ran to the kitchen. After vomiting into the sink, he rinsed it. "Strange," he told me, "I was almost overcome when I saw that that Joanna had washed the cups and placed them on a tea cloth beside the sink".

As he returned to the living room, he noticed, almost in relief, that the bedroom door had closed itself. Panic then struck. Albert said it was panic like he hoped never to face again.

He grabbed the bags and bolted down the steps. Placing the white carrier bag over the handle of the carriage, he stuck his head onto the street to look for the Wieszkowskis. The street was filled with people, people, he said, of all ethnicities but not Bronislaw and Stanie. As he pushed out the carriage, he almost collided with a small group of Chinese girls who all wanted to see the baby. He was so taken with their innocence that he pulled back the fine lace and let them see Angela, who was by this time awake but quiet.

The walk back to his flat seemed endless. Once he had reached the Parliament Building, he was confident of not running into the Poles. He slowed his pace, which gave him time to think. The baby started to cry and he picked her up. Poor Albert knew nothing about children. I remember him telling me over dinner one night about growing up as an only child with no cousins and then living as an orphan with no living relations except an uncle. "That was why," he opened up to me, "Chris and Joanna had been so central in my life". He sat on a park bench facing St Michael's College rocking Angela.

What was clear to him was that the Wieszkowskis and Chris, once they got over the shock of finding the hanging body, would immediately seek out the child. He told me he remembered a woman's heart-wrenching testimony at the St Matthias inquest. The poor woman had endeavoured to leave the cult; they did everything in their power to keep her children with them. And he feared he would experience first hand their almost pathological obsession with children, as if there was a need to pass on their beliefs. Their spiritual beliefs were genetic to them.

On the other hand, Chris knew he was flying out to Britain on Sunday, which meant they would think they had two more days before he left the country. The predicaments, the impracticalities, he counted, almost like a child, on his fingers. First, he had the two days to hide from them. Second, there was his post at Oxford, which meant a lot to him. Third, he knew nothing about children. Fourth, he was totally unfit to look after the child. But what stuck most in his mind, as he counted the fifth finger, was the image of Dr. Wieszkowski with the scalpel to his throat.

His two trump cards, as he put it to himself, were his legal status as the child's father and a degree of financial security. For the cult to dispute his paternity would render them all culpable in covering up things far worse. He reached into his pocket. He still had Joanna's letter.

Time, he realised, was running short but his heart was no longer racing. With Angela back in the carriage, he set off, but at a slower pace, towards his flat. He wanted to walk quicker but he also did not want to draw attention to himself. When Albert and the baby reached the flat, he entered his soon-to-be former home which was bare except for a bed in each bedroom which belonged to the landlord. Albert being Albert, had everything organized; his suitcases were packed; he had nothing in the refrigerator, planning to eat the last few meals out; and the list of things to do pinned to the wall in the kitchen had a line through almost everything.

When I returned home, I was flabbergasted to find Angela on Albert's bed crying. I was the eldest of four children and knew what to do and helped Albert undertake the first of his fatherly chores. In the carrier bag were several bottles of formula. Thank God, he laughed, "it isn't Pablum".

As I heated the milk in a pan which he had taken from under the sink, he told me what had happened and the walk back. The carrier bag also contained diapers, so on the hardwood floor of the flat, Albert changed his first. The soiled diaper deposited in the last garbage bag by the door, he tied it and went into the hall to drop the bag down the chute. He also went to the outside glass front door but could see no sign of anyone in the street.

Back inside the flat, he telephoned BOAC to see if it was possible to switch his flight to that evening. To his relief, it was. He then explained that his wife, who was currently in England, had decided not to return to Canada until a later date, so he would be carrying their daughter, an infant, with him. He assured them that he, naturally, had all the documentation. That too seemed not to have been a problem. There would be no additional fare for the infant. Travel, of course, was much simpler in those days.

The fight left in three hours. The phone rang. We debated about answering. I picked it up. It was Broni. He was curt and to the point: they would be over directly to pick up the child. They were meeting Chris, who was already on his way over. Chris, apparently, was beside himself with grief and remorse and was determined to get the child, his child, back.

I tried to stall them by saying there was no hurry as Albert was not leaving until Sunday but Wieszkowski rang off. I put the receiver down on the cradle but picked it up again, handing it to Albert, who telephoned for a taxi. In the next few minutes, Albert grabbed his things from the bathroom and a pair of pajamas from the bed and stuffed them into one of his suitcases. He took his suit jacket out and packed his overcoat.

Angela back in the carriage, his brief case under his arm, his two bags and the baby's bag and carrier already in the lobby, Albert turned one last time. I stood just inside the apartment. He closed the apartment door after slipping the keys into my hand. I had offered to help but he wanted me to stay inside in case they telephoned again. His last words to me I shall never forget. "My friend" he was obviously worried for my well-being, "under no circumstances open the door to anyone".

The wait outside seemed endless. Finally the taxi arrived and the driver helped him put everything except his briefcase into the trunk. As they were folding up the pram, he saw Chris running towards him, flailing his arms.

Placing the baby on the back seat, Albert motioned for the driver to get into the taxi. Before Chris could speak, Albert grabbed him by the front of his shirt. Directly in his face, only inches from his own, he spoke.

"You are too emotionally distraught to speak. We are both too emotionally distraught to speak. Dr. Wieszkowski has just phoned me and instructed that you are to meet him and Stanie here outside the building. Are you listening?"

He loosened his hold on Chris.

"Again: listen carefully. I needed to get away from Peter. He knows too much and has threatened to go to the police. As far as he knows, I am going to spend the last two nights at a hotel. I did not tell Peter the name. Actually, it is the Royal York but he doesn't know this. You must wait and then telephone me there this evening. We can meet and arrange about Angela's care before I leave on Easter Sunday."

He let go of Chris's shirt. The young man cried, turning away from Albert to lean against the wall of the building. Albert jumped into the taxi, speaking loudly enough for Chris to hear, "Royal York Hotel".

Although I did not know Albert as well as some of the others contributing these narratives like Laura, Ludovico and Cosmos, I think I knew him well enough to understand how this deception, these lies, must have grieved him. To turn away and not offer any sort of support to his friend, a man who had been like a brother and who was the father of that poor baby in the back seat, was not in keeping with everything I had come to know of his character. Chris was wailing and shouting Joanna's name, even hitting his head against the wall. I could hear him from inside the apartment.

It was the last time Albert was to see Chris alive. As he would later admit by letter he felt quite torn, part of him wanting to flee in fear and part wanting the taxi to turn back. As the taxi moved on towards the hotel, Albert watched out the window and waited until they actually arrived at the Royal York before asking the driver to drive on to the airport.

The airport, in the suburb of Malton, was quite manageable in those days; it is huge today and I avoid it whenever possible. And as I noted before, travel was simpler forty years ago. For one thing, there was no security clearance, so passengers could go directly to the gate after checking in. That meant, of course, that well-wishers and anyone else could also go directly up to the gate.

Albert, it seems, was able to check the pram as well as his two bags and Angela's. He had to carry the baby, her carrier bag and his briefcase. Canada had no immigration checkpoint on leaving the country in those days and is still be the case today. My step-dad always comments on this. "So lax these countrymen of yours my dear", as he shakes his head at my Mom, "it is so trusting, quite touching really".

This still left Albert with the worry that he had somehow been followed or that Chris had contacted the Royal Canadian Mounted Police. He tried several times to reach me by phone without luck from a pay phone. The old fashioned phone booth had a seat inside. He sat there with the baby on a bench beside it.

When he finally got through, I was crying hysterically. Broni, the woman and Chris had forced their way into the flat by saying they had the baby and that Albert was injured and needed help. Once inside, I tried to stall the trio by saying that Albert was not leaving until Sunday and I expected him back later in the evening. This, of course, contradicted what Albert had told Chris about me being aware of a hotel but not the name, which put them on the offensive.

Through a series of deep breaths and sobs, I told Albert how they had skipped their usual religious defence and got right to the brutal bit. After throwing me onto the bed, the doctor took out his scalpel and held it to my throat while the woman bound my hands with her sweater. Chris was turning my ankles until the pain made me scream. When Broni threatened to cut my throat and arrange for the blame to be placed on Albert, I capitulated and admitted that Albert was on the flight that day with the baby.

Before they left, Broni returned to the bed and made a series of slices along both of my cheeks, small nicks really, which would not require stitches but which would be painful and probably remain as permanent scars and a permanent reminder of the Wieszkowskis. The one good thing to note in all of this, the scaring diminished; sadly for me, the memory was slower to fade.

They had left me lying on the floor; they had dragged me from the bed so the blood would not stain the mattress. The woman threw a towel on my face as they left. They were in an obvious hurry by this time and in their haste did not, as one might have expected, cut the phone line.

Albert cried softly into the phone when he finally got through. He said how much it grieved him to hear me suffer so on his behalf and the child's. He thanked me and again I shall never forget, for being "his one true friend".

I told him I was leaving immediately for my parents' house and that I would be safe there. I had to get out for fear they might come back. It was the last time I was to speak with Albert. I could tell Albert was so terrified and I heard a thud as Albert actually dropped the phone. I could hear Angela crying and imagined Albert, unable even to look down, standing there with the phone dangling by its cord, circling first one way and then the other. The mind is a strange thing: whenever I think of Albert, I see him standing holding a cord with the phone circling first one way and then the other.

The details of the departure lounge as well as those of the rest of the trip, I learned later by letter. Although we did not speak again, we communicated through sporadic correspondence sent to my parents' home. That is, until Albert broke off all communication with anyone from his past. Harry told me that Mom still has the letters and offered to send them to me. But, I prefer to recall the next series of events as I remember reading them. So, in theory there is in London, in a drawer somewhere the letters. If Dr. Stevenson wants a first-hand account, he is welcome to take Mom on.

In spite of these short-comings, I have every reason to believe that the scenario, as I remember, is fundamentally true and fairly accurate. Albert might have lied, but why would he. It is, after all, all too bizarre to be fiction. Joanna was dead, I had been tortured, Albert was being pursued by religious maniacs, one of them a man with a scalpel, and there was the baby, an infant who was now screaming, and he was standing there paralysed unable to even look down at the phone dangling from its cord.

When he eventually bent over to pick up the phone and replace it in its cradle, Albert became aware of a woman standing beside him who appeared to be on the verge of picking up the baby from the seat beside the phone booth. Angela had started to cry more forcefully. Once again, he froze before willing himself to step to the side, thereby blocking her from picking up the baby. The woman, dressed in a turquoise suit with a white blouse and large chunky beads, addressed him by name.

"Dr. Stafford? Do you remember me?" She smile, "I am Deborah Rashfield".

It took a moment but when he remembered the name, Deborah Rashfield, his heart seemed to stop. He recognized her as the secretary from the bishop's office.

"The baby is beautiful. Shall I pick her up?"

"That is alright, I'll get her. She will only fuss with a stranger."

He gingerly picked up the child as if to gain time, all the while fiddling in his pocket for something to calm her, something both Albert I would have referred to as a pacifier but what Deborah Rashford call a "dummy". Albert barely managed a nervous laugh and insisted, as if to stress the point that he was used to her fussing and knew how to calm her. He sat down and held the child, as he put it "as if for dear life".

The more the woman continued to reach for the baby; the more he just kept snuggling the baby closer to himself. She, almost abruptly, changed her focus and turned her attention to a tall man who was standing directly behind Albert. She reached over and took the man's hand.

"This is my husband, Grigor. We really do need to speak with you. I suggest that we move away where we can speak quietly."

The man did not speak but reached down to pick up the carrier bag and Albert's briefcase. Albert wanted to scream but, still holding on to the baby, got up and followed the man to a quiet corner of the lounge, virtually hidden from the gate. Deborah sat, the man stood, and Albert didn't know whether to stand, sit or run. The woman spoke and what she said astounded him.

"I want to apologize for lying to you. I hate the synod office, I hate Canon Bangor and most of all I hate the fact that I lied to you. I quit my job shortly after your meeting with Bangor."

Albert sat down as she continued.

"My job was not being the bishop's secretary as Bangor said. I was just part of the stenographic pool. But my job became increasingly one of deceiving people rather than taking dictation. For you the deception was in not taking you to the bishop's office; that was on the second floor. And the bishop was actually in his office at the time of your visit, despite what Bangor said and which I did not dispute. This had happened in the past and frankly I thought it wrong, especially for a church official like that "piggish Canon Bangor".

Everything I had ever heard from Albert about Ivor Bangor confirmed that "piggish" was an apt description of the odious little man.

"I really disliked the whole process of deception, even if for 'innocent expediency' as Bangor had put it."

She touched Albert as if for reassurance before continuing.

"Canon Bangor, we used to call him Carnivore-Ivor in the pool, paid me overtime to type some letters, not to take part in make-believe scenarios. When I saw you here at the airport, I knew I needed to apologize for your not getting to see the bishop."

The man, her actual husband and no cult-member as Albert had imagined, spoke in a deep, almost lyrical voice, the voice of the Welsh, not Polish.

Mr. Rashford's thick Welsh accent resonated reassurance as he continued, "I were livid when she told me, insisted that she give her notice". He paused, "Them that was in the church, ministers and the like, didn't behave that way in the chapel when I were a youth. We are moving back to Wales in any event and I hoped never to have anything more to do with the church and that nest of vipers."

Albert noticed a woman in a blue BOAC uniform approaching him. Again, the bile collected in his throat. The official, however, suggested that since they were finishing the boarding, he might like to take the baby onto the plane. Mr. Rashford carried the carrier and briefcase to the gate. Albert handed the boarding passes to the gate attendant and a BOAC stewardess helped him and Angela as they entered the plane. They and the Welsh couple were the last ones to go on board. As he stepped through the doorway, he caught sight of two men he had previously seen with Chris and Stanie at the parish house coming into the lounge, but he hoped beyond everything they would not have the courage to confront him on the aircraft. As the door closed, he knew they were safely on board, at least for the time being.

A man travelling with an infant forty years ago is not like a man travelling with one to-day. The assumption then was the man was helpless. Little did they know how helpless Albert actually was. The stewardesses insisted on feeding and changing the baby. The woman beside him held and rocked the baby through much of the trip while Albert slept. Angela, apparently, was amazingly quiet throughout. Albert worried about the reception at immigration at Heathrow. And he imagined everyone who passed by and smiled at Angela as some sort of enemy. The anxiety briefly became more acute when the plane landed in Montreal to take on more passengers, none of whom appeared familiar or seemed especially interested in him and the child. But, Albert could not be certain. Slowly the propeller airplane taxied to the runway and left Canada for Britain.

As he waited in the long line for immigration at Heathrow, holding the baby in one arm and the briefcase and carrier bag in the other, he was approached by two uniformed personnel, a man and a woman. The woman took the baby from his arm, the man the carrier bag, leaving only the briefcase for Albert to carry. He took off his suit jacket and put it over his arm; he wrote that this was as much for something to do as to seem that everything was as it should be. A third officer opened a side door and Albert was taken into a small room and asked to take a seat. They first requested his papers, which he retrieved from his briefcase while all the while the woman continued to hold the baby.

He handed them the passport. They both looked carefully through the document before the woman spoke.

"I notice that your passport was issued in Canada and that this is your first passport. You were not born in the United Kingdom and are yet now returning. I guess my question is why are you returning to the United Kingdom with the child, who was born only very recently?"

"I have a letter here."

Trying not to shake too obviously, he reached into his briefcase and retrieved a letter with the crest of the university, which he placed on the desk. "I have been accepted for post-doctoral studies at Oxford, and am bringing my child with me."

The woman passed the letter to the man.

Albert decided to bite the proverbial bullet.

"My wife has recently died. I really didn't have anyone I trusted to care for the child until she was a bit older. And to be frank, I want to keep her with me. I expect to find a flat suitable for both of us and possibly an au pair to help with Angela — that's the baby's name."

The man leaned back in his chair. He stared at Albert intently before speaking.

"Here is your passport, Dr. Stafford. Please accept our condolences at the loss of your wife. Miss Williamson here will help you find a trolley and your luggage. He stood up and shaking Albert's hand gave a final "cheerio".

Albert need not have worried. The female official, Miss Williamson, went through a second door into the luggage area. While she held the baby, Albert found a trolley. The luggage came quite quickly after that. Officer Williamson stayed until all the luggage came through and the bags were placed on the trolley. Two other passengers opened up the pram for him and Miss Willaimson placed the baby inside. She also shook his hand and gave a farewell.

Albert was in Britain, but not for long. He pushed the pram with one hand, pulling the trolley with the other from the arrivals area into an elevator going directly to the departures level. He went directly to the Alitalia counter and asked about flights to Milan or Rome. As luck would have it, and his luck did indeed seem to be holding, there was a flight leaving in fifty-five minutes for Rome. He paid for the tickets in pounds, credit cards were hardly the norm in those days, and twenty minutes later was in the lounge waiting to board while through it all hoping the immigration officials would not chance to see him.

Just over two hours later, he was in a taxi heading to Rome's central train station.

My narrative ends here. I am still uneasy about this whole exercise. Is it supposed to be cathartic? Harry told me it was strictly for research purposes. I was fortunate in growing up with loving parents and siblings. My wife and I are close to Harry and Mom and my brothers and sister. My life with Asha and my children has been more than I could have hoped for. But there was a period of madness, religious fervour, call it what you will. Sometimes I think a drug addiction would have been easier to deal with. I came through it and have had forty years of happiness.

This exercise, nonetheless, has forced me to confront things in my past. This is not the psychoanalytical dealing with my own demons; I have done this with Asha's help many years ago. I must confront Albert. I have been not quite honest with you. I wrote that Albert cut all ties. That is not true. Albert never dropped me; I waved away our friendship. He never stopped writing; I stopped replying.

He continued to write over many years. I can justify my unwillingness to respond. I was frightened. I was frightened of Broni and Stani Wieszkowski. Could they hurt me? Could they hurt my parents or wife? Could they hurt me to get at Albert? These hypothetical questions haunted me for years. Even to this day, I find myself looking over my shoulder, walking up stairs rather than taking an elevator. Then, when Mom married Harry and she told me of his determination to cut all ties with the child and Albert. I was only too happy to go along.

But now Albert is dead. I have had a wonderful family for which I would thank God if I still believed in one. But since those days in the apartment in Toronto, I have never had a real friend. I have never felt the need to reach out to anyone. One could say, Albert ruined much in my life. That would not be true.

Peter Wilkinson
Vancouver British Columbia

# OTTAWA EVENING JOURNAL

## December 5, 1971

### BODY IDENTIFIED

The body found in a wooded region near the Ottawa River at the community of Quyon north of Hull has been tentatively identified by the Sûreté du Québec (QPP) as that of Christopher Andrew Neagle, a British student who had been studying at the University of Toronto. The police do not suspect foul play. Mr Neagle had disappeared from his flat on Spadina Avenue in Toronto, which he had shared with his sister and her child since the spring of 1968. The sister had committed suicide shortly after moving in with him and Neagle was said to have been suffering from repeated bouts of depression. According to his friend Dr. Bronislaw Wieszkowski, who was reached at his home on Manitoulin Island, Neagle had visited him eighteen months ago and told him he was planning to go to Ottawa for a job interview. Dr. Wieszkowski is a former surgeon at the Women's College Hospital who had not heard from him for several months and thought he had returned to Britain.

Christopher Neagle had been a student at Toronto's Wycliffe College and had hoped to pursue a career in the church ministry. A spokesman for his bishop, Canon Ivor Bangor, issued a statement yesterday saying that although Mr. Neagle had participated in a number of activities in the diocese, most recently at St. Helen's in North Toronto, he personally was not surprised by the suicide. He described Mr. Neagle as psychologically unstable for the ministry and doubted he would ever have been ordained.

The body was discovered by three young men cross-country skiing, who were alerted by the barking of their dogs. The body was so badly decomposed and mutilated by wolves that identification was almost impossible. His passport was found, as well as his Canadian drivers licence, several other documents, and his house keys. It appears the deceased had wandered off along the river and fallen into a small ravine. His clothes match those he was wearing when he was last seen boarding a Voyageur Colonial bus for Quyon. No reason has yet been determined as to why he was in the region of Quyon.

His friend's wife, Mrs. Stefania Wieszkowski, is expected to travel to West Quebec in an attempt to identify the remains and organize funeral arrangements.

# LAURA

## 1968–1988

I am fortunate. The others have been charged with recounting the events of different timeframes and of coordinating hearsay. I have the luxury, if that is a suitable word in this context, of writing only what I know; I have been relieved of the burden of relying on other people's conjecture. I don't know what my brothers will contribute but feel I am confident that what I write is written with a fair degree of accuracy by concentrating on these twenty years. Unlike the others, I am not relying on second-hand recollections. All for the good. It may be a function of age, maybe not, but I can remember my own observations better than those recounted to me. Granted, this makes me sound like someone in a Wilkie Collins novel, but I lived through much of what is to come; it is as clear to me as though the events happened yesterday.

You know, of course, that I am Laura Neagle Guelfi, daughter of the Reverend Swithin Neagle MBE, relict of Count Clemente Guelfi, step-mother of Count Giorgio Guelfi, mother of Luca Guelfi, mother-in-law of Larry Pearson of Los Angeles, sister of Cosmo and Harry Neagle, aunt of Chris Neagle and friend of Albert Stafford. As befits a woman of my age, and, to use an outdated word, *station*, I defer to identifying myself in terms of my relationships with men. I reside, as I have from my marriage, near the town of San Leo Tiberino in the Tuscan province of Arezzo.

I will never forget that Holy Saturday evening, dark, and time for a pre-dinner drink. Giorgio, my step-son, was away visiting school friends for the Easter weekend; my two (in addition to my aforementioned son Luca, I also have a daughter, Patricia Alba) were tucked into bed. It was a rainy cold evening. Spring had been annoyingly late in coming to the Valtiberina that year. My husband, Clemente, and I were reading in front of the fire, listening to music and enjoying a cocktail: Clemente, very Italian, *prosecco*; me, very English, gin and tonic. You see I do have an eye and memory for detail.

At about seven thirty, Riccardo, our gardener, ran into the room.

"Contessa, there is an Arezzo taxi in front with your friend."

Now, I have never had many friends, many more acquaintances and fewer of them to-day. Age has a nasty habit of dealing with acquaintances with a brutality, randomly handed out. But, Riccardo spoke as if there were only the one friend. Maybe he was more prescient than we thought.

Clemente was the one to reply.

"I will go, Laura, you stay here."

But in the end we both followed Riccardo down stairs to the door. A taxi was sitting in the drive. There, to our utter astonishment, was Albert Stafford hold a crying baby in the teeming rain. There was a carrier bag, a briefcase, two suitcases, a smaller bag, and a folded pram, which the taxi driver had deposited in the drive. Anxious to be out of the rain and get back in the taxi, the driver had just left the luggage and Albert and the baby to fend as best they could.

Clemente roared, somewhat out of character.

"Riccardo, for Christ's sake, get the luggage inside."

He had said this in English but Riccardo understood.

Then he spoke again more softly once he saw the baby.

"And who do we have here?"

Clemente had faults but was, fundamentally, a kind man, especially when it came to children, a stereotypical Italian I suppose.

Clemente, Riccardo and I each grabbed a bag. Riccardo ran back out for the pram. I took the baby while Albert took off his jacket, which was wet and dripping on the floor. He stooped to take off his shoes but Clemente wouldn't hear of it. He almost pushed the wet man upstairs to the fire where Albert collapsed into a chair and covered his face with his hands. I called Maria Pia, a local woman who was hired to help with the children, to take the baby, who was crying at this point, and prepare a bottle for it. Albert, of course, remembered Maria Pia from the previous summer. He smiled and nodded as the woman carried the infant in her arms down to the kitchen. Clemente had, meanwhile, poured Albert a bandy who sipped it but continued to shake all over.

"I can't believe I made it. Joanna is dead. I took the baby. She asked me to take the baby, I can prove it. I saw her hanging there. It was terrible, her face twisted grotesquely. She had this religious painting hanging around her neck. The trip here was a nightmare. I know nothing about babies; I hope she will be alright. I didn't know where else to come, where they won't find me and take her away."

The man just rambled.

"They want to kill me, take the baby for nefarious reasons. You are my only hope. I cannot return to Canada. They think I am in Britain so I can't go there. I beg you. I beg you. I beg you."

My Clemente, ever the businessman pragmatist, recognized that rambling at this point would not help Albert and that what the man needed was sleep.

"Bertie, all tomorrow,"

He spoke in a soothing voice.

"Riccardo has taken your bags to your room. You know you are safe and very welcome here with us. Laura and Maria Pia will look after the baby. We will talk tomorrow afternoon after lunch. Try to imagine it is last summer and you are tired from too much tennis. You will have the same room."

With that, and his no-more-nonsense expression, he took Albert's arm and led him upstairs to the second floor. Albert offered no resistance. I stayed there by the fire until Clemente returned.

"I think our family has just gotten bigger by two. But, now, Laura, you and I should have dinner."

He patted my shoulder and that was that. In many ways Clemente was a thoughtful man.

The plan had been for Clemente to drive me and the children into Florence for the Easter service at the English church. I lived the majority of my life among Italians, speak the language fluently, have tried to accommodate my lifestyle to that of my husband, and to integrate myself into country life here in the Valtiberina, but I could never change my church. Secretly, I feared my father would disinherit me or that is what I told Clemente the pragmatist. To the rest, I generally just replied, more fitting to a countess, "no thank-you; I do not wish to become a Roman Catholic".

I was more forthright when the local priests, including Ludovico, tried to influence me. "I will never kiss the ring of that old, ugly, little *stronzo* sitting on his throne in Vatican City. I'd rather kiss a toad."

And I said the same thing to my Mother-in-law, the old Contessa, but she, unlike Ludovico, never forgave me.

Clemente felt that it would be better for him to be at home when Albert woke up. Riccardo had just obtained his driver's permit so my husband asked him to drive. Poor Riccardo, he was quite nervous and kept popping the clutch, to the delight of the children. By the time we arrived home, our Easter lunch was ready. The children were enthralled with Angela and wanted to hold her. Albert was just up and looked ravenous. Ludovico, the parish priest to whom I made the disparaging yet accurate remark about the pope, arrived. Ludovico Calli, known generally as Don Ludovico, was a distant relation of my husband and, despite my cutting remarks, has remained a dear friend. He will also remain a constant throughout my narrative.

So, we all sat down, with Maria Pia feeding the baby. It was, being Easter, a rather special meal. The girls in the kitchen had prepared a veritable feast: plates of cold meats and bruschetta (using the last of the previous year's beetroot), three pastas, roast pork, potatoes, salad, cantucci with vin santo for the men, panna cotta for the children and me. It was the meal I had enjoyed every Easter since coming to live in Castello Guelfi and I never would countenance any changes to the menu. As one grows older, all the festivals tend to merge into one, so there is only one Christmas, one Easter or one Ferragosto. The memory of this particular Easter is, of course, an exception, etched in my mind with totally clear recollection. All through the meal, I wondered if it was all too much for Albert, yet he seemed to be eating with gusto. Ludovico, true to character, certainly did. At this point, he was already showing signs of corpulence. At that meal and possibly for the last time, Albert Stafford was the Albert I remembered from the summer, rather than the young man at the door standing in the rain and carrying a baby.

That mood changed in the afternoon. Clemente, Ludovico and I sat with him in the library. He sat much of the time with his face in his hands giving us the essence of what, I trust, Harry will have told you, or at least agreed to tell you, albeit from his annoyingly sanctimonious point of view. The greater part of the details I got that afternoon with the rest coming in fits and starts over the coming weeks and years.

We learned, basically, the raw details of Joanna's death, the religious madness that had infected her life and Chris's, and Albert's utter commitment to protect Angela. Much of it was not really a surprise. You will remember I was in London when my brother Harry went out to Toronto for the inquest and had seen some of the Canadian news clippings. We knew that the brother and sister had both been drawn into a religious cult but I certainly, unlike Harry, did not comprehend the degree to which this cult had affected their lives and threatened the lives of both Albert and Angela. And Harry had been reticent about the discussing the cult. He failed to mention it at our Father's funeral or at any point when our time overlapped in Oxford. Typical Harry, he was to leave us to deal with the fallout.

I sometimes understand why poor Freddie chose to leave this world as she did. Clemente took to referring to my "Brother-in-Law Pontius Pilot washing his hands of us all".

Albert was adamant that he intended to stay clear of North America and Britain. The only other place which with he was remotely familiar was Italy, and specifically with us. He was determined to keep his head down, avoid the old life and raise the child as an Italian. He begged us not to tell anyone. Our attempts to raise the possibility of any obstacles fell on deaf ears. He was serious and intent to follow a plan, a plan he seemed to have worked out on the passage out.

Easter Monday, he started. First, he wrote to Oxford, declining the postdoctoral fellowship. I don't think any of us appreciated the sacrifice, that he could so categorically abandon his life's dream. For seven years, rather like Jacob, he had worked towards this dream. A man with no family, a reticent personality, a prodigious worker, to banish it all in a letter written in fifteen minutes seemed unbelievable. He never mentioned it again after asking Maria Pia to register it and post it when she went into the village.

A second letter was composed a day later to an uncle in Canada. It involved transferring funds into an easily accessible account here in Italy. I know his first day here, he had consulted Clemente and they had gone together to the local Banca Etruria to open an account. If the bank manager found the situation of Albert's moving there unusual, he was professional. Clemente, of course, held shares in the bank which might have helped smooth things. Unlike to-day when we are overrun with English, Germans and Yanks, there were few foreigners living here at that time: an old English couple who probably only had a post office account and a Czech who seemed to live off his wife. The manager promised to facilitate everything as much as possible — not an easy thing in the Italian banking system — and surprisingly he did. Clement told me that Albert had not seen his uncle, who was also his only living relation, in a long time but trusted him to respect his wishes to remain incommunicado and to keep his whereabouts private.

The "father and daughter," as they were to be known and for all intents and purposes legally were, agreed to stay with us in the short term but began almost immediately looking for a suitable house. Clemente, naturally, held a great deal of sway in this matter as well as influence among potential sellers. Adjacent to the property of our *castello* but closer to town, in fact a ten minute walk to the main piazza, was an old *palazzione*, parts of it dating back to the eleventh century. The structure of the house was sound but in need of major renovations. Several out buildings had been used for the curing of tobacco and were totally blackened in the interior. There was an old piggery and rooms in the main house that had obviously been used for pigeons. Clemente had tried to convince him to purchase an old convent that was quite spectacular. Albert refused on two accounts: he did not want to have to rely on a car and he had had his fill of anything that smacked of religion, including abandoned church buildings.

As I previously mentioned, all this was happening before the influx of foreigners into Tuscany. Sadly, they are as often as not my own countrymen who will buy up any hovel, spend copious amounts on making it look like a London townhouse, and install enormous blue fibreglass pools. Ludovico had only one brother still living in the region, a bear of a man named Marco Calli, a notorious scoundrel on all fronts but an excellent architect. Together with Clemente's geometer, named Roberto Guarnieri, they spent hours walking the property with Alberto and poring over plans with Clemente in the evening.

In spite of the potential difficulties the buildings posed for restoration, the location itself and vista were serenely beautiful. A long dirt road, lined by traditional Cyprus trees took one down to the farm and a sharp, almost hairpin turn took one back up to the house. Albert never changed that turn despite complaints from nearly every visitor. Large fields in the distance gave way to hills of grapes and tall stands of cottonwood trees. Behind these trees towered the Tuscan hills, Apennines, some of which even after Easter still maintained their snowy tops. Every direction held views of vines, small slopes of olive trees and neighbouring farms, including to the south, our *castello*.

The millions of lire were not such a terrific obstacle. With a favourable exchange, the place was not that expensive, unlike the millions of euro it would fetch even in these difficult financial times to-day. One of the first things, Albert assured us, was the solidity of his financial situation. His parents had left him financially comfortable. His uncle, in managing his portfolio, had added substantially to his net worth. The purchase and renovation of the property would take a sizeable portion of his liquid capital but by no means all.

In all, the renovations were slated to take eighteen months. This being Italy, however, it was more like two years. We wanted them to live with us; Albert refused. While Maria Pia fussed with the baby, he walked to town each morning although it took him twenty-five minutes. He would have a coffee at the local bar. Virtually no one spoke English, but one day, an elderly medical doctor who had retired to the town some years before struck up a conversation. He had a small flat with a large garden right in the historic centre of town which he planned to sell. Albert walked along with the man and his dog, down the small streets, up steep cobbled hills, and past decaying churches.

Our village abounds in small churches no longer used for services but kept up and open for candle-lighting by elderly women. These crones are the only one to darken the doors to illuminate with their candles the treasures, such as the Della Robbias, and 12$^{th}$-century statues and frescoes. Each decade seems to provide another crop of these women; the breed never dies out. There were two such churches just by the small house with the large garden.

There was a tiny flat accessible through two doors, the first leading to a sizeable garden, which had gone to rack and ruin, and the second door leading directly into the flat. It transpired that there was also a small attached flat with a door on to a side street that could be bought separately. Albert bought them both on the spot. It was to be home to Albert and Angela for the two years of reconstruction of the country property. In the last years of Albert's life it was once again to become his home although he had managed, by that point, to buy the upper level as well.

Seven hundred years old, a large fireplace, complete with an old polenta stone, dominated the living/dining/kitchen area with its stone sink and wooden counter. That fireplace was to provide the heat in winter. The thickness of the stone walls was to provide the respite from the heat of summer. The bedroom was a good size and could also serve as a study. The second small flat, which was easily connected by the installation of a wooden door, had a living room/kitchen that he split into a small sitting room and a room for the baby. There was also a large bedroom with bathroom. Most importantly, as noted, it had a separate door leading out into the street. This was the enticement for Maria Pia to accept the offer of being nursemaid cum housekeeper for Albert. An orphan, she had never dreamed of what seemed to her such luxury, her own sitting room, bedroom and bathroom, and separate entrance. She was, in fairness, by this time devoted to Angela and since my children were past the need of a live-in attendant, I had no objections to her leaving.

The two years of living in the centre of town made a big difference in Albert's life. His first priority, it seemed, was to master the language with, if not native fluency, at least the closest thing to it. He "lived" the town. And "lived" is the only word for it. Each morning he would walk into the central piazza pushing the pram. The old English-looking pram seemed to draw attention; an attention he felt was a negative force against integration. He had Maria Pia select one of Italian design. As if the style of pram made a difference. Albert, in the eyes of all, was just an odd Englishman; but then weren't all English odd? The English widower was how they viewed him. When asked about the baby's mother, he would reply that she was dead, which, of course, was true.

He would follow Maria Pia around on market days, interrupting her in the purchases, whether vegetables or the pinafore-style aprons Italian women favour. My girls from the kitchen would always go to Wednesday market and come back to regale Clemente and me with stories of *Dottor Inglese*. Each day, he would struggle through an Italian newspaper, shout out conjugations of verbs as poor Maria Pia tried to prepare meals, and sing Italian songs to Angela. The Italian radio echoed through the garden, which he had turned into a little oasis of the sort my mother used to describe in in her mock-American drawl "a veritable riot of colour." He eschewed the Italian habit of just using pots of flowers and planted all sorts of flowers directly in the ground.

In the end, however, it was Angela who integrated them into the community. Italians love babies. A baby reared by an incompetent, albeit well-meaning, and rather formal Englishman was too much for them to bear. They would crowd around the pram, invite him to bring her to their houses to be with their children, rush over en masse to take her whenever she fussed. "*Dottore, Dottore, per favore, carissima Angela*" became a common response to her crying.

I write that he went to Mass. It seemed strange that anyone who had been through what he had back in Toronto would not have had enough of religion in general and specifically the church. Given his rationale for not buying the old convent, I was quite taken aback when Ludovico told me that Albert and Angela never missed the 9:30 said-mass.

"But no!" he said to me one day in response to my question about their attending Mass, "I would walk through the fires of Hades if it would help Angela to be one of them. Besides, Ludovico's sermons help my oral comprehension."

Well, in my opinion, Ludovico is an eloquent speaker of the Italian language, good standard Italian. His sermons are succinct and easy to follow if full of papist rubbish. He laughs to this day every time I tell him this.

Whether the sermons were of any spiritual benefit, Albert's Italian certainly did improve. In fact, it improved too well. He spoke with an almost perfect idiomatic dialect. Clemente would sit a couple of evenings every week helping him with standard Italian pronunciation. Eventually, by the time the farm was ready for them to move in, Albert could switch with ease between dialect and standard Italian, depending upon his listener. The only two with whom he would speak English were me, only when we were alone, and, of course, Angela. He wanted her to be an Italian child but an Italian child who could, nevertheless, speak English with the ease of a native speaker.

The child was a delight. I was, and remain, a woman who totally lacks in natural maternal feelings. A few years back, I sent a gift to my grandchild in Connecticut. My daughter wrote back that it was completely inappropriate and a relic of a bygone day. With Angela, things were different. She seemed to kindle some sort of maternal feeling, which I lacked with my own children and certainly my stepson, whom I quite dislike. I never tired of her visits. As a toddler, she sat on my lap and, to be honest, at times I resented Maria Pia and her unfettered access to the child.

With his small flat leased to a local clerk at the bank, Albert, Angela and Maria Pia moved to the palazzione called Fattoria Lorenzo. So Angela, of course, would have no recollection of their time in town, only life at the Fattoria. The main house had been traditionally renovated, a typical farm kitchen with open cabinets, pots and pans hanging from a wooden bar, and large stone sinks. Maria Pia loved it. In fact, she was already turning into a remarkably good cook. But mostly she was delighted to be shown into one of the tobacco outbuildings which had been turned into a small cottage just for her, especially when she noticed her own new television set. She was wedded for life to Albert and Angela, well, in a manner of speaking. Never did I hear her address him as anything other than "*Dottore*" or use a familiar verb form in his presence. I doubt the woman had the slightest romantic thought. I am more than certain, Albert held no romantic thoughts of her, poor dear.

Strange as it may seem, the only other English-speaking couple in the area were neighbours of Albert, Anne and Geoff Sparrow. Geoff had been wounded in Italy during the war and stayed on with Anne eventually joining him. Geoff farmed and an arrangement was made for him to lease Albert's fields and look after a few domestic animals. Maria Pia could see to the poultry. Even with the Sparrows, Albert was extremely formal. I never knew them to mix socially. Always polite, he addressed them as Mr. and Mrs. Sparrow, and they called him Dr. Stafford.

So in this rural and comfortable environment the *father and daughter* lived. Albert walked to town every day, eventually taking Angela by the hand to the infant school in her blue pinafore. Each Sunday, they would walk to Mass and as a treat have a *cornetto* at the bar. He would drink his espresso and she would have a Fanta. I remember her in her white First Communion dress and Albert standing there looking so much the proud father. He only seemed to smile in her presence, so much so that people would often comment to our girls, who reported back.

"Such a father; he only smiles at her. He looks a misery, except when she is there. I don't understand the English."

If they thought him English, he never attempted to dissuade them. He always feared, I think, at the bottom of his mind, some trouble, but none came. Clemente worried a bit about his intellectual state. It was all well and good to learn Italian but he needed to work. Clemente had graduated from the University in Bologna and was active on its management committees. He used a little influence to get Albert invited as an occasional lecturer in History. If Clemente got him in the door, Albert established his own reputation. Despite several offers, he refused to accept anything permanent or tenured. He would undertake no assignment that kept him away from home for more than one night. Eventually, he even purchased a small Fiat, all to get him home more quickly from the train station in Arezzo.

When she was about six or seven and preparing for her First Communion, something I had tried to dissuade Albert from permitting, Angela came to the *castello* on her own. She was running and came up to my workroom, where I was cutting out a pattern for a new dress for my daughter. You see, I did try to be a mother! She had obviously entered through the kitchen as the two girls came running up behind her. Angela was crying and gasping for breath from the long run from her house. It took me several minutes to calm her down. I remember her words so clearly. She was speaking to me in English, something she rarely did.

"Auntie, they came for me like Papa warned. Maria Pia was in the barn with the chickens and they came to the door. The English people came, just like Papa said they would."

She started to cry again and lay on my lap hugging me like a very small child.

I told the girls to telephone Maria Pia, who arrived about a quarter of an hour later. She was beside herself. She had been in feeding the chickens and saw a car in the drive. A Scottish couple were standing at the front door. It seems they had made a wrong turn down the drive and were looking for directions. Maria Pia by this point had picked up enough English from her time with us and helping Albert learn Italian to understand from them that the child had run off. She lifted Angela from my lap. I called Riccardo and had him drive them back to the Fattoria.

After this, I was concerned about the fear embedded in the child's mind. She was frightened that afternoon beyond anything I had ever seen in children. I mentioned it to Albert.

He replied rather curtly, I thought, "I just told her she must not speak to English-speaking people".

I read from his body language that as far as he was concerned this ended the conversation.

But I persisted.

"Bertie, dear, you have obviously instilled a fear, not just a caution, in the child's mind. Those people were obviously innocent Scots, not religious zealots and child-snatchers."

"We don't know that. Maria Pia said they said they were from Scotland but how would she know. They could have said they were from Arkansas or Auckland, New Zealand, for that matter. Her English is minimal."

"Surely, Bertie, you have no reason to doubt they were anything other than what they claimed."

"Laura, I have every reason to believe that they were anything other than what they claimed. Those people want the child, have always wanted the child, and will do anything to get her."

"Surely, with Chris dead, who would want her? Why would they want her?"

"You don't understand, you have never met Dr. Wieszkowski and the charming Mrs. Wieszkowski. I tell you, it is power. They controlled Joanna and Chris, "sanctified them to their inner circle", according to their warped belief.. As far as the Wieszkowskis are concerned, their child belongs to the cult. Angela is theirs by self-appointed adoption and they will stoop to any level to achieve their goal."

I had not seen Albert so distressed since that night seven years before, when he and Angela arrived. The look, the terror, was reflected again in his eyes. I wanted to calm him, reassure him.

"Bertie, how would they have any idea where you are?"

Albert turned and walked outside towards his car. He returned almost at once with an envelope. It was then that he handed me the newspaper clipping.

"I received this in the post four months ago — just the clipping in the envelope franked in Toronto, no return address."

He left the clipping on the table and walked out of the room. I still have it and am copying it out for you. It is dated January 15, 1974 and from a Toronto newspaper.

**BRUTAL MURDER SHOCKS TOWN**

> Residents of the normally peaceful Ontario town of Collingwood on Georgian Bay are shocked and confused by the death of a well-respected local doctor. The body of Dr. Robert Stafford was found in his surgery on Saturday morning by Ontario Provincial Police. He was discovered tied to a chair with over sixty-five wounds on his body and his throat slashed.
>
> Dr. Bob Stafford, a former alderman in Collingwood, was an active member of St. Andrew's Presbyterian Church. When he failed to attend a meeting at the church Friday evening, friends became concerned that something was amiss. The following morning the minister of the church went to his house only to discover his car was not in the drive. The car was still in the lot beside the surgery which was locked. Police were called to the surgery, where they discovered the body.
>
> All of Collingwood seems shaken following the grisly discovery of his body. Residents who rarely lock their doors are now afraid to go out after dark. This fear was confirmed by Collingwood Mayor Tom Downer, who went on to describe the victim as a quiet thoughtful man, well-liked by everyone. "It was impossible not to like Bob. He didn't have an enemy in the world."

Dr. Stafford was last seen alive by his nurse, Eleanor Van Stone, who left work Friday night around five o'clock. Miss Van Stone has stated that Dr. Stafford had stayed late to see a couple who claimed to be staying in a nearby hotel. A woman who had telephoned earlier in the afternoon and who had spoken with a thick European accent, asked to see the doctor about an ear infection for her six-year old son. She also requested a late afternoon or evening appointment as her husband would be back by then and could drive them.

Miss Van Stone said she had a quick glance at a couple pulling into the parking lot as she walked home along a nearby street. The woman was holding a child in her lap and the man was driving. The car, a late model Pontiac, was later reported stolen.

The murder weapon, a surgical scalpel, was found beside the body. Police have confirmed that it was not one that the doctor kept in the surgery. It appears that the victim had been tortured before having his throat slashed.

There as yet appears to be no motive for the murder. According to Miss Van Stone, the couple were unknown to Dr. Stafford or her. Nothing appeared to be missing from the surgery except a small Bible which Dr. Stafford kept in his desk drawer. The desk drawer door, left open, was the only indication that the office might have been searched.

Dr. Stafford had lead a quiet life since his wife died some years ago. His only known relation is a nephew, believed to live in Great Britain. Police have confirmed that the nephew is not considered

> a suspect. With no motive, the police are puzzled by the seeming randomness of the attack but are, nonetheless, following several sources of inquiry.

This still left open the question of feeding the overactive imagination of a child with notions of fear. I worried about its long-term effects on the child's psychological development, although we did not phrase it that way in those days. At least, the unsophisticated like we in San Leo Tiberino did not phrase it that way. Whenever she stayed over with us, which was quite rare, given that Albert liked her to stay at the Fattoria with Maria Pia when he was in Bologna, she often woke screaming in the night. I remember on several occasions going to her and the explanation as I tried to comfort her, it was always the same. Between sobs, she repeated over and over, "Auntie, the English people are back, just like Papa warned me".

I made a point of asking Maria Pia about the dreams and whatever Albert might be saying to the child to bring them on. She was so completely loyal to Albert that she refused to answer my questions. She only shook her head.

"Contessa, she was like that once but no longer. The child is so happy. And Dottore is happy."

And in that Maria Pia was probably right. Angela had a very happy childhood. We established the custom of Saturday nights at the *castello*. Maria Pia would have her night alone in her cottage with her television favourites, Angela would play grown up with my teenagers and Ludovico, and the three of us, Albert, Clemente and I, would play bridge. They would walk over; Ludovico would drive them home or sometimes Riccardo. In this routine, Angela grew, studied and was loved. I have no doubt that there was never a child loved more by her Father and that she loved us all as her family. I may have been mistaken about this, but I hold firmly to it.

* * * * *

I never knew of another incident involving these particular foreigners here in the village, certainly during those early years. As the years passed, Albert seemed calmer but he often had a furtive glance when he was in the piazza, as if always looking for someone. Whenever English people, of which there were so many fewer in those days, came to the bar where he drank his coffee, he would pick up his newspaper and leave. Of course, for some unknown reason beyond my comprehension, he read an American newspaper, so anyone seeing it would assume he spoke English. He was, quite frankly, rude, when anyone spoke to him in English. A kind man, a polite man, Albert just became paranoid around strangers.

Although I had gone along with the First Communion business, I had insisted on Angela's being confirmed in her own church. Albert was anything but keen. He perhaps, as I suspected, had become a closet Roman, I have no idea. He refused to discuss religion. I persisted. The Bishop of Fulham and Gibraltar was coming to Florence to perform the Confirmations. Riccardo drove us. Albert sat throughout the service with his furtive glancing about. Finally I whispered to him:

"Really Bertie: you look as though you expect the reredos to part any second to reveal the Red Army Brigade."

I have never forgotten his reply.

"Laura, it seems the preferable option."

But that day, as every day, his attention was on Angela. He beamed as she came to him after the service. And, of course, there was a beautiful silver hairbrush and mirror engraved with her name and the date. As always, nothing was spared for her.

He was, one might argue, overly protective of the child. But whether as a result of our conversation, I don't know, he seemed to work harder at hiding his anxiety from Angela. His house was always filled with children. He encouraged Angela to have lots of friends and she was a popular child. The small elementary school in the town suited their needs and children of all social backgrounds seemed to be drawn to the Fattoria on weekends and throughout the summer.

I sent my children away at times for their schooling, frequently to Britain. Albert would have none of that. My two were teenagers who loved having Angela with them whenever they came home. I remember one particular event, when Albert agreed to take a group of Angela's friends to the circus. He had his car and roped in Riccardo to bring my children and two others in the Daimler. Albert seemed very excited about the outing and was laughing as they all set off.

Later that evening, at dinner, Luca started to laugh. This was before he started his sullen phase which started at age sixteen and has lasted to this day. He had us all laughing as he recounted how Albert had been more "kid-like than the kids". We laughed and laughed as he regaled us with imitations of Albert eating a cone of spun candy, shaking hands with all the clowns and gazing up spellbound by the trapeze artists.

"Mamma, you could not have believed that it was old Albert who has never cracked a smile in his life."

Over time, things were calmer and Albert seemed happier and able to relax, although, in fairness, I need to add that there were activities in the village of which of which I doubt Albert was aware. One day, Ludovico was walking through the church and passed the seat where Albert and Angela usually sat. He saw something shiny. It was a surgeon's scalpel. He brought it over to Clemente and me. Clemente called in the local Carabinieri but they were unable to trace it. We agreed not to tell Albert.

It could have been, of course, a coincidence but that was not the only sign, I realize now in retrospect that someone may have been stalking Albert and Angela, especially as she grew older. At the time, we tried to pretend that they were coincidences. We certainly did not want to agitate Albert. More precisely, we wanted to ignore the signs of any unwanted attention or interest. One of the problems was that things would happen at intervals of as much as three or four years. We would assume that the Toronto group had lost interest in Angela and Albert. Then something would happen to bring back the niggling sense of insecurity.

After the visit of the "Scottish couple" and the appearance of the scalpel, both around the time of the First Communion, nothing happened for several years until the time of her Confirmation. I had done a lot of embroidery on her dress which was damaged when someone spilled wine after the service at the dinner table in the trattoria on Piazza Carmine and some got on Angela's dress. Angela was beside herself; tears streamed down her face as she tried to put on a brave face. Maria Pia had washed it carefully and put it out in the sun to bleach. Someone took it from the line. Was that a stalking incident? I didn't think so at the time. I am not so certain now.

Angela went on to secondary school in Sansepolcro with Albert driving her or, increasingly often as the years progressed, Maria Pia whenever he was in Bologna. Albert actually bought Maria Pia her own car. I can so clearly recall the little Fiat, with Maria Pia concentrating as if she were driving what my Americanophile son tiresomely referred to as "Maria Pia's own Sherman tank".

"There goes Maria Pia in her own Sherman tank," he would shout while making gestures of turning a large steering wheel. He would shout on and on and wave. In my mind, I can still see the car passing, Maria Pia driving, with Angela and three other girls from San Leo Tiberino laughing and waving back. Poor Maria Pia, I doubt she knew anything about a Sherman Tank or any other sort of tank. Luca's humour would have been lost on her.

One day I saw Maria Pia waiting by the school for the girls to come out. Riccardo was driving me home from the dentist. I waved but she didn't see me. She was too busy chatting with a couple. All I can really remember is that the man had a camera around his neck and was wearing a hooded sweatshirt. I mentioned it to her when I met her the next day at the Wednesday market and she laughed.

"Such nice people, Contessa! You should have stopped. It was the 'Scotland couple' who called at the house all those years ago, the ones who frightened Angela. They invited me for coffee but I said I would another day."

I wished I had indeed stopped. I regret that I spoke a bit harshly to Maria Pia.

"I will not tell Dottore and I suggest you do not either! Also, do not engage in another conversation with these people. And coffee is out of the question. Dottore would not like it."

"Dottore would not like it" was always a phrase designed to ensure total compliance with Maria Pia.

Over the years there were several possible sightings of the "Scotland couple." One of the more unusual occurrences involved a Mademoiselle Saint-Jacques. She was well past her Mademoiselle days, yet no one ever elevated her to the Madame status; even to-day as an old woman she is Mademoiselle St-Jacques. She was, and still is, for all the world to see, a confirmed spinster. Lucille came to Sansepolcro as a young child and so speaks faultless Italian as well as her native French and a fairly decent English. Both her parents were older when she was born. Her mother had died in the Dordogne Region of France and her father took a job as a chef in one of the smaller eateries in Sansepolcro.

Her career in life was confined to looking after her father. When he died, she was without means or occupation. This is the classic tale. Lucille could have been a character in an Edith Wharton novel or an Arnold Bennett. American novel or British novel: take your pick. She was thin, Gallic-looking, without the grooming and taste in clothing one expects in French women. She earned her living by tutoring in French. I was going to write "meager living" but that sounds too dramatic. Somehow drama and Mademoiselle do not go together, until perhaps this one incident.

We all employed Lucille at one point or other. My two went for lessons with the intent, no doubt, of tormenting the poor woman. Actually, she was the only 'expat' I recall whom Albert liked. It was hardly romantic, that is for certain, but as he once told me he "admired her spunk". As Angela pored over her notebook on a Saturday morning, Albert would sip coffee with her and chat in French. Albert spoke amazingly good French. He was the only person I ever heard use the *Madame de politesse* when referring to her.

As for me, I was not such a good linguist. But, after my children left, I would meet Lucille for coffee every few weeks to perfect what French I still retained. One day, while we were in a café, she rather abruptly switched into English. Her English, as I mentioned, was quite passable but it seemed strange, almost as if she felt people might overhear the French. This was ludicrous as it was far more likely that someone would understand English than French if, that is, anyone could possibly have had an interest in our conversation.

"Contessa, I have made the acquaintanceship of a man, an American, but it has not gone well. I have been disappointed in the affair."

I let her continue with what I hoped was a sympathetic look. Horrid as I may seem, I was quite fond of Lucille. If I am frank on the matter of friendship, Lucille, I suppose was my only woman friend then and remains so to this day.

"I met the American man in this bar. I was alone but when I went to pay for my coffee, Federico told me the American man had paid for it. I, of course, thanked him in English and he walked out the door at the same time as I. He told me that it was so nice to be able to speak English. Then he did an extraordinary thing. He asked me to dinner.

"Contessa, this has not happened to me, ever. I was going to say 'merci' but he seemed a nice man and sometimes I am lonely since Papa died."

"Lucille, did he give you his name?"

"Of course, Brian Warefield from Michigan. Michigan, Contessa, is in the middle of America."

"Lucille, of course I know where Michigan is."

She did have an annoying way of assuming everyone had lived as insular a life as she.

"He told me that he was here with his sister but they both had different interests and did not frequent each other too much."

"How was the dinner? Where did he take you?"

"Well you know, Contessa, that I am the chef's daughter. I made him dinner at my flat. After that we met every day for coffee and every evening I made dinner."

"For how long?"

"Oh, three weeks or so. Then it stopped as suddenly as it started. It was a Wednesday, I remember, as I rarely have students on a Wednesday and had made a special torte. We were having coffee after the dinner when he asked me a strange question: 'Lucille, I am coming back to Sansepolcro with my sister in the summer months. She has an adolescent child who will accompany us. It would be nice if there were an English-speaking boy or girl for him to meet. Do you know such?'

"He must have noticed me hesitate. Contessa, I did not want to involve your family. To be honest, I was ashamed for you to find out about Mr. Warefield. I was afraid you might disapprove. So I told him my students were normally Italian and that I did not mix with expatriates.

"He then said, rather nastily, words in a tone I cannot forget, 'Lucille you are not being truthful. You know Dr. Stafford over in San Leo Tiberino. There is an English child.'

"I told him that Dr. Stafford would never allow for his daughter to mix with Americans or English people. He wanted her only to be with Italians. I explained that I could not make such an introduction of the children."

I was starting to become quite anxious.

"Lucille, how did he react?"

"He said, 'Mademoiselle St-Jacques, not Lucille, I feel you do not speak truthfully to me'. Then He stood up and left. He did not come to my home again. I went to his hotel but they told me he had left with his wife. His wife, not his sister. Well, I am told such is life. But it has not been a happy time."

Another coincidence? I don't know. Probably, but I am afraid I viewed the whole thing in terms of Lucille's tragedy, not in terms of Albert's being stalked. She for her part never mentioned it again nor even mentioned seeing this Warefield person.

Then, as I look back, there was one more incident. When Angela was in her last year of secondary school, four of the girls from the school choir (including the three girls, as it so happened, who rode with Angela in Maria Pia's car each afternoon) were invited to join a mass choir to sing in St. Peter's Basilica in Rome. Albert had given it his customary "absolutely no". Angela was disappointed. She was getting to an age where her father's consistent veto was becoming irksome. She was also discovering, as youth does, that there was a larger world beyond her narrow confines. I suggested to Albert that I take Angela to Rome and we could stay at our flat not with the other girls in a dormitory. Clemente was to be out of the country on business and it would be a "girls' weekend." I could take her to the rehearsals and the concert, after which we could do some shopping. Angela needed new clothes for university. It was a gamble.

We both prevailed on him. In the end, he agreed, with a list of provisos, one of which was that we were not to take the tube. We, of course, took no notice of it. Angela, a girl who had spent virtually every day of her life in the rural Valtiberina, found the tube exciting, as did her friends. The concert was in the afternoon. I offered to take Angela and her three girlfriends out for dinner. The teacher who had accompanied the other girls was delighted at the prospect of having an evening free in Rome. I promised to have the girls back at their dormitory by nine-thirty. So, the five of us stayed on after the concert for a tour of the Vatican followed by the five o'clock Vespers.

It was raining when we left St Peter's. Taxis were in short supply. Although it was getting dark, I reasoned that the restaurant was near the Barberini tube, only four stops from the nearby Ottaviano San Pietro tube station. We dodged the pedestrian traffic, laughing most of the way. I bought the tickets and we headed down the steps. The girls were behind me. There was no one else on the stairs. Without notice, a man passed the girls and walked directly behind me. As I was about five steps from the bottom, he gave a mighty shove to my back. I flew literally down the stairs onto the platform. The girls ran after me to help me up. The man disappeared.

I didn't see him. I had let go of my purse, which slid along the platform. Although I did not see him, I heard him. As he passed me lying on the platform, knees bleeding, he called me an "old cow," not the Italian "*vecchiaccia*," but the English, "old cow".

The upshot was I had a lot of bruises, my knees were cut and bleeding, and my wrists were slightly sprained. Otherwise I was not hurt, only shaken. What was more upsetting than the aching limbs was that my purse was gone with my wallet, change purse, papers and keys to the flat. Two men in uniform helped me up as the girls, who had been so happy minutes before, took turns hugging me. My tights were torn. All I really wanted to do was get out of the station and take the girls back to the flat. I hobbled up the stairs holding on to Angela's arm and the girls found a taxi. Mercifully, I might add, Angela had enough money to get the five of us to the flat.

When the taxi dropped us off, again fortune seemed to smile; the concierge, Simone, was at home that evening and let us in. But we did not need him to let us in. When we got to our door, the keys were in the lock. Simone insisted that we wait in the hall while he checked. The flat was empty, with my purse evident for all to see on the dining room table. It sat there in the middle of the table. Nothing, moreover, appeared to be missing: money, cosmetics, identity card, driver's permit. All were as they had been when I left the house earlier that afternoon.

I didn't want the police involved, dreading the newspapers' leader: *Contessa Mugged in Metro*. And then there was Albert, whom I had disobeyed; I didn't want to have to face him. The thief had obviously not had time to copy the keys. In any event, Simone had promised to watch carefully over the flat while we went out to dinner and have the locks changed in the morning. That meant only Clemente and Giorgio need know, and I could tell them I had lost my keys. I made the girls promise not to mention it, saying their teacher might get into trouble for leaving them. Later that night as I put the chain on the door's safety lock, I emphasized again and again to Angela that it was a random attack that would only upset Albert. As far as I know he never found out.

It was only a few weeks later, when I was adding a photo to the small album of family photos I carry in my purse, that I saw what the thief had taken. Among the happy family shots, was one of Angela as a small child sitting on Albert's lap. Albert had been convinced by Clemente to dress as Father Christmas. It was so uncharacteristic of Albert to agree that I always laughed when I saw it. The photo had been ripped in half; the top half, which had a solemn white-bearded Albert, was there but the lower portion with Angela had been taken. Once again, I never told Albert.

These are the events I knew about. If Albert had any other intimations of stalking, he did not share them with me. That, however, was to have been expected. Albert's face rarely betrayed the contradictory attitudes of apprehension or tranquility. It was not in his nature. And emotion directed towards anyone but Angela seemed alien to his very being. Confidences were out of the question.

Then, before we knew it, came university for Angela, and the Fattoria, empty for weeks at a time, would suddenly become filled with university students, friends of Angela's arguing and posturing with Albert until the wee hours of the morning. As far as I am aware, nothing untoward or threatening happened throughout those university years at Bologna. After this time, of course, Angela was a woman. We, at least I, believed her out of danger.

Angela: was she a happy child? Did she have a happy childhood? A happy adolescence? Yes, in my opinion.

So I conclude my narrative. There was much happiness in those years for all of us. Happiness, however, has a way of making us unprepared for the vagaries of life. My children are estranged from me. My grandchildren exist only in the odd photograph that comes my way. Clemente's son is an uncaring brute. Clemente himself died with his mistress holding his hand. The local people address me more frequently as "Signora" than Contessa". Both of Harry's children have predeceased him. Ludovico is well past his best-buy date but refuses to step down for a younger priest. Cosmo is a lonely widower who comes out here ostensibly so we can get on each other's nerves.

I now putter about here alone, increasingly growing stout, alone at the *castello* except for faithful Riccardo who is now well into his sixties. The maids are gone, the swimming pool has been filled in, and the tennis courts where Chris, Joanna and Albert spent their days all these years ago are overrun with weeds. Whatever deference or affection the locals had for the Guelfi family died with Clemente. I don't even stay at the *castello* in the winter months. My Daimler is kaput, sold for scrap. I must now ride around in Riccardo's car.

Albert's only living relation was brutally murdered, and Albert went through a living hell for twenty years; none of us realised he was about to face another twenty.

LAURA J. NEAGLE GUELFI

# COSMO

## 1990–PRESENT

I am Cosmo Neagle, a retired bishop of the Church of England. I have been persuaded by my brother, Dr. Harry Neagle and my sister Laura Neagle Guelfi to contribute a narrative focusing on the period beginning around 1988, Angela's adult life. Much as it distresses me, I agreed to outline the events from my vantage point. I am, to be truthful, reluctant to raise this business again. After much prayer, something you may find unusual to-day, and the encouragement of my fellow cleric and friend Dom Ludovico Calli, I agreed. Had Albert Stafford been still living, I would never have consented. He is now where such recollections can no longer hurt him, or so we in the Church tell the people.

I will endeavour to provide a full account of what I know or, in certain instances, what I have been told. Much of what later occurred took place in London, and although I was not resident in London, my late wife and I were, nonetheless, in Britain. Initially, pleasure and, ultimately, displeasure brought us together with Angela and the other players involved in the London events.

My sister writes with ease; she also chats easily. Ludovico will write in precise English, subjunctive and all. Harry will write, I expect, like a pathologist. I have never written more than sermons. As a bishop, everything from communiqués to pastoral correspondence was handled by canons, administrators and archdeacons better skilled than I. My reminiscences will just run on from here, I hope in some coherent sequence.

As you know, Angela was my older brother's granddaughter. Harry's son, Christopher, and daughter, Joanna, had accompanied him to Canada when he accepted a temporary appointment at the university and stayed on for their studies after his return to Britain. Both Chris and Joanna read French Literature at Trinity College. The Provost of the college was a contemporary of mine from St.

Stephen's House in Oxford and I have been led to believe the college to be first-rate. Christopher eventually entered a more evangelical theological college than I would have hoped, but then Laura's or Harry's notes will have dealt with all of that as well as the details of my brother's estrangement from his children.

I did not agree with my brother's attitude to Christopher and Joanna. I believe children are a gift from God, not to be abandoned. And his granddaughter should not have been held responsible for the actions of her parents. None of us chooses the instrument of his birth. While I assure you my brother was and continues to be a good man in so many ways, this does not, in my opinion, atone for his behaviour towards his children. He may have grieved more than any of us believed when he lost his wife at a young age. That may have affected his relationship with his children. To-day we would probably diagnose Freddie Neagle's behaviour in pseudo-psychological popular terms such as post-partum depression and the like. Then, we just disguised the facts as accidents.

The truth is Freddy Neagle committed suicide. It might have been under the influence of alcohol and prescription drugs, but she hanged herself. I don't think Harry, a brilliant medic in his own right, ever quite recovered from the shock; his wife, quite honestly, had defeated him. He tried to be mother and father to the children, failing, I think, on both counts. When he went to Toronto that last time, he lost all patience with his children, especially over the cult and the details of Joanna's pregnancy.

I suppose, I can understand, if not justify, his reaction. My wife, Barbara, and I were never blessed with children. As old fashioned as the phrase may be, I do believe children to be a blessing. What I could never understand was Harry's refusal to have anything to do with his granddaughter. He left everything concerning her rearing to Albert Stafford, a man we in the family all knew despite what we might have wanted to believe, was not the child's father. My wife particularly in those early years came to love the child. My sister Laura did as well. Motherhood did not come naturally to Laura except, strangely, with Angela. I am, I suppose, a bit of a curmudgeon, not one to whom children come naturally. Over time, I loved Angela very much. That explains why I willingly but with a heavy heart tried to share some of the grief ever present throughout all the adult years of her life. I doubt I was successful.

Laura and Clemente together with their children became Angela and Albert's nuclear family during her early years. I don't know what, if anything, their children were told but to my knowledge no one knew that Albert was probably not Angela's natural father. You see I write "probably not Angela's father" instinctively, a force of habit for all these years. It was a wish, a day-dream, a prayer but not true. We all knew it but wished otherwise to the degree that we almost believed it. But, Chris, not Albert, was the father.

Clearly, however, no one told the truth to Angela, and I am not certain that had I been responsible for telling her, I would have done any differently. What I am certain of is this: Albert gave her a good, firm, Christian upbringing. She lived in an environment surrounded by loving cousins. This was to make the subsequent events all the more tragic.

I have always believed that the Tuscany hills are a wonderful place to rear children. One never tires of the fields of grapes and olives, the pathways, the animals — even the wild boar. The Italian countryside in Valtiberina affords a depth of peace unfathomable in a church. Does this mean in my old age, that I confess I have been a naturalist at heart all these years, a closet Green? No, I am just unquestionably an aficionado of all things Italian.

The food alone might render me apt to relocate on a permanent basis. The food, notwithstanding the ambiance of the lifestyle, is perfect. It has the four seasons: the winter can be a challenge; the summer can be unbearably hot; the spring redolent in its hope and the autumn mellow. But, in each instance, one need only look at the landscape, the hills and the colours for contrast. More than anything, it is the people: the warmth and natural generosity, the sophistication and the countrified way. Always present is this juxtaposition in the lifestyle and culture.

Angela went at Albert's insistence to the local schools. When it came time for secondary school, he or his housekeeper would drive her to Sansepolcro to the school equivalent of a grammar school in the UK. She made friends easily and had the openness seemingly lacking in Albert. They complemented each other as couples often do, as married couples often do, not parent and child. The central piazza of a small town like San Leo Tiberino is a natural gathering place for the young: boys and girls together under the guardianship of passing neighbours and shopkeepers eager to keep an eye out for problems. More often than not, Albert was the passing neighbour.

Albert, despite his total unpreparedness and unsuitability, made a good father. He never seemed to lack patience when it came to Angela. As my sister, in her obsession for such things will have pointed out, he took her to the church each Sunday, where she eventually made her first Communion in a dress made by Laura and Maria Pia, Albert's faithful housekeeper. My sister, of course, insisted that she be confirmed in the C of E and dragged her off to Florence. But Albert seemed reluctant that she venture much beyond St Leo, that was, until it was time for university.

Eventually, the University of Bologna had sought him out and he became an occasional but popular lecturer, so it seemed natural for Angela to be enrolled there. There is, in fact, nowhere better. I think in his heart of hearts he would have been more comfortable with her commuting to the University of Perugia. In fairness, I think he realized that he could not come between the girl and a first-rate education. Bologna did, at least, afford Albert the opportunity to keep an eye on her when he went up for lectures and research. He had kept a fairly good-sized flat in later years that also served as his office and library. Angela lived there. If his continual presence during her undergraduate years put any cramps in her social life, or if she was bothered in any way by his continuous presence, Angela gave no indication. In fact, Albert used to laugh that he would have to foot the bill for about eight students' dinners each time he visited. Every holiday, it seemed, Angela invited a slew of different friends to San Leo to crowd into Albert's house. Albert, reserved as he was, seemed to enjoy this.

Unbeknownst to Albert, Angela applied for a scholarship to King's College in London for an M. Phil. in Medieval English History. I know from Laura that Albert was not happy. In fact, he told me himself the summer before she left. He even went so far as to consider moving to London. I assured him that I would look in on her whenever I was in London attending to affairs in the House, and that Barbara and I would have her up to stay with us for holidays. He remained uneasy throughout the summer, as if taking Angela away from Italy would somehow harm her. I thought this irrational and I am afraid I told him so.

Several months after she arrived in London, I was invited to her flat, which was on Oakley Street in Chelsea. Albert was quite comfortably off financially, so he had insisted that she live in a proper flat and that she have no roommates. Angela had decorated it nicely. It had a large living and study area where she kept her desk, shelves of books and a sofa and two tub chairs. There was a dining room off which was a fairly well-apportioned kitchen. She was, given the cost of renting it, the only student in the flats and very much the darling of the neighbourhood.

I arrived there for drinks but it soon became evident that we were not to be alone. A young man was to join us. Angela told me that a friend from the college, Janice Hempwell, who was a Canadian, had invited her to go to a film at the Canadian High Commission some months back. There was a reception afterwards where the girls chatted to the High Commissioner, a man by the name of Roy McMurtry, whom I had met on several occasions. Angela mentioned casually that she had been born in Toronto and though her father was a Canadian she knew virtually nothing about the country. Mr. McMurtry's response was to invite both girls to a lecture on Canadian history the following week at the residence, MacDonald House, on Grosvenor Square.

The girls went and afterwards at the reception a young man approached them and spoke to Janice. She was staying at William

Goodenough, a residence for foreign graduate students on Mecklenberg Square. The young man said he was staying at London House, a residence across the square and had often seen the two of them at King's. His name was Tony Westlake and he asked the girls to join him for a drink. He was meeting a friend near the British Museum in Bloomsbury. Angela told me that she had initially begged off citing the distance back to Chelsea but the other two prevailed. Janice, however, had put pressure on her to go by saying she didn't feel comfortable going alone. In the end Angela went to meet Tony's friend, yet another Canadian named Jake Kelley.

I mention in detail all these people because they were to play significant rôles in the coming events. I came to know each one of them quite well, all, that is, except Westlake. The inevitable happened. Janice and Kelley became an item almost at once. Janice was a pleasant, if not a wholly likeable, girl. That's unfair, I suppose, as I did like her; she projected her persona, however, rather like an actress does a character. There was a sense that she was always preoccupied with her text and that someone was directing her. It was as though everything in her life was being scripted for her. The lack of natural spontaneity in one so young bothered me. This was reflected in her relationship with Jake. She was very tactile with him, always touching his hand, that sort of thing, but almost as a cat that waits pondering the right moment to jump into one's lap. But her hands looked cold, and perhaps they were, literally, because quite often Jake would start when she touched him.

Jake was the opposite, affable in every way. I often wished that he and Angela would have grown closer. They were alike, always laughing and cracking small jokes. Janice would just smile and the smile always seemed forced. Jake and Angela made Barbara and me laugh. They would behave outrageously and we would laugh until tears rolled down our faces. These times, our times together with the young people are a precious memory.

Angela, however, was slow to respond to Tony's attention but eventually they became good friends, unlike the other couple, not really an "item". Anyway, that was what Angela told me as a prelude to meeting him that evening in her flat. She also confided that she was nervous to tell Albert, who, she said, bore some sort of negative opinion of Canada. She said that he always refused to attend any social activities in the small colony of Canadians in the Valtiberina. In fact, he would barely acknowledge their presence if they encountered each other in the piazza.

About the time Tony was to arrive that first evening, he telephoned to say he was running late. She urged him to hurry as she was very anxious for him to meet her Uncle Cosmo. Apparently, he did not know I was to have been there. A few minutes later, Westlake rang again, this time to say he had been detained and would not see her that evening.

I asked her about him. Angela laughed and told me he was "a presentable young man, even by Papa's standard. He is dark like me, but tall with wavy hair, which he wears quite long"

There was no doubt that he was very clever, studying psychology. Whether it was the psychology which made her a History student uncomfortable, she said that her only reservation was his intensity of person. "Uncle Cosmo," she confided "he seems to stare too directly and at times probe in his questions, almost as though he wants to enter your mind".

This description made me slightly uncomfortable but seemed to roll off Angela like the proverbial water off a duck's back. She was just an affable young woman prepared to accept anyone on his own terms.

In deference, I suppose, to my position, she was anxious to assure me of his family's church connections. I used to have to remind her that although a bishop, I was not her Auntie Laura, the church-disciplined member of the family. Angela seemed to stress the fact that Tony's father was a church leader of sorts and that Tony was very much under his influence, writing to him several times each week and always trying to please his father.

The term passed and when it got closer to Christmas, Barbara and I invited Angela to spend the Christmas holidays with us. She asked, as Angela had always asked Albert when at university, if her friends could come as well. By her friends, she meant Janice and Jake. Tony who would have been welcomed, of course, was flying back to Canada for the holidays, she told me almost in passing. Apparently his father had insisted on a Christmas visit. Angela, strangely it seems now in retrospect, never really mentioned Tony over Christmas; the relationship, had if it ever truly existed, seemed to be over.

Angela had her first traditional English Christmas. In those days, Laura deferred to everything Italian, whether for Clemente's sake or her reputation as a *contessa*, I don't know. Albert left all the planning to her for high and holy days. Barbara, in her very English way, went all out, with crackers on the table, paper hats, goose, Christmas pudding, the works. Janice and Jake having grown up in Canada were quite used to it all, but for Angela everything was quite the new experience. Angela enjoyed everything. I can still see her laughing at the idea of holly on the table. She helped Barbara stuff the goose and boil the puddings. They all went to church Christmas morning and sang Christmas carols well into the night with Barbara playing the upright in the study.

When Angela went back to London in the new year, the relationship with Tony, which I thought over, apparently blossomed. She told me at lunch one day that he had seemed somewhat indifferent to her until he came back from Canada. He pursued her morning, noon and night. I invited him to join us for dinner on a couple of occasions but each time he begged off with a cold, an overdue assignment, always something. The other two, Janice and Jake, on the other hand, never missed an opportunity for a meal out. By this time, both Tony and Jake had moved out of London House and had taken a flat somewhere closer to the British Museum but still in Bloomsbury. Janice, apparently, hinted at moving in with Angela. Tony, Angela later told me, seconded this idea. He outlined all the advantages, but Angela had promised Albert that she would not take in flatmates. And she was still under his guidance on such matters, at least for the short term.

On February 15th, a date I am not likely to forget, Angela and I had lunch at my club. She seemed a bit nervous. She told me that Tony's parents were in town and staying at his flat. Once again, she mentioned the level of control Tony's father had over the young man's life. I assumed this was playing on her mind and accounted for her nervousness. They were to have a dinner that night along with Jake and Janice to meet them. I remember telling her about the first time Barbara had to meet my father and by the time she left for her afternoon tutorial we were both laughing.

For the details of what transpired from there I have to rely on Angela's recounting of them. There is no reason why I should believe them to be anything but an accurate account of that evening. I can hear her now and every detail seems etched in my mind. It seems her tutorial was cut short and she arrived at the flat around five thirty. Jake answered the door and whisked her into the kitchen. He told her that Tony's parents were resting in the bedroom and that Tony was out buying some wine. Jake was busy chopping up two chickens with a large knife, which he kept rinsing under the tap.

When the telephone, which actually was in the kitchen, rang, she heard Jack say that he had forgotten an assignation or something to that effect, but that he would be there as soon as possible.

"Angela," he said as he put down the receiver, "that was Janice. I forgot I was to meet her and one of her professors for a drink at the King's Arms at the corner. Could you get me out of a tricky spot and finish cutting up the chickens? We won't be long and dinner isn't until eight anyway. Please?"

Jake had an endearing way of putting a request; he made me laugh anyway, and I can assume Angela was smiling at him as he left and she started on the chickens.

A few minutes later, Tony returned.

"Angela, I thought you couldn't make it until later?"

"My tutorial was cut off early so I came right over"

"Well, all the better. I had planned a little family chit chat later, but maybe we can have it now."

The bedroom door opened and a man walked out who was the very image of Tony. It was Tony twenty-five years older.

"Dad, this is Angela."

Angela shook his hand and spoke a little nervously, as she was later to testify.

"How do you do, Dr. Westlake? Tony hasn't told me all that much about you, so I am anxious to get to know you better."

"Westlake, eh? That's little Tony-the-Anglophile's version. Me, I still have the Polish name I have used for twenty-five years, although like you I am English. But something tells me you are not English anymore."

"Italian, actually."

"Italian is it? You don't know who I am, do you? I have another name, Wieszkowski, the longer form for Westlake. I took dear Broni Wieszlowski's name and his wife, Tony's mama, after the poor Pole had a nasty accident. So, I might as well speak bluntly. Time you learned the truth. I, Angela, little Italian girl, am your Father. I am Christopher Neagle, Chris to my friends."

"I don't understand. Tony, what is this all about? What is your Father saying? Who is this Wieszkowski? My Father lives in Italy. And Neagle: that is my mother's maiden name and my Uncle Cosmo's."

"And how is dear old Cosmo these days, the three F's: fat, faggoty old phoney."

Chris was grinning at her, enjoying his own humour.

"He is your great-uncle and my plain old uncle. How charming and sweet that you call him Uncle! I never did. I suppose Laura is also your Auntie. She always was an old cow. Bet you don't call my old man Uncle Harry, or Grandpapa for that matter."

He continued to grin at her, obviously enjoying how confused and uncomfortable she had become. I shudder to think what was going through the poor girl's mind.

The man continued all the while intently "with a demonic grin," as she later put it.

"I am a Neagle; your mother, my dear departed sister Joanna was a Neagle. You are a Neagle. Tony is your half-brother and he is really a Neagle but has had to hide that. My sister Joanna and I were your parents. Only, when my sister died, Albert Stafford stole you away from me. Now you are back in the family to stay."

"You know I used to watch you. I would travel to Italy and see you coming home from school holding the hand of a woman, I heard you once call her Maria-Something. Do you remember the time we called at the farm or whatever it was and told you we were from Scotland? I had to be careful to keep a distance when Bertie was near you, but I knew he had gone up to Bologna. And you were so cute. I saw you in your first Confirmation dress from a distance with that cow, Auntie Laura fussing over you. A real treat you were, but I had to wait to meet you, wait until now."

"He is saying, Angela dear," Tony actually surprised her by smiling, "that you and I are brother and sister".

He spoke, she was to say, as though all of this was perfectly normal and confessed that the normalcy of his manner frightened her more than anything.

Angela covered her eyes so she could not see the two of them. But Chris continued.

"I give my blessing to your marriage to my son. That's what you were hoping to hear this evening, wasn't it, a blessing for a marriage? I want you back from that demon Albert. I am taking you back to Manitoulin Island, where we shall wipe the evil from your mind, the pollution of Albert Stafford. We must give thanks to God for your redemption; soon you will be pure, as pure as you were when Albert took you from my flat. Your Mother hanging there dead, and Albert, Satan's lackey, took you as if you were his, not mine."

"I am leaving."

Angela was later to say she was crying, but these were the only words she spoke through it all.

She had backed away and Tony was trying to console her.

"Darling, listen to my Dad, our Dad. Look how happy he and your Mother were as brother and sister, how they loved. You and I can do that; have babies like you and me, pure children. My father has taught me that only someone with his genes is worthy of my love. Our church teaches that brothers and sisters may marry, in fact encourages them to marry. 'Shun the evil of this world to live with the chosen in our world.' I came here to London to find you, to find my bride. My father has followed your life, at times seeing you in San Leo Tiberino and after when he discovered that you were in London.

"I followed you for weeks. When I saw you at the reception, did you know Janice had told me you would be there? Did you know I knew her in Canada? She wanted to marry me but accepted my Father and Mother's wishes. She has always obeyed the leaders; that's the nice thing about Janice. She never resists. As for Jake, he is so stupid, naïve, pliable like the rest. It was easy, except I almost met the bishop; that was close. He would have recognized Dad in me."

Tony came towards her; she shoved him away. He came back, trying to put his arms around her, but she kept pushing them down. Her right hand slid in a continuous motion from his sleeve backwards until it rested on the counter. The chicken slid to the floor but "the knife felt so light", she said. As she swung her arm back, she raised the knife, then stuck it at full force into his neck, the blood spurting from the artery all over her.

Chris ran towards her bending to catch Tony's body as it crumpled towards the floor. She brought the knife down into the older man's back towards the ribcage. He screamed. The bedroom door opened to what Angela later described as "a squat blond woman" carrying the white first Confirmation dress who ran towards her, grabbing her hand. The knife went against Angela's stomach. The woman held it there for what seemed an eternity until Angela turned it and plunged it into the woman. Angela stabbed her an additional thirteen times.

Angela later recounted that, in her fear and anger, she continued to stab the woman. Tony, she knew, was dead but not Chris. In all, she then stabbed Chris another thirty-seven times.

Janice told me shortly after the events took place that when she and Jake arrived at the flat, Angela was covered in blood, her hair, her cheeks, her clothes almost completely red. She kept hugging the white dress, which was completely saturated with blood. She was sitting on the kitchen floor, the knife still in her hand, and the three, Chris, Stanie and Tony, lay dead beside her.

Both she and Jake ran out into the living room towards the door. They then went back for her, thinking that she had been attacked along with the others. Angela waved them off.

"I killed my family; please ring the police."

Jake was later to confirm these words, what would later be taken as a confession.

The rest, according to Jake, was like any crime television show: body bags, teams of technicians and so forth. He and Janice were taken to neighbours and questioned there. Angela was taken to a hospital by ambulance, where eventually she was charged with the murder of Bronislaw Wieszkowski, Stafania Wieszkowski, and Antony Wieszkowski. Jake telephoned me at once. Barbara and I were not allowed to see her for two days and she was still in hospital, quite sedated. She refused to hold my hand but held Barbara's, although she didn't speak. Janice was not required — or refused — to return for the trial, which took place quite quickly, all things considered. Jake had stayed in Britain to finish his studies. Janice returned to Canada as soon as she was able. She never spoke to Jake again after that night. There was, on the surface, more than one tragedy to these events.

Or so it seemed. What Janice didn't add and what didn't come up subsequently at all in any report or testimony was that after Angela had said those fateful words, Janice had gone to stand over Tony, where she sobbed uncontrollably for only a short time before she turned towards Angela and spat on her. I did not learn this until sometime after and from Jake.

Janice last spoke to me a day or so before she left England. She telephoned me to thank me for the many times we had spent together. I admit that at the time, I put her strange attitude down to the pressure of trying to deal with the shocking images and, of course, the press. To-day, I expect, they would call this behaviour post-traumatic stress disorder. Everything to-day must have its psychological label. Anyway, Janice seemed almost inconsolable, but she spoke only of Tony and his parents and her loss. She continuously referred to "her loss," never once making reference to Angela or her tragedy. She did not even ask how her friend was holding up. Neither did she ask about Jake.

I rang Laura and Ludovico. It was they who told Albert who, understandably, was totally beside himself. It was probably adrenalin kicking in but Albert immediately packed and headed to the aeroport in Florence. Ludovico drove him. Maria Pia wanted to go with him. The poor darling was in shock. But, of course, she had no passport. Laura had offered to accompany Albert to London, but he managed to convince her that the press would get hold of this and it would be best to carry on normally, as if anything would ever again be normal.

Barbara and I met him at Gatwick and took him to the house in the Cotswolds. He had aged ten years since I had seen him the summer before. In my study, Barbara broke the news to him that Angela refused to see him. After my first visit in the hospital, Angela also refused to see me. Only Barbara was allowed to visit. Barbara mused that it was probably as she, relatively speaking, was a newcomer to all this. In fact, no one had ever shared the origins of Angela's birth with her. She could in all sincerity tell Angela she had no idea about those earlier events and that she had always accepted that Albert was Angela's natural father.

Angela told Barbara that she never wanted to see Albert again and that he had deceived her all these years. "Had he been honest, Barbara, none of this would have happened."

Well, I don't know that I accept this argument now, nor did I then. Angela declined all rational discussion. She refused to hear any plea for Albert that tried to put the events into any sort of context. As far as she was concerned, Chris was now her Father, had always been her Father, and she had killed him. In fact, in all her conversations with Barbara, she never once mentioned Tony or Stanie, as if they were incidental players.

Albert asked Barbara if she believed Angela to be mad. She just shook her head.

"I wouldn't, Albert, say mad," she paused searching for her words, "but singularly strange".

Well that was Barbara, always a bit vague, a tad obtuse and prone to put on a positive spin. The press, meanwhile, had a field day. Headlines raged on:

***Devil's Hereditary Priestess Seeks Revenge***
***Victim of Satanists Pleads No Contest***
***Baby Kidnapper in England***
***Bishop's Niece Unrepentant***

None of us was spared the wrath of the press. The Toronto inquest was revisited in all its glory. Reporters, or more precisely stringers, were hired to visit Toronto and San Leo Tiberino. Laura said it was awful, although Riccardo gave them short shrift, once with a tractor driven directly at them full throttle. The townspeople, to their credit, refuse to discuss the matter with any outsiders. Eventually, the reporters went away to invent stories for the British tabloids.

Mrs. Justice Joan Wilthorpe did her best to keep the more salacious elements at bay. Angela had pleaded no contest to some of the charges, but not guilty to others; all in all, there were only two charges contested, mostly dealing with pre-meditation. She insisted, against her brief's advice, and indeed a caution by Joan Wilthorpe, on taking the stand. It was from this testimony that I garnered the sequence of events I have previously outlined.

Whether her testimony helped or not I can't really say. She wore a simple dark skirt and white blouse with what Barbara called a Peter Pan collar. She wore no makeup or jewellery. Her appearance undoubtedly helped her; it seemed inconceivable that she could have committed such heinous crimes. But her manner, if not haughty, was too confident. She expressed no remorse, shed no tears, gave her testimony as if reading from a text prepared for a third person. She lost the jury.

What did help her was the evidence, at first contested as inadmissible, that Christopher Neagle and Stanie Wieszkowski had conspired for him to assume the identity of Doctor Bronislaw Wieszkowski. The possibility that they had also plotted to kill Wieszkowski was not allowed. The fact that Tony had in essence stalked her and deceived her as to his identity and intention had some bearing on the sentence. A psychiatrist testified that although Angela was of sound and rational mind, she had suffered a shock which could, — could being the operative word — have made her temporarily insane. The judge chose to ignore this in her summary.

The judge counselled the jury to focus on the facts as admitted by Angela in her testimony, which was voluntarily given. The jury did not waste time in rendering its decision. I understand that in Canada and America there are degrees of murder. Suchlike distinctions were no longer in effect in Britain by that time. Judge Wilthorpe did, however, have some discretion. She was a difficult woman to read. On the bench for ten years, she was known neither as a "hanging judge" nor a "bleeding heart". Whether she felt any sympathy for Angela, I have no idea. In the end, she imposed a tariff of eighteen years. They took Angela down.

That night, Albert had dinner with Barbara and me. That he was distraught is no overstatement. I think we all were. I remember him saying, "My God, Barbara. I didn't even share the past with you. Cosmo, I am not certain how much you really knew. How could I have told all that to a child? Everything I have done for over twenty years has been based on fear. I somehow believed that if I took her away she would be safe, that she could lead a normal life. Well, she didn't lead a normal life. I lied to her and I must face the consequences. I lived the last twenty years until the cloak of fear. The rest of my life will be under the cloak of regret."

Albert returned to Italy the following day. Laura told me he gradually resumed the pattern of life he had established when Angela first went to London, albeit a life diminished in every possible way.

He refused to discuss the case. The few expatriates in the region were always inviting him as Laura put it "to bathe in the squalor of the whole thing". He replied to all invitations that he had lost his facility in English, except for those two words beginning with the letters "F and O". The expatriates avoided him, branded him as ill-tempered, ungrateful, and totally mean-spirited. The town, however, to a man and woman, drew him closer, as if protecting him from the outside world. Maria Pia continued to look after him. And Laura and Clemente kept a close eye. The bridge games on Saturdays resumed.

And so it went for eighteen years. Albert wrote Angela faithfully every week; she returned each of the letters unopened.

* * * * *

Barbara visited the prison regularly. When she would return home, she said little except that Angela's comments concerning Albert were vitriolic. Every year, Angela seemed to hate him more and more. For the girl, I will always think of Angela as a girl, her hatred of Albert had become an obsession. This pattern continued until Barbara died.

Angela, only then, allowed me to visit once a year. We avoided all discussion of Italy and Albert specifically; it seemed best. On my last visit in prison, Angela asked me when I was going to Italy for my annual summer trek. She seemed quite intent on knowing my precise itinerary, dates and trains. It was the same routine I had taken for years: the train to Paris, three nights there and then the night-train to Milan changing for Arezzo. After I had outlined all this, she asked me a strange thing in a very quiet voice. I write "strange" because at that time I had no idea that she had been scheduled for a release. She suddenly posed a request, almost sotto voce, which, quite frankly, seemed to come from out of the blue.

"Cosmo, I want you to buy two first-class tickets with separate compartments, couchettes, to Milan leaving on your proposed departure date from Paris. And, meet me on the platform at Gare de Lyon station ten minutes before departure. Now, tell no one!"

I must have appeared puzzled. Her face changed. She seemed to smile almost mischievously.

"I can trust you, Cosmo? Can't I?"

She looked at me intently but before I could reply she said in her normal voice and volume.

"Cosmo, you really should go. We have said all there is to say. I look forward to your next visit."

Unbeknownst to me, there would not be another visit to the prison.

I worried about the whole thing of course. If she was to be released, what were the terms of the release? Surely she would not be permitted to travel outside of the United Kingdom. I am afraid I was once again worried about my position, if I could be charged with abetting a crime.

Somewhat apprehensively, according to the dates I had told Angela, I left St. Pancras Station, such a glorious piece of Victorian folly tarted up to look like a modern Waitrose awaiting delivery of tinned foods. Normally, I miss the old train from Victoria Station to Dover. I miss the swell of the Channel during the crossing. I loved arriving in Paris. This time, I just wanted to get to Paris as quickly and effortlessly as possible. And I can't say that I enjoyed my time in Paris in the least. The train departure for Italy loomed ahead. In fact, I even had strange dreams about the Gare de Lyon station, a sense of pending entrapment.

I arrived at the station about 11:30. There she was on the platform, looking every inch the middle-class European woman of a certain age. She had obviously been shopping and was wearing a Chanel-style suit. She carried a small leather purse. There was a largish bag, also good quality leather, over her shoulder and she was pulling a small black suitcase. Her hair had been cut fairly short with just a hint of curl. She smiled at me from under dark glasses and through expertly applied lipstick. No one could possibly imagine for an instant that she was a murderess released from prison only a few days previously.

"Cosmo" was all she said as she took my hand. She had not called me Uncle Cosmo since her arrest.

Later she said the passport had not proven a problem. Her lawyer had taken her photo and obtained the application for an Italian passport. He still had her old one which was, of course, under the name of Stafford. The murderess had been incarcerated as a Neagle, the name on the registration of her birth. His secretary dropped the forms off at the Italian consulate and waited while they checked it. They questioned the dates. She told them that Miss Stafford had married in England and not travelled in recent years. The secretary went on to explain that Miss Stafford now wanted to return home to the safety of her family and never again return to England. I guess lawyers' secretaries are not bound to the same code of ethics and the truth as their employers! Anyway, she evidently hit a sympathetic cord with the clerk and the new passport arrived at the lawyer's office a few days later.

"Why ever would they check me out? The British, of course, would be shirty about it. But the Italians!" She laughed.

We ate a light meal. She smoked a cigarette afterwards before announcing that she was off to bed. She would not take breakfast but meet me on the platform in Milano.

I slept surprisingly soundly. By this point, I understood that the train would not be stopped. The Schengen Agreement eliminated any border controls. The following morning, Angela looked extremely attractive. She was wearing the same suit but had the jacket open to show a white blouse and a pearl choker. We boarded the first class compartment Inter-city for Florence but spoke little during the journey. The train to Arezzo did not leave Florence for thirty minutes, so we drank a coffee and she ate a cornetto. I had been up early and eaten a full breakfast in the dining car. There was no first class compartment on the train to Arezzo. Angela sat across from me facing in the direction the train was travelling. She opened the window and let the air blow on her.

Riccardo was waiting when we arrived at Arezzo. He was driving a rather smart Audi which he told me was his own. He had confessed to me the autumn before that he had refused to drive Laura's old Daimler any longer anywhere other than around the village. Eventually, she had agreed to sell it to a collector. He also had asked me not to mention the Daimler to Laura; it was still apparently a sore point. If he was surprised to see Angela, he did not show it. He greeted her as he would have twenty year ago when he might have picked her up from university. She took his hand and shook it, coldly.

Actually, I was quite taken back by the manner in which she spoke to Riccardo and that she spoke to him in English.

"Please phone the Contessa to tell her I am here and will join her for lunch. Also, have her invite Dottore Stafford to join us."

The tone in her speech, not really haughty but, nonetheless, stinging in its indifference; this from Angela to a man who had played with her and looked after her as a child. It upset me. If it bothered Riccardo, he didn't show it. His English had obviously improved since she went away to England.

Angela showed no interest in the changes around her: the new highway, suburban-style houses on the outskirt of the villages, the new-style Italian motorcars. Thirty-five minutes later, we pulled up at the Castello. Laura was there waiting but Angela waved her back.

"I need to think a bit. I will wait in the stable. Tell Dottore he can speak to me there in private. She left her purse and suitcase in the car but, taking her leather bag, walked quickly and, I could almost write, in light of things to come, resolutely, to the old stable.

I went inside the Castello. Laura had set the table for four. I thought, once again, there was no question that Riccardo was to join us even after all these years. Albert arrived about ten minutes later. He came into the house. Laura hugged him as he held my hand. Laura told him Angela wanted to see him in the stable. His face literally shone, tears ran down his face as he bolted towards the stable.

Seconds later we heard screams, short piercing screams. The three of us ran with Riccardo arriving first. He tried to block Laura from entering. Albert was on his knees screaming the same words over and over.

"Joanna! Joanna! No!"

It was not, of course, Joanna this time. It was Angela hanging from the rafters. Albert wailed and writhed on the floor. He kept screaming. Laura, always in control, told Riccardo to telephone the police and Ludovico. She knelt down beside and held Alberto as one would a child. I had climbed up to cut her down but knew it was hopeless. She had bitten her tongue; her face, which had seemed so elegantly made-up minutes ago, was a grotesque caricature of humanity, the lips red and smeared, the pearl choker pushed up by the rope until it rested under her ears.

Beneath her were several large white papers and a butcher's cleaver. Albert was holding the papers, which I took from him. Even in the horror of the moment, I read them. The writing was printed and child-like in appearance. She had written:

> Dottor Stafford: I cannot call you Papa or even friend. You more than anyone deceived me. I understand that I grew up in a den of vipers but you were the worst. As he lay dying, dying by my hand, my true Father whispered to me that you were the evil one. He asked me to swear that I would kill you one day as I had killed him. My Father was right. You destroyed my Mother, my Father and me. I was abandoned, not by my family, but by you. I came back here to this place of sin to kill you with this cleaver. I know, however, that you will suffer more on this earth if I die. I die here today, dead as surely as by your hand. Meditate on this for the rest of your life.
>
> Angela Neagle

The madness of the next days I cannot easily remember with any sense of chronology. And I doubt poor Laura could be any clearer. I am glad that it is I who write the account of Angela's death and not Laura. She loved Angela in a way she had never been able to love her own children. The situation was as surreal as anything I have known. The doctors sedated Albert only for one day. He refused any further assistance after that. The body was held by the medical examiners. As soon as it was released, the funeral was held. Technically, I suppose the church could have refused to bury Angela's remains. She had, after all, committed suicide. But the medical reports and police reports stated that she was clearly not of sound mind. How they could come to such a conclusion, I don't know. With this verdict, how could Ludovico refuse? Not that I think for one moment he would have refused.

Albert, wearing a dark suit, stood in the church, The *Prepositura,* the largest church and the one where Angela made her first Communion. He was perfectly composed as he shook the hand of practically everyone in the town. And the town came, not in the ghoulish guise of piety, morbidity, or curiosity, but out of concern for a girl they had watched grow in their midst and the reserved foreign gentleman who was always polite and had made such an effort to assimilate into their lives. Albert insisted on sitting alone in the front pew, erect, stoic, I don't know the word. Laura, Maria Pia, Riccardo and I sat behind him. Georgio, Laura's step-son declined to attend.

The procession to the cemetery was slow. Since it was situated just below the town, we approached it by walking the kilometer down through San Angelo's gate and on to a winding country path. It was a glorious day and the wildflowers abounded on each side of the path, the red of the poppies almost shattering into the yellow broom. First in the procession was Ludovico reciting the rosary over an amplifier, then the black hearse with the undertaker and his men beside it. Albert followed, alone and upright. I took both Laura's and Maria Pia's arms. We were followed by the townspeople responding to the rosary.

Albert remained, as in the church, silent throughout, neither reciting the prayers nor responding to liturgical ceremony, that is, until the moment for lowering the casket. He lurched towards it, fell to his knees in the dirt and held to the wooden box as one would hold a body. He would not move. Minutes passed; there was silence. It was Maria Pia who went to him, lifted him up.

"Alberto, we must go home."

She took his hand and led him, as one might a child, past the graves, out from the cemetery and up the hill to the town. I doubt if there was a dry eye in the cemetery. They watched the man who had taken the little girl by hand to the piazza every week for a Fanta being led up the hill by his housekeeper, who addressed him as "Alberto" for the first time in forty years.

And so, you know the rest. He lived another few years, playing bridge every Saturday night, attending Mass on Sundays, standing there ever stoic but never really participating, reading his *International Herald Tribune* every morning at Gianni's bar on the piazza, meeting the odd academic, and playing chess with me when I came for visits. So he lived until he had that unfortunate motor accident in Città di Castello, when he began his physical and mental decline.

* * * * *

Not long ago, I received a visit from a young woman. In order to tell you about the unusual visit, I must confess to venturing into an area where I must break a confidence, one I would normally consider as sacramental. Barbara told me the story as she lay in the hospice dying of a painful pancreatic cancer, wanting me to know yet begging me to keep her secret. I held her hand and promised. It probably seems old-fashioned and not in keeping with the image I expect you have already formed of me, when I confess that I have prayed about what I am about to write. I am about to break that promise, which I gave that good woman, who stood by with all my faults, or rather in spite of them. As, she lay dying Barbara confided Angela's story in fuller detail than I really wanted to know.

Barbara, of course, visited Angela regularly in prison. She would tell me afterwards that each visit had been like the last. Angela rarely mentioned anyone, although once or twice she did ask about Maria

Pia. Angela once said that she would send her a letter but knew that he — meaning Albert — would get hold of it and take it out on the poor woman. This was preposterous but Barbara said it was not possible to reason with Angela about Albert; she didn't try. Otherwise, Angela seemed normal. She read a great deal, kept in shape physically and even taught language and literature classes to her fellow inmates. Barbara said it was strange but Angela seemed well-liked. She lived among every sort of violent criminal but showed no fear. Perhaps having murdered three people so brutally, albeit in a passion rather than in cold-blood, gave her some sort of status within the prison world.

Once Barbara died, as I previously mentioned, Angela allowed me to visit once a year, which I did. I offered to come more frequently but she said once annually was enough. She would discuss world affairs but never the past or the present to the degree, at least, that it affected any of us. She aged which was natural, and by the end of her sentence looked a youngish forty-year-old matron.

Barbara was a kind woman and a good wife; we were never blessed with children, an out-dated expression I have already admitted. Despite what has been written about my youthful transgressions, I opted for a heterosexual life; I could have gone either way. I chose the path I chose and held back no secrets from my wife. She loved Angela from the time she was a small child, when we visited in Italy. When Angela came to study in Britain, Barbara was ecstatic.

I think the Christmas when Angela came with her two friends was the happiest of our married life. I also believe the feelings were reciprocated by Angela. Laura, with all her fine qualities, had lovingly hovered over Angela as she was growing up, but she was never a mother-like person. I don't think it is in her blood. And Maria Pia, who undoubtedly loved Angela, always worried about pleasing Albert first and foremost. Angela loved Barbara from childhood, and it was perhaps natural that she was the only one permitted to visit her and become a confidante of sorts.

During the period awaiting the verdict, when Barbara was making one of her visits to the gaol; this was, of course, before she was transferred to Holloway Prison where she would spend the next eighteen years. Angela seemed distressed about something other than the pending judicial ordeal. Finally, she tapped at her stomach and Barbara understood at once. On the next visit Barbara did not shy away from a discussion of Angela's condition. Through all the stages of the judicial process, Angela showed no sign of her pregnancy. It was only in her eighth month that it became even slightly evident. She had, moreover, withheld the information from both her solicitor and her barrister. That is why she had, against their advice, pleaded no contest to the major charges, to advance the trial date.

Barbara's reaction was immediate.

"But surely the court, especially the jury, would have shown more leniency, had it been known that your half-brother had knowingly fathered your child. Your anger at the discovery would have seemed more justifiable."

Barbara told me she just shrugged, confiding that her only concern was to get rid of the child as soon as possible and have it grow up without any connection to her or anyone from her past. She wanted her child to have a clean slate. For this reason, she declined Barbara's offer to take the child. She was adamant.

"I don't want the child to hate you, Barbara, at some point in the future, as I now despise Albert Stafford. I need you to help me organize an institutional arrangement, not an adoption."

Those were her very words: "institutional arrangement" not an adoption. What choice did Barbara have?

The days of orphanages are pretty well a thing of the past in Britain. There are, however, one or two places where children can be reared from infancy, at least there were twenty or so years ago. One was a charming country home run by the Sisters of Saints Agnes and Monica. Barbara was able to use her church connections — or rather mine unbeknownst to me — to arrange a placement. At any one time, there were about forty children living there for longer and shorter periods. The child was to live there until an age when she could be sent to boarding school. She would return there in the holidays. By the time the child was a teenager, however, the facility was closed, but she continued to return for holidays; she was, understandably, quite attached to the few remaining elderly sisters.

Barbara had accompanied a social worker from the prison system to the convent, where the child was christened in the chapel as Maria Barbara. She was to be reared under the surname of Neagle, not Stafford, which of course still remained Angela's legal name. Barbara admitted that it was difficult to leave the child and especially to promise Angela that she would never visit. Angela never referred to her again. Nothing more was to be known until this girl, now a woman, arrived at the door one evening at my house in the Cotswolds.

Maria Neagle was by no means attractive. Her hair was flat and just hung over her ears with a fringe in need of a trim hanging on her forehead. She was about ten kilos overweight and wore a loose-fitting, flowered-print dress, relatively long for the period, which covered legs that were bare down to red socks. There was no makeup on a pale face dominated by heavy eyeglasses under thick eyebrows. She carried a large purse and a Waitrose shopping bag. Frankly: she was the type of woman one imagines frequents supermarkets for an outing.

She asked for me by name and if she could come in to discuss a matter, as she put it, "of a certain delicacy".

My housekeeper was there that evening, so I asked the young woman into my study, something I dislike doing when I am alone. Before I could speak, the young woman began what seemed a rehearsed statement.

"My name is Maria, and I think you and your wife placed me in the convent when I was a baby. Sister Rita Holter told me a bishop's wife had brought me there with another woman, but everything was kept very secret. She said she recognized the Bishop's wife from when she had attended a confirmation and there was a tea afterwards, but couldn't remember her name. As I said, she is very old, in fact, the oldest sister. Mother Superior refused to tell me anything, but Sister Rita felt sorry when she overheard me pestering Mother about my past. After Compline one night, she took me aside and told me about the bishop's wife. She made me promise most solemnly not to say who told me. I think you can help me find my mother."

All this in almost one breath.

I waved her to sit down and said I would have tea brought in. I went to the kitchen to ask Mrs. Burnett, my housekeeper, to bring tea and cakes. No doubt, I went into the kitchen as much to collect myself as anything. When I returned to my study, Maria was sitting in a leather chair in front of my desk with her hands folded in her lap. I suggested we first wait for tea and I would answer her questions, but first she must tell me what she knew of her past.

Maria confessed that she knew virtually nothing of her origins. She had spent all her early years in the convent, and even after the child-centre closed she stayed on. There was a nearby girls' boarding school where she attended, but she had not been a good student and returned to the St. Agnes and St. Monica sisters at age sixteen. In fact, she had planned to join the order, but recent events included a plan to marry, though first she wanted to know about her parents.

"I am just not very good with the computers and Internet. One day, I typed in Neagle, my name Neagle, I saw there was a bishop, I thought it might be you and that you were related to me. I looked you up in the sisters' Crockford and it said you had a wife named Barbara and gave your address. In fact, before I got up my courage to come, and when I was still planning to become a sister, I thought you might be my father and your wife wanted to hide it. Imagine, I thought, Sister Maria, a bishop's daughter. It is silly, I know."

Mrs. Burnette arrived with the tea and poured us each a cup before leaving the study door slightly ajar.

I waited until I heard Mrs. Burnett was back in the kitchen. I had to answer the woman but struggled with how to explain that she had been born in a prison infirmary, that her mother had abandoned her at birth, that her mother was a murderess who had killed her father and upon release from prison committed suicide. Most of all, I hated to tell her that her parents were brother and sister as had been her grandparents. I didn't lie but manipulated the truth whether, I question now, to protect her or save me from a responsibility for her future care. I wanted her gone.

I sipped my tea and explained that both of her parents were dead. Her father, of Polish extraction with the name of Wieszkowski, had died before she was born and her parents could marry. Her mother who was my niece had asked my late wife, Barbara, to place her in a suitable religious home. So far: no lies. Her mother had died in Italy and had never had a chance to reconcile with her child. My wife had acted in charity in fulfilling her mother's wishes. I had avoided lying until I said I was her only relation and a distant one. I omitted nearly everything.

A lack of education, a life sheltered among naïve women, an old-fashioned deference to male figures, especially in the church, a mental simplicity through massive inbreeding, whatever it was, or maybe it was all of them: Maria asked no additional question. With her hands still in her lap, she said only, "Well, now I know".

She stood to leave, gathering her bags, which had rested all the while beside her chair. I wanted to give her something, anything which might give her a sense of family, heritage, lineage — I don't know what to call it.

"Your great-grandmother was the daughter of a viscount, you know." It was a ridiculous thing to say but she actually smiled, "Really".

Again, she made as to leave, "Thank you, my Lord, for your time. You have told me what I need to know. I am sorry your wife is dead. We shared a name; I am Maria Barbara. I should like to have met her; she knew me all those years ago."

I gestured for her to sit down.

"Please, you must finish your tea and cake and tell me before you leave of your plans to marry."

She seemed reluctant to sit down but eventually did, placing her bags, once again beside her. I poured her another cup of tea. She told me how she had met her fiancé, an American from northern Michigan.

"He was much better than me on the Internet. I am hopeless. He found my name on an old list from my boarding school and tracked me down through one of the other girls. He thought that we might be closely related. Now I know that is not the case. You have assured me of that. But he was certain, as his mother told him before she died that he should find me. She said she dreamed that we must meet and that we were related. Apparently she belonged to some mystical organization or faith, although my boyfriend is not at all like that."

I had a terrible premonition before she even continued.

"His name is Jan and, isn't it strange, his father was also Polish, although he has his mother's Christian name, except, of course, a man's version. Jan laughed when he told me his name sounded Polish, but he really thought his mother named him after herself, Janice. Then she reached into her purse and handed me a photo that frankly chilled my blood; there was no mistake.

Angela's friends, Janice and Jake had broken their relationship, as I mentioned, well before the trial. Janice had returned to Canada after the killings and was not called to testify. Jake, of course, had to make a formal statement in the courtroom. Defence had made no effort to counter what he had said. I met Jake on the street several years later. He elected not to return to Canada and was living with his wife in a small house they had recently bought in Camden Town.

I thought it odd at the time that when I asked him about Janice he replied, "I am convinced she only used me to get closer to Tony whom I suspect she had known, quite probably intimately, back in Canada". He took a deep breath, looked away and continued, "I am not certain, to be honest, this intimacy did not continue here in London".

"The night before, when we met Tony's parents", Jake added, "Janice had called them Stanie and Broni immediately, as if they were already acquainted. I confronted her with this later and she brushed me off saying I was jealous."

I know now that Jake's suspicions had been more than accurate. Tony was Maria's father as well as her fiancé's.

Maria then reached into her purse and pulled out a Bible. She smiled as she looked at it before handing it to me.

"His family Bible. Well, in a way his family Bible. Jan got this Bible from his mother. She had received it from his father, who got it from his father. Jan gave it to me. He wanted me to have it and carry it with me all the time. So, I do."

She handed me the Bible. It was a red-covered King James Version. I opened it but what I read sent shivers down my spine. There was a presentation certificate inside the cover.

**PRESENTED TO DOCTOR ROBERT STAFFORD**
**CHAIRMAN OF THE BUILDING COMMITTEE**
**ST. ANDREW'S PRESBYTERIAN CHURCH**
**COLLINGWOOD ONTARIO**
**JUNE 15TH 1947**

On the first page facing the certificate was handwriting, the first inscription was printed in large bold letters, whereas the one beneath was crafted in small, neat cursive penmanship:

> FOR I THE LORD THY GOD AM A JEALOUS GOD, VISITING THE INIQUITY OF THE FATHERS UPON THE CHILDREN UNTO THE THIRD AND FOURTH GENERATION OF THEM THAT HATE ME.
>
> *To Janice with love from Tony. September 9, 1988. May we ever remain united in the task which awaits us.*

I was a coward. I handed her back the photograph and the Bible and told her I wished her and her fiancé "every possible happiness". Maria placed them both back in her purse and zipped it shut. I called for Mrs. Burnett to show her out. I just wanted her out of my house as swiftly as possible.

Then, Maria did something which has haunted me since. She turned back, set down her Waitrose bag and purse as she got to the front door, and asked if I would give her a blessing. Mrs. Burnett was smiling. Maria actually knelt there. Mrs. Burnett bowed her head. I have no idea how I got the words out. She rose and left. I tasted bile.

I have never felt such shame. I betrayed everyone. I was complicit with everyone against Albert. Ludovico loved me and I easily abandoned him for my career disguised as a vocation. I was an incomplete husband to Barbara. I continue to use my sister as a mere convenience. I am a hypocrite in condemning my brother. It is many, many years since I have treated my vocation as anything but a readily available means to social standing and a seat in the House of Lords. As a priest and a bishop, I am a charlatan. I have never come up to the mark and, in every way, my priesthood has been a compete fraud. Never, however, have I behaved as unworthily as I did to that unfortunate young woman, my own brother's great-grandchild.

COSMO ST. J. L. NEAGLE +

# Laura

2012

It is six weeks, my dear Doctor Stevenson, since I posted my narrative and I gather a similar time for the others. I am now sending one last narrative, a coda, as it were, to the quartet concerto already played. This one, unlike the previous, I may not share with my brothers and Ludovico. I cannot speak for the others, but I might start by writing that the recalling of these events has not only been cathartic but has also, in a strange sense, allowed each an opportunity to take stock of our own lives. The whole exercise undoubtedly did so for me, forcing me to make substantive changes in the way I live.

The changes in my life bear no relationship to the events hitherto related except, I suppose, to the degree that everything in our lives has been formed, one could write tarnished, by the events that took place in Toronto, London and San Leo Tiberino all these years ago.

Well, I shall "bite the bullet" as my son used to say so tiresomely as a child. I have left Italy for the last time and returned to Oxford to our Father's flat. It was left jointly to Harry and me, and he kindly signed over his share to me when he married his Canadian wife, Helen, some years ago. They have a flat in St. John's Wood in London large enough, I am told, to accommodate her various children and grandchildren when they come to Britain. I have never met Helen. The house in the Cotswolds went to Cosmo; no doubt, our dear Father felt that Cosmo, a cleric, would someday need a proper home of his own. The *castello* is now in the full possession of my stepson, Giorgio Guelfi. He finally has my home and all my money; I hope he will be happy.

This may come as a surprise, certainly it will be to my brothers when they learn the news which they must be told whether I send them this narrative or not. I have remarried. After having him as a lover for forty years, I decided to make an honest boy of Riccardo. We were married a few days ago at the registry office, not a church, here in Oxford. Not in a church, how unlike me! Shall I say it was a matter of different religions or allow you to surmise what you will?

So, having come clean on that account, I must now confess that, despite my assurances to the contrary, I was not fully honest in my earlier narrative. Most of what I am about to tell you is known only to Ludovico; my brothers know nothing of what I am about to recount. They are not complicit in any sort of cover up. But if Ludovico is guilty of colluding with me to deceive, he did it at my bidding, for my sake and that of my children. He is, in a sense, my true brother, the one I have always turned to when I needed help. Perhaps underneath we are birds of a feather.

As you might have surmised, I am not especially close to my two offspring. They both live in America with their spouses and families, one on the east coast and one on the west. They used to come to Italy every two or three years with their children in tow; I never had a desire to visit America. I went as a university student to New York but am not interested in seeing the quaintness of their New England or the brashness of Los Angeles. I doubt they will care what I write. They have, I well expect, written off their mother as a toffee-nosed Brit posturing about as an Italian aristocrat, at best; at worst, they think of me, if they ever do, as an uncaring bitch. Yet, in a snobbish way, they, along with their egalitarian spouses, will react with horror to learn of my marriage to Riccardo, their childhood friend of the working variety.

I now know that both Cosmo and Ludovico have admitted candidly in their narratives to their youthful indiscretions. They had hinted as much their intention to do some serious revealing, but it took courage. I doubt if either one of them has had a serious career as a shirt-lifter but they have left themselves vulnerable, should you, our Canadian friend, choose for some reason to extend this study of the Toronto business to include all the vulnerable underbellies. So, as the expression goes: in for a penny; in for a pound. If their dirty underpants are to be hung out on the line, why not put out the dirty camisole and knickers as well?

Joanna was not the only one to give birth in that winter of 1967 although my child preceded Angela's by some months. While they were all glued to their seats at the enquiry in Toronto, I was delivered of a third child in Oxford. As I previously wrote, I went to Britain to look after our dying Father, while Harry flew off to Toronto the day before I arrived at the Oxford flat. My poor father, born in 1884, was past discerning very much, so I doubt he noticed my shape. When I left for Britain, I was showing only slight signs of pregnancy; I had shown very little with my first two. Whether Clemente noticed, or cared, I have no idea. By this time, he had set up housekeeping with his latest mistress in our Rome flat. If he suspected, I think he probably thought I would have an abortion while in Oxford.

Perhaps it was the idea of vanished youth, I can't really say, but I was overcome with a strange jealousy of Chris, Joanna and Albert that summer so many years ago. Clemente was a good husband, as far as that goes, but he was older by some twenty years and already seeking out other, younger interests. The three were so youthful and even Albert exhibited, at times, a carefree attitude. I had not yet started to bed Riccardo; he was a still a tad young; my odious stepson was far too young. Ludovico, as we all now know, was preoccupied with my brother. My child's father was Chris. I seduced my young nephew on more than one occasion without, I am proud to write, drawing the suspicion of anyone in the house. He might have been a latent religious nutter but he was a randy, oversexed young man.

The child was born almost three months prematurely, yet surprisingly quite robust, three days before my father's death, which prompted Harry to return to Britain. So Harry, or Cosmo for that matter, never knew. Our dear Father, albeit by all accounts a simple country parson, was also a financial wizard when it came to the stock market. It was his financial acumen, not the church, which garnered him his MBE. When he died, in addition to the properties, he left the three of us a great deal of money. I was a relatively wealthy woman, well, for a short while. Giorgio has seen to that; little by little, penny by penny, he has sequestered it all. Fortunately, he did not know about the Oxford flat, or I fear it too would be gone. Now, Riccardo and I can live in the flat, thanks in no small part to his Italian state pension and his lifelong ability to save his wages. We actually drove to Oxford in his Audi.

I had the money to pay for the child's keep. Even with such a short deadline before Harry's return, I was able to find the services of a retired nurse willing to care for the child in return for a very smart flat and not inconsiderable stipend. As to whether she had any affection for the child I cannot say with any degree of certainty. I have no doubts whatsoever that it was well cared for and she seemed a decent sort of person. Clearly, she was qualified and competent, with the best of references. I was just relieved not to be saddled with the problem.

As I lay in there, with the midwife fussing about in the flat, with my Father dying in the next room, my mind played strange tricks. To pass the time of the labour, I quoted Latin; in a bizarre way it had a soothing effect. I had read Latin at Lady Margaret Hall, which was an all-women college in those days, taking a reasonable second in Classics. The Greek was of little practicality but the Latin served me well in Italy. As the child was finally ready to be pushed out, I was — and I know this seems totally absurd and you will think me a wacko if you already don't — reciting from memory random passages in Latin and not the original Greek from the *Iliad*, actually Book XXII, which I had learned by memory. The baby actually popped out to:

> *Ne me mori sed non sine nixor, quod per palmam,*
> *certamine maxima pugna quae postea dicetur.*[3]

It did, of course, lead to the child's naming. I knew he would have to be strong in the world to counter the obstacles, other than money and solvency, which might plague his childhood, not the least of the lack of both father and mother. I also recognized that if there was to be glory or struggle in his life, it would come down to him with little input, support or credit from me.

---

3 Well let me die—but not without struggle, not without glory, no, in some great clash of arms that even men to come will hear of down the years!

Over the next four years, I made periodic trips to Britain with the excuse of seeing to my Father's estate or meeting with financial advisors. Clemente never objected. He probably thought I had a lover. Matrimony Italian-style, well for a certain class. I would spend time with the child at the leased flat. By the age of two, I had started to notice deformities in it. At first, I blamed it on the fact Chris and I were aunt and nephew. But, pediatricians, to whom I never confided the affinity between its parents, diagnosed Achondroplasia. Hector was a dwarf.

The plan had been for Hector to live with the nurse until old enough to go to school. I had already made enquiries about enrolling "my ward" at Harrow. As I said, at that stage, money was not a consideration. Clearly with the diagnosis, the symptoms of which were very much evident by the time he was four years old, public schools were not an option. Public schools can be very brutal.

My other options were limited. Understanding as Clemente was, I doubted he would welcome the child at the *castello* or even countenance any sort of connection or affinity if Hector were to be placed nearby. Some plans had to be made and, although Italy increasingly became the preferred option, the timing had to be perfect. I may have been an uncaring mother but my sense of maternal timing was impeccable.

Clemente's mother, Alicia, had lived in South Africa for many years before her timely death, well timely for me. She never approved of me. The "dowager Contessa" was an expression I used to use in her presence since I never spoke to her in Italian. She hated it. Anyway, the Guelfi family had extensive holdings in both the Orange Free State and Cape Colony for two generations. She met a business associate of her husband not long after the old Count died and up and married him. They lived, happily or otherwise, in Port Elizabeth. Clemente was travelling to South Africa, *sans* mistress, and thought it a good opportunity to take the children for a month to see their Nonna. I had my window.

I told Clemente that I planned to stay in England during their absence to visit my brothers. I returned to Italy with the child at the first opportunity. It cost a bit to satisfy the "grief" of the nurse at the parting from her charge. Her grief was eventually assuaged when I paid her rent for the smart flat, up front, for the following five years. When Hector and I arrived at the *castello*, it was basically closed up, except for Riccardo, whose trust and loyalty I never had reason to doubt, even then.

Riccardo had moved up the ladder over the years from apprentice gardener to full gardener. He was Umbrian, which did not initially sit well with the old gardener Giuseppe or for that matter the other staff members. Giuseppe complained to Clemente that he "talked funny". Riccardo could charm the proverbial pants off anyone, quite literally in my case. With his personality, and through hard work, Riccardo won the heart of the old man who insisted he be made head gardener when he retired, despite the boy's age. And upward he was to move over the years until he became estate manager. Riccardo was there alone when we arrived with only a few rooms opened all of which faced on to the back of the house and not the drive.

Riccardo came from a large Umbrian family centred in Città di Castello. His father was the eldest of eight and Riccardo himself the eldest of many, many cousins. One uncle, Luigi, was a widower and childless. He was about to return from living in Sicily where he had buried his wife. He may have had questionable business dealings but who was going to enquire. One never knows with these people. They all, regardless of *professional associations*, eventually return home from Sicily. A doctor friend of Ludovico facilitated the legal transfer. Paper work in Palermo, like placating Luigi himself, was expensive but not onerous. Financial incentives aside, however, Luigi loved the boy the moment he set eyes on him.

The one proverbial fly in the proverbial ointment was Giorgio. He was not expecting me to return to the *castello* for several weeks. Expecting me to still be in Britain and disliking Riccardo so much that he hoped, no doubt, to find him out in neglecting the estate, Giorgio drove up from Rome. He was not alone. Arm in arm, he entered the *castello* with a stunningly beautiful young woman and a perfectly featured young man with what intent I never ascertained. And, of course, he discovered my secret. The price of his silence has been virtually all of my money. I am penniless. Again, fortunately, he never knew about the Oxford flat or that Riccardo had saved so much over the years. The Riccardo whom to this day he disdainfully addresses as Ganovelli. The little prick.

On the rare occasions that Riccardo drove me to church in Florence when the children were away at school or otherwise occupied, we would swing by Città to check on the child's progress. In the eyes of neighbours and family who might be dropping by — and the Ganovellis were that sort of extended family — how natural it seemed for Riccardo to drop in to visit his uncle; how condescending for Riccardo's employer to take an interest in his little deformed cousin.

Hector had easily integrated into this large, albeit somewhat shady, family. I went for the last visit on his seventh birthday, although I still continue to send him a card each year, postmarked from England of course. He spoke to me initially in English but I could tell he was more comfortable in Italian so we switched. As I was getting into the car that last time, he ran and hugged me, holding on for several seconds before running back to the football game with his cousins.

Judge me as you will. It is good for all of us to have everything out in the open, at least among ourselves, and of course for you, my dear Doctor Stevenson. The frightening events that were spawned by the death of that poor girl in Toronto have infected all our lives for over forty years. The demonology which had its genesis in the St. Matthias's group and then morphed in to the Wieszkowskis' dogma of bodily possession by outside forces of evil, is rubbish as far as I am concerned. What I do believe, more precisely have come to believe, is that some of us are inherently imbued with the gene of evil.

All of the Neagles were evil to some degree, infused genetically with some innate need, call it passion, to love, then drain another of love, and, in the end, be cruel, all the while feigning obliviousness of our evil and secretly proud of the hurt we cause. How easy it has been for us to convince ourselves over the years of our righteousness! Judge for yourself. You have read the narratives.

It was Albert in his declining days who spoke to Cosmo of "deceit and abandonment", but Albert was the only one who was neither deceitful nor capable of abandoning those he loved. Yet, each of us Neagles — Joanna, Chris, Harry and his step-son, Cosmos, and Angela — has practiced to deceive and then abandon poor Albert.

I was the last in a long line of inflictors of deliberate cruelty by denying the veracity of Albert's happiness, so imaginatively expressed in that journal composed in his dying summer. Albert and my son. Albert and Ettore. I tried to expunge the record written by Albert in his garden while surrounded by his dreams and friends. I pretended even the real was not real and, in doing so, failed to decipher the beauty and truth that shone in Albert's vision of life, a vision he shared with my son. Albert and Ettore. To each, I have been deceitful. And, I also, in the end, abandoned both Albert and Ettore. I must be clear on this point.

Laura Jean Ganovelli

# ACKNOWLEDGEMENTS

Doug Casey made me write the book. I ought to clarify this: he encouraged me beyond endurance to return to my writing. If a reader is dissatisfied with the book, direct you annoyance at him and not me. My serendipitous acquaintanceship with Mrs. Diane Glasgow at Holt Renfrew, lead to a first-class editing. Given my sloppiness, this was a big feat. For any dissatisfaction on this score, however, direct your annoyance at me. Guy Parent helped me in my philosophical understanding of Father Guy Paris and Polish spiritualism related to St. Mary Faustina Kowalska. Ruth Honeyman spurred me on. And Mary Morican led me to publication with Code Workun from my publishing house holding my hand as I tiptoed through the vagaries of actually publishing a book. Of course, I must give thanks for Jill Moll of Books on Beechwood who actually proved the book will hit the shelves.

Finally, Karen Bissell Evans produced the sketches of Ettore and Barbara Nettleton proved the photos for the jacket cover from her collection of Tribunale dolls found in an abandoned church nearby my home in Anghiari; and she also oversaw the design work; Barbara, in fact, would have been "at home" in Albert's garden.

Mark Curfoot-Mollington
Anghiari, Toscana

# ABOUT THE AUTHOR

Mark Curfoot-Mollington was born in Toronto and graduated from Trinity College at the University of Toronto and Carleton University in Ottawa. He is a widower living in Italy and frequently back in Ottawa.

CPSIA information can be obtained
at www.ICGtesting.com
Printed in the USA
LVOW11s0136290917
550325LV00001B/8/P